Finally, Rae-Anne got a good look at the limo driver's face.

And without warning, her whole world split apart around her.

He turned around only briefly, after negotiating a steep turn and easing the limo into another long stretch of road. The countryside was getting less and less familiar, and Rae-Anne was certain now that they were nowhere near the church, and that something was going on that she didn't understand and couldn't control.

But all of those mysteries faded away as the driver met her eyes and she found herself caught and held in the darkly suggestive glare of the man she had loved and mourned as dead a decade ago.

Dear Reader,

Once again, we've got an irresistible month of reading coming your way. One look at our lead title will be all you need to know what I'm talking about. Of course I'm referring to *The Heart of Devin MacKade,* by award-winning, *New York Times* bestselling author Nora Roberts. This is the third installment of her family-oriented miniseries, "The MacKade Brothers," which moves back and forth between Silhouette Intimate Moments and Silhouette Special Edition. Enjoy every word of it!

Next up, begin a new miniseries from another award winner, Justine Davis. "Trinity Street West" leads off with the story of Quisto Romero in *Lover Under Cover.* You'll remember Quisto from *One Last Chance,* and you'll be glad to know that not only does he find a love of his own this time around, he introduces you to a whole cast of characters to follow through the rest of this terrific series. Two more miniseries are represented this month, as well: *The Quiet One* is the latest in Alicia Scott's "The Guiness Gang," while Cathryn Clare's "Assignment: Romance" begins with *The Wedding Assignment.* And don't forget Lee Magner's *Dangerous* and Sally Tyler Hayes' *Homecoming,* which round out the month with more of the compellingly emotional stories you've come to expect from us.

Enjoy them all—and come back next month for more excitingly romantic reading, here at Silhouette Intimate Moments.

Yours,

Leslie Wainger
Senior Editor and Editorial Coordinator

Please address questions and book requests to:
Silhouette Reader Service
U.S.: 3010 Walden Ave., P.O. Box 1325, Buffalo, NY 14269
Canadian: P.O. Box 609, Fort Erie, Ont. L2A 5X3

THE WEDDING ASSIGNMENT

CATHRYN CLARE

Silhouette

INTIMATE™MOMENTS®

Published by Silhouette Books

America's Publisher of Contemporary Romance

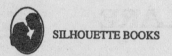

SILHOUETTE BOOKS

ISBN 0-373-07702-5

THE WEDDING ASSIGNMENT

Printed in U.S.A.

CATHRYN CLARE

is a transplanted Canadian who followed true love south of the border when she married an American ten years ago. She says, "I was one of those annoying children who always knew exactly what they were going to be when they grew up," and she has proved herself right with a full-time career as a writer since 1987.

"Being a writer has its hazards. So many things that I see—a car at the side of the road, two people having an argument, a hat someone left in a restaurant—make me want to sit down and finish the stories suggested to me. It can be very hard to concentrate on real life sometimes! But the good part of being a writer is that every story, no matter how it starts out, can be a way to show the incredible power that love has in our lives."

For L. D. Huff—
college buddy
Texan tour guide
fellow teller of tales
and an awful good old boy.

Prologue

It was his least favorite dream.

He was always standing on the shore of a lake, looking across the water. It wasn't anyplace he'd ever been in his waking life, although he'd dreamed about it enough over the years that he'd started to think, *Not this damn place again,* whenever it turned up in his dreams.

There was a small child—sometimes an infant, sometimes older—playing on a beach on the other side of the lake. Sometimes Wiley could see a pail and a shovel and a tall sand castle. Sometimes the sand castle even had little flags waving bravely from its turrets.

Sometimes he couldn't tell what the child was doing. But he knew beyond any doubt that he was supposed to be over there, too, looking after the kid, keeping an eye on things.

And he couldn't get there. The shore was overhung with trees in both directions, and even though he could see the child in such detail, for some reason it seemed to be too far to swim.

So he always ended up just standing there, cursing his own uselessness and kicking at the water that lapped at his feet. He didn't know who the child was. He didn't know why he was so sure he was supposed to be there. He just was, and the knowledge of it built up in him like a head of steam, threatening to blow him apart.

That was it. That was the whole dream, just standing around on the shore of a lake feeling frustrated beyond his limits.

He'd been having it since he was a kid himself. And he'd long since given up trying to figure out what the hell it meant.

Chapter 1

If he squinted hard, Wiley Cotter could just make out two pairs of broad shoulders in the dense clouds of smoke from the oil drum.

"Hey, Wiley." That was his youngest brother, Sam. "What if that old lady two houses over calls the fire department again?"

"We'll just offer them a plateful, same as we did last time."

Wiley heard his brother Jack's soft chuckle. "Doesn't Austin have laws about bribing fire department officials?" he asked.

"Good barbecue is above the law. You ought to know that." Wiley dipped his brush into the bowl of sauce he'd spent an hour making last night. Some of it mixed with the grease dripping off the ribs on the grill, making the flames in the drum barbecue sizzle and jump a little higher. The cloud of smoke darkened and grew.

"Whoa." Jack stepped back a pace or two. "'Come on over for a couple of beers, some barbecue, relax for a while,' you said. I distinctly remember the word *relax*. There was nothing about natural disasters when you invited us."

"This barbecue thing is getting to be an obsession," Sam put in. "Ever since you heard about the joint across from the office going out of business—"

"'Obsession' is a mite strong." Wiley gave the ribs one more pass with his brush, then closed the hinged lid of the drum. "I'd settle for 'quest.'"

"*I'd* settle for a big bucket of water and some breathable air," Jack said. "I've been in the hot seat all week long, big brother. I don't need it on my days off, too."

As the smoke slowly thinned, Wiley looked at his two brothers. Like himself, they were dark-haired and broad-shouldered, with skin that tanned easily and eyes that were accustomed to looking at the world with a certain amount of suspicion.

All three brothers, too, tended to layer their speech with mockery, which Wiley knew was a way of keeping their distance from most of the rest of the world. Given the way the three of them had grown up, it wasn't surprising.

He always knew, though, when Jack or Sam was being serious about something. And there had been a bitter edge to Jack's voice just now that caught Wiley's ear.

"Who's got you in the hot seat?" he asked, as the three of them moved away from the barbecue to the small deck Wiley had built onto the back of his house.

"A big wheel out of San Antonio named Rodney Dietrich." Jack accepted the beer Wiley offered from the ice chest on the deck. "Heard of him?"

"Yeah. He used to own a development company that was on the sidelines of that last DEA investigation I did."

Wiley didn't go into details. He'd never really confided in either of his brothers about the final case he'd worked for the federal Drug Enforcement Agency.

Hell, he still didn't like to think about it himself, even though it had been serious enough to sour him on his job and prompt him to go to work as an independent investigator. He wouldn't have minded sharing that with Jack and Sam, but there was no way to tell the whole story without mentioning the woman he'd had to walk away from in the process. Wiley had never even come close to forgiving himself for that, and it had kept him silent on the subject for almost ten years now.

"So what's Rodney Dietrich up to these days, now that real estate didn't work out for him?" he asked, reaching for a beer from the cooler.

"Well, according to Rodney, he's running his family's hotel chain and doing just fine at it." Jack took a sip of his beer. "In reality, though, he's operating a money-laundering network that processes most of the illegal gambling proceeds in this great state of ours. The FBI's trying to shut down the gambling end of things. And I'm supposed to shut down Rodney, if I can."

"Why are you sounding so glum about it?" Sam wanted to know. All three Cotters had gravitated toward law enforcement, Jack as an FBI agent and Wiley and Sam as private investigators. After the helpless uncertainty of their childhoods, they seemed to have developed a shared taste for unraveling mysteries, clearing up chaos, righting wrongs.

"Because I've nearly got him where I want him, except that clear out of the blue he's decided to take some time off to get *married*, for Pete's sake."

Wiley grinned at the look on Jack's face. Another thing the Cotter brothers shared was a baffled wariness about the state of matrimony and everything that went with it.

"So you're stuck waiting for him to get back to work," he guessed.

"Right." Jack's expression got more serious. "And I'm stuck looking for another inside source in his operation, too. The last one we had just met with a sudden 'accident' on a fishing pier down in the Gulf."

"Heck of a coincidence," Wiley said.

"It's not the only one. There's a certain amount of evidence to suggest that the guy even rigged the accident that killed his first wife. Seems the lady had been asking some inconvenient questions about his business."

"Sounds like a nice guy," Sam commented.

This was interesting, Wiley thought, but hardly earth-shaking. In fact, his mind had started to drift slightly, lulled by barbecue smoke and sunshine and concern that maybe he hadn't basted those ribs quite liberally enough. And then Jack dropped his bombshell.

"Why any sane woman would want to hook up with a man like that is beyond me," he said. "I wonder if Ms. Rae-Anne Blackburn has any idea what she's getting herself into."

Wiley had just popped the top off his beer bottle and was raising it to his lips. At Jack's words he went stock-still.

"Rae-Anne Blackburn?" He repeated the name slowly. He must have misheard it, he thought. He'd just been thinking about Rae-Anne, that was why. The memories of his last DEA case had brought her to mind, and now he was imagining that Jack had said her name.

But Jack was nodding matter-of-factly. "You sound as if you know her," he said.

Wiley wasn't aware of getting to his feet. But suddenly he was standing up, pacing to the other side of the deck, peering into the blue pall of barbecue smoke as though he was looking back through time.

"I used to know her." His voice grated over the words.
Rae-Anne... dear God in heaven...

"How well?"

"Well enough."

Well enough to know she deserved better than to marry a slick operator like Rodney Dietrich. Well enough that the thought of her marrying anybody at all made Wiley half-crazy inside.

"Think she's honest?" Jack was asking.

"I know she is."

Did he? He and Rae-Anne had once understood each other so instinctively, so quickly. Did he still have the right to claim he knew her that well?

Suddenly he didn't care. What Wiley already knew about Rodney Dietrich's reputation wasn't good. What Jack had just said made it a lot worse. Rae-Anne couldn't marry a man like that, not without listening to the other side of the story first.

"What's up, Wiley?" Sam asked. "You look like you're hatching a whopper of an idea."

It had taken Wiley a lot of years to find his brothers again. Most of the time it felt good to have them around, to be with people who knew him well.

Occasionally, though, it could be a real pain. This was one of those times.

"I might be," he growled.

"Well, if it's about talking to Rae-Anne Blackburn, it's the best news I've heard all day," Jack said. "It turns out she actually works in Rodney's hotel chain—she's a bartender."

"She always was." She'd said the tips weren't as good as when she'd been waitressing, but the advantage of having a bar between her and the greedy hands of her customers had outweighed the financial angle. He could practically hear her saying it, could imagine the edge of laughter in her voice as she'd spoken.

"So she could be a source of information, if she's willing to talk to us," Jack went on. "If you'll have a shot at it—"

Wiley didn't answer. He was trying to stay calm, but it wasn't working. Suddenly, after long years of holding them at bay, images of Rae-Anne were flooding his mind.

That red-gold hair of hers, always looking as though it had just been kissed by the sun.

Her blue eyes, trusting, alive with the emotion of the moment.

Her skin, eggshell white, eggshell perfect.

That gentle voice. That dazzlingly sexy smile.

He couldn't stop the memories that were washing over him. Rae-Anne leaning over the bar to tease him into laughter at the end of a long day. Rae-Anne in his arms, breathless, astonishing him with her openness and seeming just as astonished by it herself.

Rae-Anne marrying a man who was crooked at best, dangerous at worst.

"*Damn* it...."

The vehemence in his voice surprised him. Both his brothers looked startled by his tone, and by the belligerent way he put his beer bottle down on the deck.

"I do believe," Sam said, "that Wiley's forgotten all about his barbecue."

Wiley glared at him. "Think you can ride herd on the office for a while, little brother?" he asked abruptly.

Sam's smile vanished. "I'd rather not," he said.

Wiley knew the reasons for that. Sam had had his own disastrous experiences with love, and Wiley had always been considerate about not forcing his brother into daily contact with the woman he'd loved and then lost.

But this was too urgent to let Sam's old hurts stand in the way of it. "I know you'd rather not," he said. "I wouldn't ask you if it wasn't important." He turned to face Jack without waiting for Sam's answer. "When exactly is Rodney Dietrich's wedding?" he demanded.

"Next Saturday afternoon. Am I hearing the possibility that you'll talk to Rodney's bride and see if she knows anything we might be able to use?"

Wiley took a long swallow of his beer, as though it could quench all the feelings that had begun to smolder inside him at the mention of Rae-Anne's name. "You're not hearing a damn thing," he growled, "until you tell me everything you know about this case, starting right now."

It was eighty-five degrees out, and Rae-Anne Blackburn was freezing.

Nearly everyone else had left the long, low ranch house by now. Renee, Rodney's longtime housekeeper, was scurrying toward her car, her arms full of flowers. The photographer was packing up his gear, having taken Rae-Anne's picture in the elegant oval foyer. It had seemed to take forever to get the shots set up, what with arranging her veil and touching up her makeup and swirling her train around her among the bouquets on the black-and-white marble floor.

She'd felt cold then, too, although she hoped it wouldn't show through the bright, artificial smile she'd managed to come up with for the photographer.

Better not use up all those smiles too early, she told herself as she rearranged the big skirt and started toward the door. She had a feeling she was going to need a whole lot more of them to get through the rest of the day.

"Oh, my dear, you look a little pale." That was Rodney's old aunt, Lindie, who claimed she hadn't missed a family wedding in sixty-five years and had flown in from

Phoenix at short notice for this one. Rae-Anne had lobbied for a quick ceremony at the registry office, but Rodney had a strong sense of family, and although the Dietrichs seemed to have spread themselves all over the country, a surprising number of them had responded to Rodney's last-minute invitation.

"Just because we planned the wedding in a hurry doesn't mean you don't get a proper welcome into the Dietrich clan," he'd told her, and she'd given in because it was such a novelty to think of being welcomed into anyone's family in such a permanent way.

"Let me dab a little more blush on your cheeks," Lindie was saying now, reaching into her handbag. "Poor Rae-Anne, are you having last-minute jitters? *Everybody* gets them, dear. Just keep taking deep breaths from right down below your diaphragm—like this—" She hauled in a couple of noisy breaths and let them out again in windy sighs. "And you'll be all right," she finished. "Of course—"

Lindie craned her long neck toward the door in a pose that reminded Rae-Anne suddenly, hilariously, of the way Rodney's old hunting dog looked whenever she remembered the bird-chasing glories of her long-ago youth. *I can't laugh,* Rae-Anne thought. *If I start to laugh, it'll be all over.* She started to rub her nose, thinking the gesture might ward off the half-hysterical giggle inside, but then she remembered the fancy makeup job the hairdresser's assistant had applied this morning and stopped herself just in time.

"Of course, if you want company in the limo after all, I'd be more than happy to go with you," Lindie was saying. "I think the driver's waiting out there now, so we could just—"

"Thanks, Lindie, but I'd really rather go by myself." Rae-Anne spoke quickly, wondering why her heart was beating so hard all of a sudden. She could feel it at the base of her throat like a finger tapping insistently on her collarbone.

"I understand, dear. I'm sure your parents would have been so proud to be here today, but as it is—"

Rae-Anne didn't want to talk about her parents. Her mother had died five years earlier in a plane crash while hopping from one high-powered diplomatic assignment to the next. And her father had been dead since Rae-Anne was three, victim of a disease that might have been cured in time if the family had been living in a country where the medical technology to save him had been available.

Rae-Anne clasped the little heart-shaped locket she wore around her neck—a gift from her father on her third birthday—and fought off a wave of bitterness at the way her mother's career had always had to come first. It had robbed Rae-Anne of so much in those early years.

She squeezed the little locket harder, and then let it go, telling herself this was no time to indulge old resentments.

Someday she would pass this locket on to a child of her own—a child who would be raised with love and respect, never shunted aside or made to feel second-best.

But before that happy day arrived, Rae-Anne had a wedding to get through. And if she was going to get her nerves and her thoughts under some kind of control before she walked up the aisle, she knew she needed to be alone.

But if Aunt Lindie thought she wanted to be alone in the limo to think about her parents, so be it. Rae-Anne was willing to do whatever she had to to make this trip to the church by herself.

"It's okay," she said, ushering the little henna-haired woman gently but firmly toward the door. "If you go with Renee and Abel, you can help them carry the flowers in when they get to the church. And I'll be right behind you in the limo. All right?"

It was a little like urging a benevolently drunken patron out the door after last call, she thought. Lindie talked all the way to the front steps, and then only got going because Renee was waving at her and Abel was honking the horn.

Rae-Anne waved at them and watched the photographer's van follow Renee and Abel's station wagon down the long curve of the driveway toward the road. The autumn weather had been dry, and the two vehicles left a tall plume of dust that rose gently into the blue Texas sky.

"Dear Lord," she muttered, inspired by the thought that the dust looked like a prayer wafting heavenward, "if You let me get through the next couple of hours without fainting or being sick, I'd be much obliged to You."

She shouldn't be feeling this way, she knew. She should be happy that so many of her barely admitted dreams were beginning to come true. She was marrying a man who loved her, who had pursued her with single-minded devotion for nearly two years. He was offering her things that had been missing from her life for as long as she could remember, things like security, and love, and a family, and a home that was all hers.

Rodney's hill-country ranch house was luxurious, but not lonely like some of the embassy residences where she'd spent her childhood and youth. She should be happy about that fact. She should be lighthearted. But instead, she felt . . .

Trapped.

It was just the dress, she told herself. And the dainty little shoes. And the gloves, and the veil. It was the fact that she'd let Rodney talk her into a dress-up church wedding in the first place. The last time she'd worn elbow-length white gloves had been at an embassy party in Hong Kong when she'd been seventeen. It had made her feel like some kind of fashion doll then, too.

She pulled the front door closed behind her and set the alarm code, pushing the buttons carefully with one gloved fingertip. The gloves were trimmed with delicate seed pearls, and as the afternoon sunlight touched her hand, Rae-Anne wondered why the pearls had suddenly started shimmering.

It took a moment to realize that it was because there were tears in her eyes.

Again.

"Damn it," she muttered. "This is getting worse instead of better."

The long white limo sat implacably next to the bottom step, like an ocean liner she wasn't sure she wanted to board. Rae-Anne was a little surprised that the driver hadn't come to hold the door for her, but she wasn't sorry to have another few seconds in the sunshine to try to warm her chilly hands and collect herself.

"You've gone over and over this, Rae-Anne," she told herself out loud. "What else are you going to do? Hit the road again? Start over in some new place? You've been doing that for so long, and look where it's gotten you. Rodney loves you. He wants to have children with you. You'd be crazy not to go through with this now."

Every time she got to this stage in her chain of reasoning, her stomach gave a horrible lurch of panicky protest. She waited for it now, and clutched her hands over her still-flat belly when she felt it arrive.

This lurch was worse than the last one. Rae-Anne closed her eyes and tried to pull in a long breath of the clear hill-country air.

Her stomach wouldn't let her. Her stomach, in fact, seemed to have gone on strike completely a couple of days ago, and all of Rodney's coaxing and Rae-Anne's own common sense hadn't been able to get it to eat or calm down or do any of the things it was supposed to do.

"Fine," she said now. "*Be* jittery, then. Aunt Lindie says that's what's supposed to happen, and Aunt Lindie's clearly been to enough weddings that she ought to know."

Without waiting for the driver any longer, she negotiated the four shallow steps between her and the waiting limo and opened the rear door for herself.

The car was about the size of a regulation football field. Inside, it was dim and cool. The air-conditioned breeze pumping out of the vents near the windows immediately canceled out the soothing warmth of the sunshine outside.

"Do you think you could turn the air-conditioning down, please?" she asked, leaning forward so the driver could hear her.

That was good, she thought. Her voice had sounded firm, almost as though she really *was* the same Rae-Anne Blackburn who'd always prided herself on her ability to fend for herself, on her independence and her certainty.

The trouble was, one of the things she'd been most certain about was that she was never going to settle down until she met the man of her dreams.

And yet here she was, doing just that.

"Oh, hell," she said, and felt the treacherous tears starting to spill over again.

"Ma'am?"

The driver thought she'd been speaking to him, she realized. She cleared her throat and leaned forward a little, wishing the stays at the sides of her bodice didn't cut into her ribs as she moved.

"Let's get moving," she said, trying for the authoritative tone she'd managed a moment ago. "You know which church it is, right?"

That was better. Her voice hadn't quivered at all that time.

But she was still cold, although the driver had adjusted the control on the dashboard. She was about to walk up the aisle with the man she'd promised to marry, and it was all she could do to hold back her tears.

The worst part was that she knew exactly why.

It was because of Wiley Cotter.

Rae-Anne had learned early in her life that it didn't pay to pin too much on your dreams, especially if those dreams depended on other people. But there were a few secret hopes that she'd hugged in the secret recesses of her heart all these years.

She had always hoped that someday she would meet a man who would stir her body and soul in a way too powerful to resist. She hoped that after so many years of restless traveling, she would find a place that felt like home. And— assuming dreams number one and two were possible—she had a deeply buried hope that someday she might be a mother to children of her own in a way that her own mother had failed to be to her.

Well, Wiley Cotter had taken care of the first requirement in a way more spectacular than Rae-Anne had ever even let herself imagine.

And then, instead of turning magically into Mr. Right, he'd become Mr. Disappearing Act. And even before he'd vanished from her life, he'd made it very clear that he wasn't the man to fulfill the rest of Rae-Anne's secret hopes.

Rodney was. Rodney had always wanted children. And he was as settled and secure on his ancestral hill-country property as it was possible to be.

But Rodney had never turned her heart to pure flame the way Wiley Cotter had once done. And *that* was why she had cold feet—hell, cold everything—on her wedding afternoon.

Wiley was dead, and there was no use thinking about him now. But her mind kept confronting her with thoughts of that tall, lanky, heart-stoppingly handsome Texan who'd swept her heart away, with memories of the way his laugh could fill a whole room. And in spite of everything, in spite of the fact that she was about to become Mrs. Rodney Dietrich and a respectable and wealthy hill-country matron, Rae-Anne couldn't stop thinking about the way Wiley had made love to her, wicked as sin and as sweet and hot as her wildest dreams.

The limo was passing the tall limestone gates now, and gliding onto the road that led to New Braunfels, five or six miles away. Rae-Anne settled herself against the upholstered back seat and tried to clear her mind of Wiley's ghost, the way she'd tried to clear it in the early days of pain and grief when she'd first heard he was dead.

She wanted to arrive at the church composed and confident and untroubled by any of the unhappiness in her past. That was why she'd needed this last ride by herself, away from Aunt Lindie and all the other well-wishers who thought it was just wonderful that dear Rodney had finally chosen a bride. She took in as deep a breath as the restrictive bodice would allow and tried to calm the fluttering in the middle of her body.

It wasn't working. As the limo started to pick up speed on the winding road, Rae-Anne clutched her hands together in sudden panic. *It's too late now,* she thought. The words hit her hard, compounding the chill she was feeling inside.

Was she really doing the right thing? Wouldn't it have been better to be completely honest with Rodney, to say, "We like each other, but that's not enough"?

She could still do it. They weren't married yet. It would cause a stir, but it wouldn't be the end of the world. She could be free again to live her own life, with those improbable dreams of hers hidden but still intact. She could be her own woman, as she'd always been.

Except that that wasn't possible anymore.

The answer came from inside her almost as if the new life forming in her belly had heard her thoughts and disagreed with them. It wasn't anything as tangible as a small body stirring, not this early in her pregnancy. But she could feel *something,* some certainty that she wasn't alone in this body of hers anymore, that she would never quite be her own woman again, because there would be this child to share herself with.

And at that thought, all her wild ideas about cutting loose and running evaporated into the still-cool air inside the limousine. Rodney Dietrich might not be the man of her dreams, but it was still his child she was carrying, and he was offering—gladly, eagerly—a home and a family for the baby to be born into. No amount of dreaming about Wiley Cotter could ever provide that.

And Rae-Anne was determined that her child would never know the constant uncertainty and uprooting of her own childhood. She pressed both gloved hands over her stomach again and wondered if it was just her overexcited imagination that made her think she felt an answering flutter under her quivering fingertips.

"You're a bit young yet to be a ring bearer," she murmured. "But we'll go up the aisle together just the same."

She smoothed her hands over the white expanse of the skirt, feeling the swirling patterns of the seed pearls under her fingertips. She felt a little calmer now, or at least she did until the driver's voice startled her.

"Did you say something, ma'am?"

Rae-Anne lifted her head suddenly. The driver's voice was deep and husky, with a slow drawl in it.

Of *course* it reminded her of Wiley, she told herself. He'd been lurking in her thoughts all week, inviting himself in, making himself hard to forget, the way he'd done when she'd first met him. It was no big mystery that men she didn't even know were starting to sound just like him.

Still . . .

Rae-Anne frowned and tried to get a look at the driver's face in the rearview mirror.

She couldn't. The limo was too long, and she was stuck at the very back of it, miles from the driver with the sexy drawl.

"I was just muttering to myself," she said. "I do that, when I get worked up about something."

"Yeah, I know."

She must be losing her grip, she thought. She was almost sure she heard him snort, a familiar, earthy sound that had her heart pounding before she realized it.

She was almost sure she saw the edge of his profile quirk upward in the kind of lazy, tilted smile that sometimes got into her dreams.

She was less sure—but not completely unconvinced—about his muttered answer.

I know.

That was exactly what it had sounded like.

She made herself sit still for a few minutes, but her curiosity kept building, especially when she remembered that there'd been some last-minute snafu about the car. Some change of limousine companies, or something.

She hadn't paid much attention, because Rodney and his assorted aunts and cousins had seemed happy to take over all the details of running the hastily planned wedding. It was

Aunt Lindie who had sorted out the last-minute misunderstandings, like the flowers being delivered a day early and no one thinking to tell the restaurant that the groom's godmother was allergic to seafood.

But now she wished she'd been a little more attentive to the arrangements about the limo. There was something funny about switching companies at this late date, wasn't there? And why did the dark-haired chauffeur seem to be taking such care that she didn't get more than just a glimpse of his profile? She slid sideways on the wide back seat, trying to get a better look at the man behind the wheel.

"Are you sure this is the right way?" she asked sharply. "I don't recognize this road."

"It's a shortcut."

The driver muttered the words, as if he didn't want her to hear him clearly. And he was keeping his head tilted so she couldn't see him, either.

They were still cruising through the open, scrubby landscape of the hill country, but this wasn't the main road into New Braunfels. They must have made a turn while RaeAnne was too preoccupied to notice. The realization kicked her nerves into high gear again, and her imagination started churning out all kinds of alarming possibilities.

She was about to marry an extremely wealthy man. She remembered the elaborate security procedures she'd lived with as the daughter of a diplomat, all the warnings about not making herself a target, not taking any chances. Dear Lord, she thought, what if some idiot had read the announcement of her wedding and decided that absconding with her would be a good way to make a quick million bucks?

The word *kidnap* spun into her thoughts before she'd realized the idea was even there.

She leaned forward again, silently cursing the formfitting gown she was fastened into. If there *was* something going on—if she had to give a description of the man—

He had a map out, she noticed. The sight of it brought her fears even more sharply into focus. Didn't limo companies hire people who knew their way around? Suddenly all her prewedding uncertainty magnified itself into a sense of dread, a feeling that she had gotten herself into a place she really didn't want to be. Without realizing she'd done it, she put her open hands over her stomach again, hugging the invisible new life inside her with sudden, protective strength.

She looked at the door handle closest to her right hand and wondered what would happen if she jumped out of the car. They were going at least forty miles an hour. Was it an impossibly dangerous idea for a pregnant woman to be entertaining? And even if it wasn't, how far was she likely to get, wearing this tight-fitting white dress with its outrageously long skirt and train, and shoes that were made for tiptoeing, not running?

The idea didn't appeal to her. She was stuck, trapped in a Titanic-size limousine with a man who was being extremely careful that she didn't get so much as a glimpse of him.

Well, there was always the direct approach. Rae-Anne could be tactful when the occasion called for it, but this one didn't seem to. As clearly as she could, she said, "How far are we from the church?"

He didn't answer her. She repeated the question, but it was like talking to a stone statue.

Rae-Anne felt panic starting to erode her nerves again. *Think, Rae-Anne,* she told herself. *Don't lose your head.*

The direct approach had failed, and leaping out of the car seemed foolhardy at best. She was going to have to try something else.

Wherever they were, they were following a fairly straight road at the moment, and it wasn't hard to keep her balance as she got to her feet. She wished she had something more practical on her feet than these fairy-tale slippers, but even with the slight swaying of the car from side to side, she managed to reach the small jump seat directly behind the open partition without having to cling to the door handles for support. The rustling of the layers of crinoline under her wide skirt sounded harsh and dry as she moved.

She saw the driver's head flick upward and realized he'd seen her approaching in the rearview mirror. She didn't like the sudden tightening of the corner of his mouth or the quick *thunk* of the automatic door locks closing.

But at least she wasn't just sitting at the back of the car feeling as though she was stuck in the end zone while the play was going on at the other end of the field. Rae-Anne had always hated sitting and waiting for things to happen, and at least now she'd done something, even if she wasn't sure where it might lead.

Finally she got what she'd been after—a good look at the driver's face. And without warning her whole world split apart around her.

He turned around only briefly, after negotiating a steep turn and easing the limo into another long stretch of road on the other side of it. The countryside was getting less and less familiar, and Rae-Anne was certain that they were nowhere near New Braunfels and that something was going on that she didn't understand and couldn't control.

But all those mysteries faded away as the driver met her eyes and she found herself caught and held in the darkly suggestive glare of the man she had loved and mourned as dead a decade ago.

Chapter 2

He should have found a way to do this more gradually, Wiley thought. He should have eased into it with a comment or two, maybe a suggestion that she should get herself ready for a shock. He didn't like the sudden pallor of her face, or the way her blue eyes had gone wide and unblinking. She looked as though she'd retreated inside herself and might not come back out.

He growled a soft expletive and turned back to the road. He hadn't exactly had a lot of time to practice being a limo driver, and it was trickier than he'd imagined to maneuver the long vehicle around these little hill-country turns and hollows.

And he'd had shock of his own to deal with, damn it.

He'd been trying to get to see Rae-Anne for the past several days, but the Dietrich place was a virtual fortress—that's what came of having all that money, he supposed—and crawling with relatives and guests, as well. Even Wiley's carefully timed attempt at posing as a florist's deliveryman hadn't gotten past the eagle-eyed old lady who seemed to have appointed herself keeper of the castle.

It was lucky Wiley had had the benefit of the FBI's contacts in San Antonio. Getting himself hired as a limo driver at the last minute had taken a lot of string-pulling, but the bureau had finally managed it. He'd barely had time to find a uniform that fit his oversize frame, to check out a couple of usable escape routes and to rehearse a few carefully chosen phrases for getting his message across to Rae-Anne.

And his very first sight of her knocked him speechless.

In her wedding dress, she was straight out of his most secret fantasies. The small pearls on the bodice glittered in the sunlight as she stepped out of the house, and Wiley caught his breath, hard, at the way the design outlined the body he remembered so well.

The dress left her shoulders bare, revealing skin that was still unimaginably fair and smooth. The way the lacy veil swirled around her made Wiley weak in the knees. He could almost *feel* the gentle brush of it across her arms and back. He'd touched Rae-Anne Blackburn's skin so many times himself, his own fingers as feather-light as the gossamer lace of that veil, all his senses lost in wonder that such a strong and stubborn woman could turn so soft and responsive in his arms.

Her eyes seemed wider, bluer than they ever had. Maybe it was because of the way she wore her hair. She'd usually pulled it into a ponytail or a loose braid when he'd known her, and it was strange to see her thick, exuberant auburn mane disciplined into a tight French braid. The pearl-edged combs that held it in place didn't soften the formal style much. Wiley had felt an urge in his fingertips to let her hair loose, to see its highlights glistening gold in the afternoon sunlight.

Her hairstyle wasn't the only thing that startled him. He recognized the quiet, mutinous look in her eyes, too, the look that meant Rae-Anne wasn't happy with something.

He knew that look so well—knew *all* her expressions and moods so well, he thought, although it had been ten years since they'd seen each other. Did Rodney Dietrich realize there was something troubling his bride on her wedding morning? Did Rodney have any idea how restless and complicated and maddening Rae-Anne could be when she put her mind to it?

Wiley had been so intent on the logistics of getting to speak to Rae-Anne alone that he hadn't foreseen his jealousy taking over like this. Maybe Rodney Dietrich *did* know those things. Maybe Rodney was the man Rae-Anne had been waiting for, after all. Maybe she was only looking troubled because she was worried about the caterer screwing up or some damn thing.

It wasn't until they were well clear of the ranch house that he'd had himself under control enough to turn and face her. And even then it didn't work quite the way he'd planned.

"I know this is kind of a surprise, honey," he said, keeping his eyes on the road. "But it's important, or I wouldn't be doing this to you."

He waited, but she didn't answer. In the rearview mirror he could see her impossibly blue eyes, looking for all the world as though some kind of magic spell had frozen them into that wide-open stare.

He plunged ahead, because he couldn't imagine what else to do. "If you'll pardon my saying so, you haven't exactly been looking like the picture of a blissful bride back there since I picked you up," he said. "Are you sure you really want to marry this guy, Rae-Anne?"

She finally spoke, but he could barely hear the words. It was only because he saw the slight movement of her lips in the mirror that he caught what she was saying.

"You're supposed to be dead." It was whisper-soft, as if she was speaking to herself. "Wiley—"

Her face had gotten even paler under that fancy makeup job. Wiley was struck by how vulnerable she looked as she folded her arms tightly around herself. "Hey, don't get all faint on me, honey," he said quickly. "I can explain about being dead. But I'd rather wait until I don't have to drive at the same time."

Her silence after he'd spoken was not reassuring. Neither was the fact that when he glanced in the rearview mirror this time, her eyes were closed and she seemed to be swaying more than the car's motion would account for.

"Rae-Anne." His voice was sharp, and her eyes snapped open at the sound of it. "Listen to me. I wouldn't be doing this if it wasn't important. There are some things about Rodney Dietrich that you have to know, and I couldn't find a way to tell you about them before now. If you can hang on just a few more minutes, I'll pull over and we can talk. But it's going to take a few minutes. Okay?"

He saw her nod and reach out a hand for the armrest on the door nearest to her.

"Not thinking of bailing out on me again, are you?"

His words seemed to startle her out of the fog that had settled over her. She frowned and said, "How did you—"

"I saw you thinking about it a while back. I know you, Rae-Anne. You'd jump off a moving train if you discovered it wasn't going where you wanted it to."

Her forehead furrowed slightly, and a little bit of color came into her too-white face. "Damn it, Wiley—"

He turned his attention to the road just in time. He'd chosen this route deliberately because it was seldom used and there would be less chance of the white limousine being noticed here. But the road was also an obstacle course of sudden bends and dips, and Wiley had nearly missed negotiating one of those. With an effort he wrenched his concentration to his driving and away from the distracting, beautiful, bewildered woman sitting just a few inches away from him.

"Save the questions, all right, Rae-Anne?" he muttered, as the limo careened a little too close to the ditch between the road and the rocky hillside. "I've got my hands full at the moment."

Maybe this wasn't happening, Rae-Anne thought.

She closed her eyes again, trying to remember when she'd last eaten a full meal. There'd been so much going on this week—the party at the main hotel with her fellow workers, Rodney's employees in the San Antonio-based chain, then the surprise shower the Dietrich cousins had thrown for her when they'd arrived, and the get-together with the neighbors from the ranches near Rodney's family home. Then there had been dress fittings and all the arrangements about packing up her own apartment so that she would be ready to move in with Rodney next week after their brief honeymoon.

She thought it might have been breakfast yesterday—she dimly recalled Renee fussing over her, and Rodney making careful comments about how she needed to eat. No one besides Rodney and the doctor knew yet that Rae-Anne was pregnant, although it had almost seemed, from Renee's motherly urgings, that the housekeeper might have guessed their secret.

In any event, she'd been subsisting on too little food for what suddenly felt like too long a time. And so she supposed it shouldn't be surprising if she was having hallucinations.

She settled back against the upholstered wall of the stretch limo, her fingers curled around the armrest to keep her steady. Wiley couldn't be here because Wiley was dead. She had conjured him up from the depths of her imagination, from the longings that should have died with him but hadn't. If she'd eaten more, if she'd been less distraught, this wouldn't be happening.

In a moment she would see the broad limestone church in New Braunfels appearing ahead of her, with Aunt Lindie waving from the steps, telling her to hurry. All she had to do was sit in this surprisingly gentle haze and wait for the world around her to start making sense again.

It was almost calming to watch the familiar hill-country scenery rolling past the windows, with the live oak trees tossing lazily in the autumn breeze and the hot sun beating down on the dry grass and the prickly pears that dotted the landscape. It was by far the most soothing thing that had happened to her for weeks, and even if it was just a hallucination—

"Rae-Anne?"

She realized with a start that the limo had stopped. She focused her eyes with an effort, and saw that the vision of Wiley Cotter's face hadn't disappeared. He was leaning toward her through the open door next to her, holding out his hand.

"Come on," he was saying. "You look like a ghost. Some fresh air will do you good."

She started to argue with him, started to tell him that *he* was the ghost, not her. But somehow the effort of speaking was just too great. She took the hand he was offering her, startled by its warm, living strength as his fingers curled around hers.

"I should have had breakfast." She murmured the words as she got cautiously to her feet. "Or dinner."

"Is *that* why you're so damn pale?" Wiley didn't sound like a ghost, or feel like one, either. It was all too absurd, though, too impossible, for Rae-Anne to believe it was really happening.

But then, as she stepped clear of the limousine, her wobbly knees buckled on her, and she felt herself suddenly being gathered into the strong circle of Wiley Cotter's arms.

And then she had to believe he was real.

There was nothing on earth that had ever come close to the way she felt when she was close to Wiley. Even his tailcoat and white shirt couldn't hide the formidable muscles of his upper body, and she almost laughed at the easy way he pulled her against him.

It was so familiar—it was *all* familiar, the sudden lowering of his dark brows and the enticingly masculine scent of soap and skin and the way his long fingers closed around her waist, around her shoulder.

"Wiley—"

His name turned into a question, almost a plea, as she spoke it.

"Shh." He was holding her closer now, smoothing one big palm over her back. She could feel his fingers easing their way over the swirling rows of pearls. The heat of his hand seemed to melt whatever had been keeping her so cold, and the feeling of his cheek rubbing against her temple sent a bolt of awareness straight through her body.

"It's all right." That bear's growl of a voice was as rough as ever, but it had softened to a murmur, and she closed her eyes as the pleasure of hearing it again wrapped itself all the way around her. "You're all right, Rae-Anne. Even brides who *do* eat breakfast tend to get a little wobbly, I'm told."

She was trying to rally her wits, but it was simply too sweet to be standing here with Wiley in the breezy afternoon sunshine with no sound around them but the rustling of leaves and grasses in the warm wind.

Wiley was alive. The thought was finally beginning to sink in. *Wiley Cotter was alive, and holding her in his arms.* She took a deep breath, feeling her whole frame shudder with it. At some point she had wrapped her arms around his waist, and she found herself holding on as though she'd been drowning and Wiley was her only hope of rescue.

And then reality hit her, all at once and with nothing to cushion it.

She hadn't been drowning. She'd been on her way to get married.

And Wiley had waylaid her, for some reason he still hadn't bothered to explain.

Back in New Braunfels—wherever the heck New Braunfels was from here—Rodney and seventy-five of their friends and his family were waiting for Rae-Anne to show up so the ceremony could begin. And she was standing in the middle of nowhere in her wedding dress, clinging with undeniable pleasure to a man who was supposed to be dead.

"Wiley." Her voice was stronger this time, and she managed to lift her head without feeling as though it might whirl right off her shoulders. "You've got to let me go. We've got to get back—"

She could feel the reluctance in the way he eased his grip. Was it her imagination, or did he linger before sliding his face away from hers? Was it possible that the gentle sensation she felt at her temple—hardly more than the touch of the breeze—was his lips touching her skin, lightly, fleetingly, before he stepped away?

Rae-Anne felt her heart pounding at her collarbone again, the way it had just before she'd forced herself into the limo at the ranch house. Her thoughts were clearing finally, although her limbs were far from steady and she wasn't quite ready to let go of Wiley's supporting hand as he led her to a bench she hadn't noticed before.

They were in some kind of picnic area, she realized. There was another car here, too—a blue sedan—but it appeared to be empty.

"Have a seat," Wiley was saying. "Let me see what I can salvage from breakfast."

She wasn't sure what he meant, and her efforts to figure it out were sabotaged by a sudden vision of how the two of them must have looked as they crossed the sunny paved area by the side of the road. Rae-Anne's pearl-encrusted dress was eye-catching enough on its own, and with Wiley taking her arm, standing tall and handsome as ever in his tailored morning coat and crisp white shirt, she knew they must look like some kind of fairy-tale prince and princess, or at the very least a brand-new bride and groom pausing on their way to their honeymoon.

The contrast between that and the reality of the situation made Rae-Anne want to laugh, or cry, or both. She closed her eyes as she settled herself on the wooden bench and waited to see what Wiley had meant about breakfast.

"Feeling any better?" He was back almost immediately with a thermos bottle and something in a fast-food wrapper. "This might help. I think it's even still cold—I squeezed it fresh before I left this morning."

The thermos was half-full of orange juice, and after an initial lurch from her stomach, Rae-Anne discovered that she was actually hungry after all. She took a sip of the juice and frowned as Wiley held out his other offering.

"Half a breakfast biscuit probably isn't as fancy as what Rodney had lined up as a wedding dinner," he was saying, "but maybe it'll put some color in your face, if you can eat some."

Rae-Anne did, and was surprised at how good it felt. *You're not just feeding yourself—you're feeding the baby now, too,* she could hear Rodney telling her. She took another bite and a second sip of orange juice, and felt the world coming into focus more reliably this time.

Things had seemed unfocused for weeks, ever since her discovery that in spite of the precautions she and Rodney had taken during their occasional lovemaking, she had managed to become pregnant. Everything had happened so fast after that—first Rodney's insistence that they should get married, then the whirlwind wedding plans and the whole new future she had suddenly found herself facing.

And now this.

By the time she had finished the orange juice and polished off Wiley's leftover breakfast, she was feeling strong enough to deal with the unexpected sight of her lost lover and with the oversize force of his personality. Her mind seized on his last comment, about Rodney and dinner.

"Rodney was offering me a lot more than just dinner," she pointed out. "He probably still is, come to that. And I intend to take him up on it. How far is it to the church?"

Wiley shook his dark head. "We're not going to the church until you've listened to what I have to tell you."

"The hell we're not." It was amazing how much better she was feeling, she thought. Was it just the sudden boost in her blood sugar, or something else? "You have no right to derail my life like this, Wiley—no right at all."

"I'm not derailing it. I'm helping you get it back on track."

"By making me miss my own wedding?"

"By opening your eyes about the man you were going to marry."

He stood up again, tall and imposing in his tailored suit. Rae-Anne watched as he tossed the fast-food wrapper into the nearest trash can and screwed the top on the thermos. Her frown turned to puzzlement as he began closing and locking all the doors of the limousine, ending with the driver's side. His final gesture before slamming the last door was to toss his uniform cap onto the front seat, raking his free hand through his thick dark hair as he did it.

She knew that gesture of his so well. It meant he was restless and uncertain but determined not to let anyone know it.

Rae-Anne had always been able to see through Wiley's defenses that way, just as he'd seen through hers. It had made them more vulnerable to each other than either one really liked to be. But it had also made them equal partners, evenly matched whether they were making love or wrangling with each other about anything that was handy.

They'd done a lot of both in the few months they'd spent together. And Rae-Anne knew—suddenly, achingly—that *that* was why she was feeling so much clearer and more alive again.

It wasn't the orange juice or the fresh air. It was Wiley. It was the fact that for the first time in what felt like forever, she was facing her natural counterpart, the sparring partner who'd brought out her strengths without even trying, the man who seemed to understand her instinctively and immediately.

And the man who'd broken her heart so that it had never really mended again.

She got to her feet, pleased to note that her knees felt steady and strong this time. "So you won't take me to New Braunfels?" she asked.

"No." He wasn't looking at her as he spoke.

"Fine. I'll get my own ride, then."

She expected him to argue, but he didn't. She expected to hear the heels of his expensive leather boots clunking toward her across the hot pavement of the parking area, but the light rustling of the live oak leaves was the only sound that followed her as she headed for the side of the road.

It was a farm road they'd been following, one of hundreds of narrow, winding routes that crisscrossed the hill country. Some of them were pretty remote, but they all led somewhere eventually, and after a moment's hesitation, Rae-Anne decided that going on would be smarter than going back. She *knew* there was nothing behind them but miles of empty territory, but there might be a town, or at least a ranch, just around the next bend.

So she walked, or tried to. Her satin slippers kept wobbling underneath her, and she knew it wouldn't take long before they started raising blisters on her feet. The pavement, which had felt smooth under the cushioned ride of the limo, turned out to be much rougher than she'd expected. Her ankles kept turning on loose stones she couldn't see under her wide skirt, and more than once she caught herself just before she fell.

But the important thing was that she was free, and moving under her own steam. She gritted her teeth and told herself blisters didn't matter and pushed herself to a slightly faster pace.

It was strange that Wiley still wasn't coming after her in the limo, she thought. She'd been sure he would follow her immediately, but he so far hadn't.

When she reached the crest of the first hill, she turned briefly and looked at the picnic area. Wiley had opened the driver's door of the blue sedan and seemed to be taking off his dark tailcoat before he climbed inside.

The blue car must be his, she realized. He must have left it in this isolated spot, knowing that a long white limousine would be far too easy to spot once the general alarm went out that Rae-Anne had disappeared on the way to her wedding.

She still couldn't imagine why he'd gone to all this trouble, or what his veiled remarks about Rodney had meant. She felt her curiosity building inside her, but the urge to keep moving was even stronger, and as Wiley got into the sedan and slammed the door, she started walking again. The sound of the car engine starting up reached her faintly on the wind that was snaking over the top of the rise.

"Good try, Wiley," she said out loud. "Get me out in the middle of nowhere, figure I'll sit around waiting to see what you do next. You seem to have forgotten a thing or two that you used to know about me."

Talking out loud was a way of taking her mind off the increasing pain in her feet. She'd *known* the slippers were slightly too small, but there hadn't been time to custom-order a pair in the right size. And it hadn't seemed to matter so much when she'd only expected to walk up the aisle in them and to take a single turn around the dance floor.

The thought of all the preparations in New Braunfels prompted her to walk even faster. She would get a ride to a telephone, she thought. The first driver to come by would be bound to stop for her, if only to find out why a bride in full wedding regalia was hiking along the side of a farm road in the middle of the hill country.

The car behind her was getting closer. Rae-Anne closed her hands into fists and realized she was still wearing her elbow-length gloves. Impatiently, she tugged at the fingertips of one of them, feeling suddenly hemmed in by her fancy clothes. Her whole body felt lighter when she had pulled the gloves off and let them fall by the side of the road. If Wiley tried to drag her off, she was going to give him a fight, and that was going to be easier to do without beaded elbow-length interference.

She nearly turned her ankle again, and cursed quietly as she caught her balance. The car behind her slowed, then came on until it was just behind her.

"You issuing a challenge, Rae-Anne?"

She glanced over her shoulder and saw that Wiley was holding her discarded gloves. He was grinning, too, the son of a gun. She turned away from him.

"Because if you are," Wiley went on, "I accept. Why don't you get into the car and we'll talk about it?"

"You must be kidding."

"Actually, I'm very serious."

He didn't *sound* serious. But then, he almost never did. Unless you knew how to listen to him, unless you could see through that mocking exterior of his, it was easy to think that Wiley Cotter was just another urban cowboy, long-legged and glib and out for a good time and not much else.

Rae-Anne knew better—had always known better. For a confused couple of seconds she felt her grip on time slipping away from her, whirling her out of the present and back to the days when she and Wiley had plunged headlong into each other's lives as though yesterday and tomorrow didn't even exist.

His voice was so familiar. And at the very back of it, beyond that ironic tone, beneath that deep rasp that had shocked her into silence when he'd first spoken to her in the limousine, Rae-Anne could hear the same old buried hunger that had always touched and stirred something far, far inside herself.

Oh, God, Wiley, I've missed you . . .

The words spun out of her unconscious mind, leaving an ache behind them that startled her. She forced herself to walk faster, as if she could outdistance the feelings that were starting to wake inside her after all these years.

"Leave me alone, Wiley," she said, as firmly as she could. "You've caused enough problems for me already today."

She thought she heard him snort, but decided to ignore it. If he preferred to discover all over again how stubborn she could be, she was happy to let him do it.

She didn't know how much territory they actually covered, with Rae-Anne striding as steadily on as she could and Wiley just behind her in the blue sedan. She *did* know that by the time she finally heard another engine approaching, her feet were burning with fresh blisters and she was beginning to wonder if anyone ever used this road at all.

It was a pickup truck, a red one. She could see it coming down the slope of the next hill. She hoisted her unwieldy skirt a little higher as she stepped into the middle of the road and raised an arm to flag the truck down.

But it only slowed and gave her a wide berth. It took her a moment to realize that she wasn't the only one waving.

Behind her, Wiley had raised both his hands from the steering wheel in a "what can you do?" gesture that seemed to generate immediate sympathy from the two men in the pickup. Neither of them rolled down their windows, but both grinned at Wiley. One of them even gave him a thumbs-up sign, clearly wishing him good luck.

"You son of a bitch." Rae-Anne stopped walking so suddenly that Wiley had to stomp on the brakes. "What are you trying to do?"

"I'm *trying* to get you to get into the car with me. And I'd appreciate it if you'd do it soon. This is wasting a lot of time." He looked unrepentant.

Rae-Anne's annoyance grew as she listened to him. "Hey, if you've got plans for the day, don't let me keep you," she said. "Me, I only had one thing scheduled, and I'm just interested in getting back to it as soon as I can."

Wiley put the sedan in gear again as Rae-Anne began to walk. "Aren't your feet getting kind of sore?" he asked.

"That's my problem, not yours."

"Oh, yeah, I forgot. You're the one who can always handle any situation she gets into, right?"

She dimly recalled telling him that when they'd first met, one night when she'd had to pacify a couple of noisy drunks at the bar and Wiley had wondered out loud why she hadn't chosen an easier line of work.

"That's right." She muttered another curse as her ankle turned under her, and told herself it wouldn't help if she sprained something and had to resort to standing here, helpless, waiting for the next truck to drive by.

The silence between them was punctuated by the purring of the car engine and the light, irritated tapping of Rae-Anne's slippers against the pavement. The breeze was still whistling by, tugging at Rae-Anne's veil and making her aware of all the finicky little hairpins that were holding her hair tightly in place.

It felt like a long time before Wiley spoke again.

"You work at one of Rodney Dietrich's hotels, right?"

"How do you know that?" She didn't like the feeling that there was a lot going on around her that she hadn't been aware of. Whatever Wiley was doing here, it was clearly part of some larger scheme she knew nothing about.

He headed off her question with another one of his own. "How much has Rodney ever told you about how his first wife died?" he asked.

Chapter 3

He'd caught her, he could tell.

Until now, even when she'd been half-woozy with hunger and shock at the picnic area, she'd been wearing that stubbornly mutinous look he remembered so well. She'd been resisting the idea that Wiley was even here, and refusing point-blank to listen to what he was saying.

But now he'd touched something in her that looked like genuine interest. She didn't stop walking, but her voice sounded less defiant.

"He doesn't talk about Danielle much," she said slowly. "Why are you asking?"

He cleared his throat. Somehow he hadn't expected this would be so difficult.

But then, Rae-Anne had never wanted things sugarcoated. And maybe there wasn't a way to sugarcoat this particular piece of news, anyway. "There's a certain amount of evidence to suggest that Danielle Dietrich's death wasn't exactly an accident," he said.

She frowned but didn't say anything, and Wiley went on. "How much do you know about how Rodney's hotel business is financed?"

Once again he saw the slight flicker in her blue eyes that betrayed her interest, in spite of the impatience in her voice. "I wish you'd stick to one subject at a time," she told him.

"It's the same subject. Rae-Anne, Rodney's not just the well-to-do good old boy he seems to be. He inherited a lot of money when he was twenty-one, but he lost it all in some real estate venture that went wrong—"

"He's told me about that," she said quickly. "It wasn't his fault. His partner walked out on him and took all the money along."

"I know. The point is, he took over running his family's hotel chain when he had no more money of his own. And then he expanded the business too far, too fast, and ended up scrambling for financing when times suddenly got tighter again."

He waited, feeling a little hypnotized by the way Rae-Anne's veil was floating out behind her. Her strides were angry and determined, but the veil kept catching the rhythm of her body and translating it into a gentle, wafting motion.

That was Rae-Anne all over, Wiley thought—taut and confident and ready to fight on the one hand, and almost magically gentle on the other. She was the most maddening combination of toughness and vulnerability he'd ever encountered.

"What are you telling me, Wiley?" she demanded.

"I'm telling you that your fiancé only salvaged his business empire by letting the mob into it in a big way."

He couldn't tell if her silence was due to shock or to the fact that she was thinking hard. Her fine auburn brows had drawn together, and he wondered if his words were making more sense to her than she was willing to admit.

"And I'm also saying that Rodney's first wife, Danielle, got wind of what he'd done and didn't like it. When she challenged him on it, and threatened to divorce him and claim half their assets in a settlement, she just happened to die accidentally. The divorce claim would have exposed his real source of income, and Rodney couldn't risk that."

"I don't believe it." Her words were quick.

"I think you do."

He knew he was right when he saw her pace falter slightly, as though she suddenly couldn't decide whether she wanted to keep walking. He could see the struggle going on inside her and could almost feel the effort of will that kept her moving ahead.

He'd only caught a glimpse of her shoes when she'd come down the broad stairs from the front door of the ranch house, but he was pretty sure they weren't doing her feet any good on this rough road. And she'd been close to fainting half an hour earlier. The fact that she was still moving at all was proof of just how tenacious she could be.

But she was smart as well as stubborn—smart enough, Wiley hoped, that she'd already been entertaining a doubt or two about the man she'd been going to marry.

"I think you've been wondering about this, Rae-Anne," he told her. "Otherwise you would be telling me I was full of hot air and you'd be obliged if I'd just drive off a mountaintop at the first opportunity. Right?"

The exquisitely fair skin of her forehead creased into a frown. "I don't know why you're not dead like you're supposed to be, Wiley, but if you've been this irritating to everybody over the past ten years, it's a wonder *somebody* hasn't tried to kill you."

"Oh, people have tried."

And nearly succeeded, he didn't add. It had been an attempt on his life that had forced him away from Rae-Anne in the first place, but this wasn't the time or the place to be talking about that. Until she was clear of Rodney Dietrich, there was no possible point to discussing their past or imagining that they might have any kind of a future.

"How about a guy named Ellis Maitland?" he asked. "Did you happen to know him?"

"Of course I knew Ellis. He was one of the courtesy van drivers for the hotel chain."

"Then you know that he met with a little accident not long ago."

"It wasn't just a little accident, Wiley. He died, for heaven's sake."

"Do you know how?"

"He was fishing." She sounded less than certain about it. "A big wave swept him off a pier, I think."

"Well, that's the official guess, anyway." Wiley eased his foot down a little lower on the gas pedal to keep up with Rae-Anne's quicker steps. She seemed to be trying to outpace what he was saying, and he was inclined to take that as another sign that she suspected he might be right about all of this.

"Would it surprise you to learn that old Ellis was working for the mob as well as for Rodney?" he asked. "Or that his real job, under cover of driving that courtesy van, was to pick up illegal gambling cash from mob runners and get it to Rodney, who's in charge of laundering it through a network of bank accounts he's set up? Ellis got nailed for a moving violation a while ago, and decided that rather than take a chance on going to jail, he would testify about what went on at Rodney's hotels. And then—what do you know? He has an accident on a fishing pier."

"Money laundering?" She seemed to be testing the words out, asking herself whether they made sense.

"That's right. That's Rodney's *real* job, honey. That's what he does for his silent partners in exchange for all the money they pumped into his hotels. All Rodney really wants is to go on leading that hill-country-gentleman existence of his, and he's willing to do whatever it takes—"

"Stop it!" She stopped and turned on her heel suddenly. "I don't know why you're doing this, Wiley, but I don't want to hear any more."

He'd expected anger from her, and resentment, and opposition. He hadn't expected the anguish he saw in her face, or the desperation that had shot through her words.

And he didn't understand why she was wrapping her arms so tightly around her rib cage. It almost looked as though she was in physical pain. Her face had gone pale again, pale enough that even through the porcelain finish of her makeup he could see a faint hint of the freckles that had always dotted her cheeks and the bridge of her nose, a legacy, she'd once told him, of her red-hair-and-freckles youth.

At least she didn't look as though she was going to keel over. But this was almost worse. She looked, he realized suddenly, as though she'd been pushed to some limit he hadn't known was there, or maybe a little beyond it.

The thought was disturbing. Had he been misreading her after all? He'd been so certain he was touching on doubts that had already formed in her mind, so certain that he was doing the right thing in opening her eyes about Rodney Dietrich. But her posture, tight and held-in and defensive, made him think there might be something in this whole situation he'd missed.

He pulled the car quickly to the side of the road and cranked on the hand brake. "How far are you intending to walk in that getup?'' he demanded, as he got out of the driver's seat.

She looked at her fairy-tale white skirt. When she met his eyes again, he was shocked to see that the tiny pearls on her dress weren't the only things glistening in the sunlight. There were tears in Rae-Anne's eyes, making her look younger and more frightened than he'd known she could be.

He'd never seen her cry. The realization shook him. He'd seen her furious plenty of times, and breathless with passion, and engulfed in laughter. But the helpless expression on her face wasn't one he'd ever associated with Rae-Anne Blackburn.

''Rae-Anne, I'm sorry.'' He started across the road but paused. The tight, protective way she was holding herself was somehow like a physical barrier between them, warning him away. ''I still think you need to hear all this. My God, honey, you can't possibly want to marry a man who's capable of doing half of what Rodney's done. He's involved with some very dangerous people, and I just don't want to see you stumble into the middle of a situation you don't understand.''

She didn't answer right away. The tears in her eyes trembled slightly but didn't fall. Wiley could tell how hard she was working at holding them back. The breeze was still lifting her veil gently to one side, tossing it up and down, the way someone might lift a baby's hand to teach it to say goodbye. The motion looked forlorn, almost mournful.

Wiley shook his head. Where the hell had that image come from? He didn't usually indulge in fanciful thinking, and he certainly didn't intend to say goodbye to Rae-Anne this time until he was absolutely certain she was safe and happy.

''You haven't given me a single shred of proof about any of this,'' she said finally.

"I will."

"When?"

"As soon as we get to somewhere a little more comfortable."

"What if I don't want to go?"

"What are you planning to do instead?"

She looked around her. They were halfway up the long slope of a hill, with cattle pasture on both sides of them. One of the ranchers had been cutting deadwood and piling it up next to the fence, and the tall stack of weathered gray roots and branches seemed to catch Rae-Anne's eye for a moment.

In the distance Wiley could hear the sound of a cow lowing, and an even more distant one answering. He'd never been wild about the countryside, having spent far too much of his childhood staring out the window at it, wondering when the better future his parents had promised him was ever going to arrive.

But he knew Rae-Anne loved the Texas landscape, especially the hill country. He saw her blue eyes scanning the tree-dotted fields and the long curve of road ahead, and wondered if she was trying to think of a way to fade into the scenery, free of Wiley and the questions he'd raised.

Before she could answer his most recent question, though, Wiley caught the grinding noise of an engine laboring up the far side of the hill. Rae-Anne's face lit up with renewed hope as she heard it, too.

"That'll be my ride," she said, with more energy. "And about time, too. Excuse me, would you, Wiley?" She stepped farther away from him, into the very center of the road.

"Rae-Anne..."

She didn't answer, but kept her gaze on the crest of the hill.

"Rae-Anne, I'm not sure climbing into a truck with some stranger is a great idea."

"It's not your problem. And if you hadn't given those guys in the last truck the high sign, I'd have gotten a ride and been on my way to a telephone right now."

He felt a sudden tug of panic somewhere deep inside him. She wouldn't just walk away on him, would she? After all they'd once meant to each other, after the disturbing scenario he'd just outlined for her—

But that seemed to be what she intended to do. Wiley didn't want to have to drag her bodily into his car if he could avoid it. But he'd be damned if he was going to let her disappear into the sunset, either, just because she didn't like what he was saying.

There had to be some middle ground, something between brute force and quiet submission. And suddenly Wiley knew what it was.

"Sorry about putting the kibosh on that last ride for you, honey," he said, making his voice sound as unconcerned as possible. "I was just reminding those guys of the cowboy's code of honor. You know—never mess with another man's woman."

He saw her blue eyes flash and felt a sense of relief that she'd gotten past the helplessness he'd glimpsed a moment ago. He hadn't known what the hell to do with that new, unexpected side of Rae-Anne. But this one—the spitfire, the scrapper—was as familiar to him as his own face in the mirror.

"I am *not* your woman!" She flicked her billowing veil out of her way with one hand as she answered him. "And I've waited tables and tended bar in enough little joints to know all about cowboys, thank you."

"Then you should have realized that folks around here aren't given to interfering in each other's business." Wiley moved to his car and leaned against the hood with his arms crossed, looking just as casual as he could. "Although if you want to try again, I guess that's up to you."

The truck he'd heard approaching had cleared the top of the hill, and the driver was slowing down as he took in the sight of Rae-Anne in her wedding dress waving at him from the middle of the road. Wiley could see the surprise on the rancher's weather-lined face even before the truck had slowed to a halt.

"I need a ride," Rae-Anne was saying. "How far are we from the nearest town?"

"Well, now." The man tipped his hat back from his face and surveyed her from veil to hem. "It's kind of a ways."

"Does that mean a mile? Ten miles?"

"Closer to ten, I'd say."

"Can you take me there?" Wiley saw her eyes flick in his direction, daring him to interfere.

He didn't bother. He just held his pose—resigned, patient, puzzled. The rancher was taking it all in, looking more and more dubious.

"Bit soon to be having a parting of the ways, isn't it?" he wondered out loud.

"We're not married." Judging by the tightness of Rae-Anne's tone, she realized just how unlikely her words sounded to the stranger.

"That so?" The man appealed to Wiley, who shrugged.

"Somebody told me it was bad luck to try to see the bride before she walked up the aisle," he said. "Guess I should have listened."

"Well, I guess so." The driver chuckled, but there was something pitying in the sound. "Your car working okay, mister?"

Wiley nodded. "Car's not the problem," he said, looking significantly at Rae-Anne.

She was looking at him with her blue glare turned up to its full voltage. The setup had worked perfectly—the rancher had come across an arguing couple, apparently newly married or just about to be, and he wasn't about to get into the middle of what was clearly a complicated mess.

"Well, as long as you folks aren't stranded out here, I'd better be getting on," he said.

"Wait a minute—"

"Sorry, ma'am." He touched the brim of his hat in apology. "But this is between the two of you. Hope you get it sorted out."

He eased the protesting gearshift into first and the truck chugged away along the winding road.

Rae-Anne stood looking after it in silence for almost a minute. She seemed to be replaying the scene in her head, trying to figure out whether there was anything she could have done to counteract the impression she and Wiley were bound to leave on people's minds. He saw her look at the wide, glittering skirt of her own gown and shake her head slowly.

"Don't you *dare* say I told you so," she warned him.

Wiley uncrossed his arms and held his hands out palms up. "Am I saying anything?" he asked.

"You're *thinking* it. And you're thinking that the same damn thing is going to happen no matter who comes along this road. And now the sun's starting to go down—"

Her voice faltered a little over her last words, and Wiley felt a renewed twinge of alarm at the sound. He'd spent a lot of time this past week imagining this scene, but it had always featured a Rae-Anne who was as feisty and combative as she'd been when he'd known her ten years ago. The thought that she might be on the verge of falling apart on him was one he wasn't sure what to do with.

But she seemed to have gotten herself in hand, although she'd crossed her arms over her belly again in that protective gesture that seemed so unlike the Rae-Anne he knew. "Do you have anyplace definite in mind to go?" she asked him abruptly.

"Yeah."

She didn't ask for details. He watched her look around at the fields on both sides of the road and saw her frown into the early twilight that made it hard to focus on the scenery around them. Was she actually going to get into his car and come with him?

Not without one last attempt to do it her own way, she wasn't. She started to sigh but suppressed the sound and turned in the direction the pickup truck had come from. With her shoulders set at a square and determined angle and her veil drifting out behind her again like a gentle cloud, she started to walk.

It was nearly ten miles to the next town, the driver had said. It was at least that far to the last settlement they'd passed on their way here, and even ranch dwellings had been few and far between along the route. But Rae-Anne was walking again anyway, seeming determined to keep moving under her own steam if she could.

The problem was that she couldn't. She'd only taken a few steps when he heard a low exclamation of pain, followed by a quiet curse. She paused, then started again. But this time it was clear that she was hobbling awkwardly, and that the cause of it was the pain in her feet.

They must be badly blistered, Wiley thought. She'd covered at least three miles in those ridiculous little fairy-princess slippers on a road that wasn't designed for foot traffic in the first place, unless you were a cow. He couldn't blame her for limping.

He wondered how long she would keep it up. As it turned out, it wasn't long.

She was halfway to the crest of the hill when she turned around. Her expression, or what Wiley could see of it in the quickly dimming light, was defiant.

"Now I know exactly how Cinderella felt just before the clock struck," she said.

Wiley chuckled. This was the Rae-Anne he remembered, all right. He slid into the driver's seat of his car and caught up with her in seconds.

"Will you take me someplace where I can use a phone?" she asked.

"I'll take you someplace where we can finish the conversation we started about Rodney. If you still want to call him when we're done that, you're welcome to."

She considered it, and seemed to decide it was the best she was going to do at the moment. She nodded without speaking, and Wiley was out of the car and striding around to hold the passenger door open for her almost before she had completed the gesture.

"Your coach awaits, your ladyship," he said.

His relief was making him flippant. But he almost wished he could take the words back when he saw the look that crossed Rae-Anne's face. He wondered whether she'd been going up the aisle to meet Rodney Dietrich because she'd hoped he could give her all those fairy-tale things—like love, and contentment, and happily ever after—that Wiley himself had never promised her. If that was the case, his news about Rodney must be hitting her hard.

And Wiley was no more able than he'd ever been to offer promises about anything at all. The only thing he could promise Rae-Anne was his honesty and a ride to where they were going.

And she seemed to know that. Her voice was sharper as she said, "I know this kind of coach, Wiley. It's the one that turns into a pumpkin when you least expect it. Let's get on the road before that happens, all right?"

It took a while for her to fit the folds of her wedding dress into the small space of the car's front seat. Neither of them spoke as she was doing it. Wiley closed the door gently on that creation of lace and satin and pearls and headed to the other side of the car without any idea what was going through Rae-Anne's mind. And they both stayed silent as he got into the driver's seat and drove toward the darkening western sky.

The cabin looked small from the outside, but it had two bedrooms and a huge bathroom behind its log exterior.

"And no phone," Rae-Anne pointed out.

"The phone's in the office. We're supposed to talk, anyway, before you use the phone, remember?"

"I remember."

She didn't sound any too pleased about it, either. She seemed happier about the news that Wiley had brought a change of clothes—"Assuming you're still the same size," he'd told her—and that there was a pair of sneakers as well as some jeans and a T-shirt in the small overnight bag he had stowed in the trunk of his car.

It was disconcerting to think about Wiley standing in a women's clothing store trying to remember the exact shape of her waist and hips, but she didn't tell him that. And she certainly wasn't about to mention the fact that her old size wasn't likely to fit her for too much longer, anyway.

For the moment it was enough to know that she could get out of her wedding dress and into some clothes that would make her feel more like her real self. Darker thoughts about

Rodney kept nudging at her, and so did all her unanswered questions about Wiley's reappearance.

But she'd decided, on that windswept, lonely stretch of farm road, that there was no way she could sort everything out all at once. The smartest thing she could do was to take one step at a time. And the first step involved getting out of her wedding dress.

Unfortunately, as soon as she tried it she discovered that it wasn't something she could manage without help.

The dress had a long row of buttons that ran down her back from mid-spine to below her waist. With her upper body hemmed into the tight bodice and her arms restricted by the short off-the-shoulder sleeves, there was no way she could twist her arms far enough to undo the buttons.

She tried anyway. She contorted herself every way she could think of, and then invented a couple more, but the dress stayed firmly in place. The only thing she accomplished was to come up with some very unkind ideas about what to do with the guy who'd designed the thing in the first place.

Asking Wiley for help was out of the question.

But so was spending the rest of her mortal life trapped in her wedding gown. And the more she thought about herself as a prisoner, the more uncomfortable and fidgety she felt inside the satin-and-pearl casing that Aunt Lindie and Renee had buttoned her into this afternoon.

It would have been much easier to march into the next room and say, "Wiley, I need help," if she hadn't still been fighting off the memory of the way his arms had felt closing around her.

And the scent of his skin.

And the dimple that had creased his tanned face once or twice while he'd been needling her this afternoon. He'd always looked unbearably sexy with that dimple showing. The accompanying dazzle of his smile and the glint in his dark brown eyes had never hurt, either.

How the hell was she supposed to walk out there and ask for his help undressing when her whole body felt invaded by memories that she'd managed to suppress for so long? Wiley's hands on her body... Wiley's dark, devilish grin curving against her bare skin... his hoarse cry of delight as they'd met and joined each other in a passion that had never been matched in Rae-Anne's experience or even in her imagination...

It was impossible. And she couldn't think of any way around it.

She pressed her hands over her belly again and fought for sanity. If Wiley wasn't dead and Rodney wasn't who she'd thought he was, what on earth could she rely on?

The answer came quite calmly out of some hidden corner of her mind. *You can rely on yourself, the same as you always have.* The words were quiet but definite, and she felt herself listening hard, hanging on as hard as she could to this much-needed scrap of wisdom.

She *had* to rely on herself, now more than ever. There was another human being depending on her, counting on her to do the best thing for both of them. It was amazing how the knowledge of that tiny, unformed life inside her was able to cut through her confusion and put her fears into some kind of perspective.

It made it easier to see, for example, that she was going to have to get out of her wedding dress one way or another, and that she had only one option for assistance. Limping badly on feet that had become far more painfully blistered than she'd realized, she went to the front bedroom that Wiley had claimed as his.

"I'm sorry," she said, trying to sound matter-of-fact. "But the plain truth is that this dress just isn't designed for solo operation. It took two people to get me into it, and if I'm going to get out of it again, Wiley, you're going to have to give me a hand."

Chapter 4

Wiley had turned on the lamps around the front room, and the place looked unexpectedly cozy after the darkness outside. The red blanket on the double bed glowed warm in the light, and the carpet on the floor was soft under Rae-Anne's blistered feet.

The look on Wiley's face, though, was anything but soothing. He was giving her a head-to-foot assessment, deliberate and thorough, and his eyes were darkening from brown to nearly black as he looked at her. Rae-Anne felt something inside her responding to the change in him, something primitive that kept getting past all her efforts to prevent it.

"You're sure about this?" he asked slowly.

"Believe me, I'm sure." If she could just hold on to this matter-of-fact tone, she thought, she would be all right. She half turned, sweeping aside her veil so he could see the little row of buttons at her back. "I can't reach these buttons, no matter what."

She let the veil fall again, shivering slightly as its light folds settled themselves over her bare shoulders. "Let's just do it and not talk about it, all right?" she added.

It seemed to take him forever to answer, but maybe that was because of the way time seemed to have slowed down since she'd entered his room. Something strange was happening, Rae-Anne thought, something unsettling, almost magical. She could feel the quiet solitude of the cabin wrapping itself around her like a cloak, closing her in with all the unresolved memories and desires that Wiley's disappearance had left in her life.

It should have been that disappearance, that betrayal of their love, that was uppermost on her mind as she waited for him to come to some kind of decision about helping her with her dress. But it wasn't.

It was the buried hunger in his eyes as she turned to meet his gaze again.

And the way her heart seemed to be beating in unison with the pulse point at the open collar of his white shirt.

Rae-Anne swallowed hard. *Think about Rodney,* she ordered herself. *Think about the fact that you're wearing this wedding dress because you're engaged to another man. Think about why you're engaged to him.*

It should have worked.

But it didn't.

The part of the world that had Rodney in it seemed a million miles away from this isolated cabin. Out there, somewhere, was a storm of questions and decisions and realities that Rae-Anne knew she would have to deal with before long. But right now, right here, none of it seemed to matter.

What *did* matter was the look in Wiley's dark eyes. Was it frustration or desire that she was seeing there? Or, like Rae-Anne herself, was he in the grip of both at the same time, held together by a restless current that was oddly and unexpectedly exciting?

All of those things came through clearly in his voice, cutting through his words as he said, ''Wouldn't it be easier to take the veil off first?''

''Maybe.''

She'd left the veil on because without it her gown suddenly seemed much more daring than she'd intended. The low bodice followed the curves of her breasts in a long, revealing line, and despite the small sleeves, her arms and shoulders were bare.

But Wiley was right about it being in the way. Rae-Anne leaned her head forward slightly and raised her hands to the complicated arrangement of pins and clips that held it in place, wishing her fingers were steadier and her heart wasn't starting to thud at her ribs so insistently.

There was something far too suggestive about removing her veil for Wiley like this. And the suggestion escalated into outright temptation when she realized what he'd really intended.

He'd stepped close to her before she'd seen him move. All of a sudden she felt encircled by him, the way she'd been this afternoon when they'd stepped out of the limo.

''Let me do that,'' Wiley said. His voice was soft and rough, and his fingers, where they curled around her wrists, felt warm and strong.

''I don't think—''

She couldn't get the rest of the words out. It didn't seem to bother Wiley.

''I can see the top of your head, and you can't.'' His words were surprisingly practical, and for a moment Rae-Anne let herself relax a little as he let her arms go and turned his attention to her veil. She would feel calmer, she told herself, as soon as all this wedding paraphernalia was out of the way.

Her moment of relaxation didn't last. Wiley broke it—casually, it seemed—with one of the many questions she didn't feel like tackling this evening.

"So how long have you been engaged to Rodney Dietrich?" he asked, dropping the first pin onto the bedside table at his side.

Rae-Anne swallowed. "Not long," she said.

"But you've known him a while."

It didn't sound like a question. In fact, it sounded suspiciously as though he already knew the answer.

"What makes you say that?" she demanded.

He shrugged, his big shoulders blocking her vision entirely for a moment. "I keep my ears open," he said.

"No kidding." She shifted to try to look him in the eye and winced as one of the pins holding the veil dug into her scalp.

"Hold still," Wiley ordered. "Why can't they just tie these things on with string or something?"

Rae-Anne snorted. "Hardly high fashion," she said. "Monsieur Antoine would not approve."

"That who did your hair?"

"Yes."

"You should have had him check with me first. I'd have told him it doesn't look much like the réal Rae-Anne Blackburn."

Wiley had always done this to her, Rae-Anne remembered with sudden clarity. She'd never been able just to be angry with him, or just disappointed, or just *anything*. He'd always called up too many emotions in her all at once, and he was doing it again now.

She shook her head at him, ignoring his muttered curse as he lost his grip on her veil. She took a couple of steps away from his oversize presence and raised her hands to finish what he'd started.

"I couldn't ask your opinion about my hair," she said pointedly, "for the very good reason that I believed you were dead." How *had* Monsieur Antoine attached this thing, anyway? Rae-Anne felt her fingers shaking with frustration as she tried to find the hidden pins.

Wiley was standing his ground, although she could tell by the set of his shoulders that he wasn't any happier with her line of questioning than she'd been with his.

"We had a date one night about ten years ago," she went on. "You probably don't remember. We were going to go to a movie." She found one of the recalcitrant pins and pulled it free. "I waited for you, but you never showed up. I called your apartment and you weren't there. I called you at work the next day and they wouldn't tell me anything. I couldn't imagine what else to do—"

She was never going to find the final pin at this rate. She made herself stop talking and took a deep breath before she started again.

"I kept calling the DEA until they finally told me you were dead—killed in the line of duty, the guy said. By that time I'd gotten through to your immediate boss, so I figured he would know what he was talking about. I guess I was wrong."

She couldn't keep the bitterness out of her voice. She'd known Wiley's job was dangerous, but somehow she'd never let herself imagine the awful possibility that he might die doing it. And the man she'd talked to had hardly been sympathetic. "It happens," had been his blunt comment, as though it were no big deal that he'd just shattered Rae-Anne's whole world.

And maybe it really *was* no big deal. She'd seen happiness beckoning to her before, only to have it disappear when she reached for it. But with Wiley, she'd really believed her dreams had been coming true at last.

And then they hadn't.

She waited for him to speak, suddenly not trusting her voice. His answer was slow and surprising.

"I didn't know," he said finally. "When you were trying to find out what had happened to me, I was in an intensive-care ward under an assumed name, with a whole lot of knife holes stuck in me."

Rae-Anne drew in a quick breath. She'd always hated this side of Wiley's life, even before it had come between them.

"My boss didn't know who you were," he went on. "Nobody knew I had a girlfriend. And since nobody knew you, and I wasn't around to ask, the boys followed standard procedure in a case where the agent's life is endangered."

She didn't like the official tone that had come into his voice. "In other words, they lied to me," she said bluntly.

"Yeah." She'd expected his usual mocking grin, but his face stayed very serious. "Rae-Anne, I swear to you that if there had been a thing on earth I could have done to keep it from happening, I'd have done it. Hell, I never meant for you to be hurt like that. And when I went looking for you—"

"You looked for me?"

"Of course I did. Looked all over the map. Where the hell did you get to, anyway?"

"I worked as a stewardess on Caribbean cruise ships for a couple of years. It was a way to...keep moving."

"And to keep hidden. By the time I gave up looking for you, honey, I was an expert in missing-persons searches. It was about the only good thing that came out of that whole mess."

Something sudden and hopeful fluttered in Rae-Anne's chest. She tried to tamp it down and concentrated on her veil again instead of on Wiley's dark gaze. She found the last pin and pulled it free. The white mist of the fabric swirling between them was as ghostly and elusive as her memories of the love she and Wiley had shared and lost.

When she met his eyes again, she could almost feel the heat of his gaze. He seemed to be thinking that they might actually salvage something out of the bitterness of the past, some warmth from the fire they'd always ignited in each other. That must be why he'd interrupted her wedding day and carried her off like a knight on a white horse rescuing his lady from a dragon.

For a knight, his timing was rotten. And the dragon he'd snatched her away from was the father of her unborn child and a man she was actually quite fond of.

But Rodney had never made her feel the things Wiley could. And even if there was nowhere for this unlikely rescue attempt to go, it was still exhilarating to know that he *hadn't* just walked away from her coldly, without a second thought. That he'd bothered to look for her after she'd hit the road again.

And that he'd cared enough to come back for her now.

"Wiley," she said, picking her words carefully, "what, exactly, are you doing here?"

He looked at her for a long moment, and she felt the dangerous tug of his gaze drawing them together. *No,* her mind said firmly. *There are too many reasons not to let this happen.* But her body was pulsing unmistakably in places that only Wiley had ever stirred into life.

"At the moment," he said matter-of-factly, "I'm waiting to help you undo those buttons. Or have you changed your mind?"

She almost said yes and fled to the safety of her bedroom. But it wasn't like Rae-Anne to back down. And besides, she really did want to get out of her dress. She took a determinedly deep breath and turned her back to Wiley.

He started briskly at the top of the row, twisting the tiny pearl buttons free of their satin loops. For a minute Rae-Anne hoped that she was the only one feeling any reaction to their closeness, and that Wiley might just finish what he was doing and let her go. But then he paused.

She couldn't tell why. She only knew that his sudden stillness had a charged, erotic quality to it, and that she was startled to realize she'd been letting herself revel in the heat of his hands so close to her skin.

"Something wrong?"

"I don't know."

His voice was a slow growl, nothing more. Rae-Anne held herself very straight, hoping he didn't notice her breathing was quickening.

She wished she could see his face, his hands. He seemed to have paused with one of the buttons half-undone. She could feel his knuckles just barely brushing against the skin of her back, touching her as lightly as her gossamer veil.

"It's been occurring to me," he murmured, "that you can't be wearing much underneath this dress."

"You're right." The huskiness in her voice astonished her. "There's a strapless bra. You'll come to it soon."

"I think I just did."

"Oh."

Rae-Anne had always prided herself on knowing what to say in even the most difficult situation. She could strike up a conversation with almost anyone, defuse a brewing fight with a well-placed word or two, cut to the heart of an argument with sharp-edged clarity.

She never found herself saying *oh* like a blushing school-girl. But Wiley's comment had stopped her.

He stayed still for what felt like an eternity, while the heat at the center of Rae-Anne's body spread until it had touched every part of her. She could tell him to stop, she knew. She could insist that he finish undoing her buttons and let her go, and he would do it.

But she couldn't bring herself to say the words.

He had come back to her. However ill-timed and unwel-come his reappearance was, she couldn't deny her pleasure at knowing he was alive and knowing he cared enough about her to come back. Surely, just for one sweet, stolen mo-ment, she could let herself savor the thousand sensations Wiley sparked in her soul and her body.

It was almost as though he knew what she was thinking. As she drew in another long breath, he let out the breath he seemed to have been holding and eased his fingers slowly inside the edges of her gown.

He found the clasp of her strapless bra on the first try and flicked it open with wordless efficiency. Rae-Anne reached a hand out as though looking for some way to steady her-self, but the only fixed point in her world at the moment was Wiley, silent and absorbed at her back, exploring her smooth skin as though this was a new delight and not one he had discovered a hundred times before.

"Wiley—"

"Shh." His voice was as gentle as his hands. "Don't say anything, honey. Not now."

"We can't—we shouldn't let this happen."

"Are you telling me you honestly want to stop?"

She couldn't say it, not honestly. By the time he'd re-sumed his progress down the row of buttons, Rae-Anne's blood was thundering in her veins, and her knees felt weak for a whole set of reasons that had nothing to do with how much she'd eaten or slept recently.

He'd reached the small of her back now. Rae-Anne closed her eyes, remembering how he'd once kissed her all over, resting his face in that warm, curved hollow and murmuring that he could happily spend all of eternity without ever moving again.

"I have a question for you." His voice was rough at her ear.

Was he going to ask her about Rodney? Rae-Anne felt her body tense slightly, unwilling to let all the complicated realities of her life intrude into this moment of sensuous peace.

"What is it?" she asked. The words wouldn't come out any louder than a whisper.

"I've been looking at you for hours now, Rae-Anne, and I still can't believe how beautiful you are." He raised his hands as he spoke, cradling her shoulders in his palms so gently that she wanted to lean back to feel the warmth of his skin meet hers more fully. "I thought I remembered everything about you—how blue your eyes are, and that little place where your pulse beats at the center of your collarbone, and the way you hold yourself up so straight when you're so tired you want to fall down."

Rae-Anne had given up disguising the quickened pace of her breath. The idea that Wiley had been thinking about her this way was almost as seductive as his hands on her skin.

"But somehow I forgot just how beautiful you really are." He raised one hand, sliding a long forefinger along the soft curve of her jaw and then cupping her chin with gentle possessiveness.

"You said— You had a question." She dredged the words from somewhere.

"I know." His hand swirled over the intricate arrangement of her hair, and then down to the back of her neck. The warmth of it made Rae-Anne's body ache to feel his touch everywhere, arousing her as only Wiley had ever known how to do.

"I was just wondering—whether I had any right to ask to kiss the bride."

She didn't know what to answer. This was all wrong—it shouldn't be happening. There was no way to still the storm in her blood as she remembered the pleasure the two of them had always been able to give each other.

"Wiley, you son of a bitch . . ."

His name came out on a half-pleading note, and he laughed as he heard it. "Why does it sound so good to hear you say that to me?" he rumbled at her ear.

"Probably because you deserve to hear it." His laugh had broken the tension that had been gripping her, and she laughed with him. She was still smiling as she turned to meet him, and the gleam in his dark eyes struck something inside her that gave off a whole shower of sparks.

Sparks turned to fire as Wiley recaptured her face and brought it up to meet his. Her laugh seemed to release something in him, too. Or maybe he'd just reached the end of his willpower.

That was what she could taste on his lips—an almost desperate need for her kiss, for her admission that she was rocked by the same longings that were tearing him apart. His request to kiss the bride had been slow, almost formal. But his kiss was something very different.

Rae-Anne parted her lips and met his mouth with a desperation of her own. He felt so good, so strong, so *right*. Everything else was going wrong around her, but just now, just for this moment, there was comfort in Wiley's arms, and more passion in his kiss than she'd ever hoped to know again.

His arms had tightened around her almost convulsively, and she had to struggle to free herself far enough to wrap her arms around his neck. He smelled of soap and fresh air, and when she closed her eyes and let her hands drift into his thick, dark hair, she felt swept away into a world colored by her own senses, where the familiar masculine scent of Wiley merged seductively with the heat of his skin and the slickness of his tongue alongside her own.

His mouth was explicit, demanding. And Rae-Anne suddenly couldn't imagine wanting to hold back anything from this man who had always seemed to know her so intimately, so completely. She urged the kiss deeper, capturing his lower lip between her teeth and tugging it gently, suggestively. The feeling of his slanted grin blossoming under her lips turned her half-liquid inside.

"This beats any receiving line *I* ever stood in," he growled, and Rae-Anne laughed again, light-headed with delight.

Her laughter turned to a gasp as she realized what had been on his mind in breaking the kiss. His hands were at her hips, and her wedding dress, with its buttons finally undone, was gaping open along her back. Wiley took hold of the pearl-encrusted fabric and slowly began to ease the dress toward the floor, freeing Rae-Anne at last.

Wiley followed the dress downward, pausing just long enough to shed his own clothing in the process of helping Rae-Anne out of hers. He kissed the spot where her pulse pounded at the base of her throat and then moved lower to the soft hollow between her breasts. He paused long enough to tease each pink nipple into taut attention, leaving Rae-Anne trembling in his strong grip, not certain how much longer she was going to be able to rely on her legs to hold her up.

Wiley's warm breath fanned across her belly like the sun's embrace, and she threaded her fingers once more through his hair. This *couldn't* be wrong, she thought dizzily, not when her mind and her body were so united in pleasure and crying out for the all-embracing comfort of Wiley's presence. It had been so long since she'd felt this whole, this certain. Everything in her life was so tangled up right now—surely, just for the moment, she could reach for the one thing that seemed simple and right.

She wanted Wiley Cotter. And he wanted her. Did anything else really matter, just now?

Very quickly, the only thing that mattered was the fact that Wiley had finally pushed her wedding dress all the way to the floor, making a billowing pile around her ankles. She felt like Venus rising from the waves, or maybe like a mermaid granted the gift of a human lover for one stolen night.

And when Wiley's kisses followed the long curve of her inner thigh and then rose without warning to heat the juncture of her legs, she felt engulfed by something she had needed for what suddenly seemed like forever—something primitive and powerful, beyond words, even beyond thought.

"Wiley—"

She cried out his name and heard—or maybe felt—the low moan of his answer. Her whole body was quivering, shaken by the force of her desire and by Wiley's masterful caresses. The heat of his hands on the backs of her legs made her want to lean into him, but the warm focus of his lips kept her trembling upright, caught on a single point of pleasure even while her whole body was overrun with sensation.

She wasn't prepared for the tremor that rocked her from within, or for the way it seemed to shake all her emotions loose inside her. She twisted her hands involuntarily in Wiley's hair as she felt the first convulsive quaver, and then cried out with a long, astonished note of release that seemed to go on and on.

When the room around her finally eased into focus again, Wiley had closed his arms around the middle of her body, his face pressed into her belly as he shook his head slightly against her warm skin.

"Nothing," he was murmuring, almost to himself. "There is nothing in the world like loving you."

She felt him kissing her navel, his long fingers splayed against her ribs and then traveling upward to glance over the still-taut centers of her breasts. Rae-Anne gasped and eased herself fully into his arms as he got to his feet, carrying them both onto the double bed.

She was aching to feel him inside her, uniting them completely. And Wiley's whole body felt so good under her hands, so familiar, so strong.

Then why, as she ran her palms along the rise and fall of his rib cage, was he suddenly looking at a spot just above her eyes? Why, in spite of the undeniable hunger in his face, did he seem thoughtful, almost angry?

"What is it?"

The question came out in a gasp as the hard length of his arousal moved against her belly and the rough strength of his legs glided against her smooth skin. She wanted him inside her, she thought urgently, wanted to hold him in an embrace that could keep at bay everything that had come between them.

The split second before he replied was just long enough to let in the thought that he might be worried about her getting pregnant. She hadn't had time to come up with an answer when his answer knocked her off-balance from another direction.

"Your hair."

"My *hair?*" At first she couldn't imagine what he meant.

"We have to do something about it."

"Why?"

"Because no matter what Monsieur Antoine may think, it just doesn't look like you."

He let go of her wrists and leaned closer to her. The warm weight of his big chest was pressing her into the bed, chasing away all of her less immediate concerns, and that included any concern about her hair.

But he was refusing to give in to the way she arched against him. She could feel him holding himself back while he threaded his fingers through her hair and tried to make sense of the fancy combs and pins that held it in its elegant wedding style.

"Leave it, Wiley." She heard the pleading sound in her voice. "It doesn't matter."

"It damn well *does* matter." Rae-Anne winced as he pulled a strand loose, his hands awkward among the careful braids and swirls the hairdresser had taken so long to create. "I'm not making love to some illustration in a bridal magazine, Rae-Anne. I'm making love to *you.*"

"Oh, Wiley..."

The worst of it was that she knew he was right. It *wasn't* her—not the fairy-tale dress, the formal church wedding, the fancy hairstyle that suddenly felt so tight and uncomfortable. It wasn't like Rae-Anne to let herself be talked into things she didn't want to do, but she'd been scared, damn it, and more uncertain than she'd ever been in her life.

And now she wasn't. Now she felt stronger, more like herself. And she knew exactly what Wiley meant about her hair.

"Here. Let me do that."

She moved against Wiley until her arms were over her head, and took over the job of disentangling the combs and undoing her French braid. Her shift in position left their bodies even more intimately coiled around each other, suggesting erotic possibilities that would have made Rae-Anne blush if they'd occurred to her in broad daylight.

How was she supposed to keep her mind on the combs in her hair when she could feel Wiley's flat stomach and strong hips and insistent arousal so close against her? She wanted to lose herself forever in the feeling of her breasts against the curling hairs on his chest, in the warm strength of his skin against hers. Concentrating on her hair was an almost impossible task.

But she finally managed it. She shook her head and felt her hair loosening into a halo on the blanket beneath her. Wiley's long sigh, as he watched her, was a kind of caress in itself, a silent tribute that suddenly made her feel more beautiful than she'd remembered was possible.

"Rae-Anne." Her name was a breath, a whisper, almost a prayer. "Now you look like Rae-Anne again. Like *my* Rae-Anne..."

She murmured his name, and he captured the end of the sound with his mouth. Her soft cry of longing was cut off by the sensation she'd been aching for, of Wiley's hand at the soft junction of her legs, Wiley's knowing fingers finding the liquid core of her once again.

She could feel his whole frame trembling above her, as if the effort of reining himself in was about to shake him apart.

She knew exactly how he felt.

"Please, Wiley..." She ran her hands one more time over the hard muscles of his shoulders and back and finally pushed her fingers into his hair, forcing his head up. His eyes, when they met hers, were as black as midnight.

"We did the wedding dress." It was all she could do to get the words out. "We did the veil. We did my hair. I don't know how much more of this I can stand...."

Her voice rose in a gasp as Wiley moved against her. He slid inside her so easily, so smoothly, that Rae-Anne suddenly couldn't remember how or why they'd ever been apart. Her whole body welcomed him, clutching him with a strong, involuntary spasm that made both of them cry out in astonishment.

Rae-Anne tried to call Wiley's name, not sure whether her voice was working or not as she closed her eyes and curled her fingers into his hair. Under her palms she could feel his face twisted in what almost seemed to be pain, and the sound of his voice—ragged, almost desperate—made her think that whatever was hurting him came from somewhere deep inside.

"Rae-Anne—"

Any hope of holding back was gone the moment they joined together. They moved with a rhythm that came from the depths of the earth itself, fierce and yet somehow gentle. Rae-Anne felt herself rocked by it, caught up in its power, driven wherever the pulsing in her body took her.

It took her faster and faster toward the release she wanted so urgently. She wrapped her arms close around Wiley's big frame and held on to him as if he was the one fixed point in a universe that was starting to come apart around her.

When it did, she felt rather than heard her long shuddering cry, and clasped Wiley even harder as the same primitive spasm shook his body, as well. For a long, soundless moment there was nothing in the world but the two of them and the spell they had cast with their loving.

And for a long moment, that was enough.

Chapter 5

"Rae-Anne."

Wiley pulled the curtain open just slightly, letting the morning sunshine brighten the big bedroom.

"Come on, honey. We need to get moving. Company's coming."

He'd never known her to sleep this hard for this long. She'd always been a light sleeper, like Wiley himself, and quick to wake up in the mornings.

But she hadn't even stirred since Wiley had eased out of bed an hour earlier. The sound of the shower hadn't wakened her, and neither had the smell of the coffee Wiley had brought from the office after using the phone.

He stood watching her now, still reluctant to disturb the sleep she so obviously needed. The morning sun coming through the window glinted off the small gold locket around Rae-Anne's neck, the one item she hadn't taken off in last night's sensual free-for-all.

He remembered the locket. It had always seemed to have sentimental associations for Rae-Anne, although Wiley wasn't sure what they were. He was perversely glad the ornament she'd chosen to wear to her wedding was something of her own, not a gift from Rodney Dietrich.

The locket wasn't the only thing that caught Wiley's attention. He couldn't help noticing the faint purple smudges under Rae-Anne's eyes, clearer now that most of her fancy makeup had worn off.

Several times yesterday afternoon he'd had the impression that she was holding herself upright by sheer force of will. Maybe this deep sleep was just her body's declaration that force of will couldn't keep a person going forever.

He could see one of her hands just above the edge of the blanket. It was clenched into a fist, protective, childlike. It made him want to curl his fingers around it, to climb into bed beside her and wrap her sleeping body with his strength.

Good, Wiley, he told himself silently. *Then you can move on to other productive, professional kinds of behavior, like making love to her again even though that's the one thing you swore you weren't going to do.*

Actually, it wasn't the only thing he'd promised himself.

He'd sworn he wasn't going to touch her, too.

Or kiss her.

Or even *think* about kissing her.

That one had gone by the boards the first moment he'd seen her on the steps of Rodney Dietrich's ranch house. And he hadn't wasted his time getting past the others, either.

Face it, Cotter. He knew his expression was grim as he pulled another curtain open slightly to let a little more morning light in. *Promises aren't your thing. You should know that by now.*

He *did* know it. He'd avoided promising anything at all to Rae-Anne when they'd been lovers before, for the very good reason that he'd known his job could drag him away from her without any warning. Wiley wasn't in any position to give Rae-Anne the things she'd wanted—a permanent home, children of her own, the security of knowing that the man she loved would always be there for her.

Rodney Dietrich *was* in a position to promise Rae-Anne those things. And the fact that she'd made love with Wiley last night didn't change that.

Hell, they'd both been swept away by the moment, overrun by old longings that Wiley, for one, thought he'd conquered once and for all. Last night, anything and everything had seemed possible.

But it was morning now. And in the bright light that crept around the curtains he'd drawn, it was easy to see that making love couldn't change a damn thing between him and Rae-Anne.

"Rae-Anne." He leaned over the bed and shook her gently but insistently. "We've got visitors on their way. And my guess is you'd prefer to be dressed when they get here."

She awakened slowly, blinking her eyes in protest against the light. Her auburn hair was tangled across the pillowcase, a dark contrast to the white linens and Rae-Anne's porcelain-fair complexion. Wiley watched her turn her face halfway into the pillow and then go suddenly still.

She seemed to be thinking hard. Her forehead was creased, her expression serious.

"You in there, honey?" he asked.

Her blue eyes flew open wide at the sound of his voice. She looked almost afraid, and her voice, when she said his name, had a note of something very like despair in it.

"Oh, God," she said. Her words were half-muffled by the pillow. "Wiley. It *is* you. It really happened."

"It wasn't all a dream, if that's what you're thinking." It was an effort to sound nonchalant about it, but Wiley didn't trust himself to do anything else. Letting himself get close to Rae-Anne had been a bad mistake last night. And aside from the personal possibilities for disaster if he let it happen again, he needed to keep his head clear for Jack's arrival, which should be any time now.

"Oh, God." Rae-Anne sounded at least as remorseful as Wiley felt. It was enough to bolster his resolve and keep him moving until he was standing several feet away from the bed. Getting close to her last night *had* been a mistake. The look on Rae-Anne's face only confirmed it.

Then why, he wondered fleetingly, was the dismay in Rae-Anne's blue eyes making him ache this way inside? It wasn't simple desire he was feeling, not by a long shot. It was something more like—

Disappointment. He'd actually been hoping, in some hidden corner of himself, that she might wake up with that languid, contented look on her face, that glowing smile that told him she was still wrapped in the pleasures of some warm fantasy world and wasn't at all averse to the idea of easing back there and taking Wiley with her. He hadn't realized until this moment how much he'd missed seeing her look at him that way.

Dream on, Wiley, he told himself. The days when Rae-Anne Blackburn would smile at him that way were long gone. Nothing between the two of them could be the way it had once been. The best he could hope for was to get her free of the man she'd mistakenly gotten tangled up with, and then to bow out of her life a little more gracefully than he had the last time.

So he clamped down hard on the disappointment inside him and told himself it was a *good* thing Rae-Anne seemed so troubled and distant toward him this morning.

"What did you mean about visitors?" she asked, frowning at him, gathering the red blanket around her bare shoulders. "Where *are* we, anyway, Wiley? What's going on?"

"It's a long story."

"Well, if you'd deign to let me in on it—"

"I will. Or maybe I'd better let my brother do it. He knows more about this case than I do."

"Your brother? What are you talking about?"

"My brother Jack works for the FBI. That's how I happen to know so much about your friend Rodney."

She sat up, tossing her thick auburn hair out of her eyes. Wiley felt another little clutch low down in his belly at the thought of smoothing out those dark red tangles with his fingers, and watching Rae-Anne's hair catch the morning sunlight and turn to gold.

He growled a silent warning at himself and moved a little farther from the bed.

"This is the FBI's case, not mine," he said bluntly. "I'm only along as a favor to Jack. He's on his way here now, with a couple of colleagues. That's why I figured it was time to wake you up."

He didn't like the way Rae-Anne's silence stretched on, or the lost look that had come into her blue eyes. She seemed to be grasping at one thought after another and not feeling reassured by any of them.

She started to speak, then caught herself. There was something unbearably vulnerable in the way her eyes had widened, and it was all Wiley could do to hold his ground on the other side of the bedroom. If he took one step toward Rae-Anne, if he let himself answer the unspoken plea he saw hovering on her parted lips, he would be lost, too, and that wouldn't do either of them any good.

"Come on, honey," he said. His voice had roughened with the effort of keeping himself still. "Jack and his boys could be here any time now. I suggest you get into some of those clothes in that suitcase I brought.''

He watched as her gaze swung toward the spot on the floor where her wedding gown had been. Wiley had gathered the big, billowing pile of satin and lace into his arms earlier this morning. He'd hung it carefully in the closet next to his chauffeur's suit, fighting off the shaking in his fingers as he'd done up the pearl buttons that had turned into such a wildly erotic prelude to seduction last night.

It was better to have cleared away that graphic reminder of their lovemaking, he told himself. Did Rae-Anne see it that way, too, or was there something else behind the sudden, unsteady breath she drew in as her eyes met his again?

"Oh, God." Her eyes seemed bluer, more enormous than ever. "You didn't—come back because of this?"

"This" was the rumpled bed they'd been sleeping in. And Wiley knew without asking that it also meant the passion of their lovemaking last night.

He couldn't let that get in the way of what he was really here to do. And so he summoned up as much willpower as he could muster and said, "We both got carried away, honey. It happens. But this morning we've got to get down to business."

For a long moment she just stared at him. Then she slid to the edge of the bed and stood up without speaking. Wiley tried to order himself to look away, but it didn't work. He didn't miss a single detail, from the way she winced when her blistered feet hit the carpet to the feminine sway of her hips as she headed for the other bedroom. His body had responded immediately to her loveliness, her nakedness, and it took a moment to register that she had closed the door between them with a very definite click.

Good, he told himself. That's what he wanted.

Then why, when he heard the car pull up outside the cabin a few minutes later, was he still rooted in the same spot, still listening for faint sounds inside the other room as though they might answer all the questions Rae-Anne had left unspoken between them?

The room was full of people.

At least, that was her first impression. Furious though she was with Wiley, she at least had to admit it was a good thing he'd wakened her and suggested that she get dressed. It would have been awkward as hell meeting these strangers without any warning at all.

It was hard enough to keep her thoughts straight as it was. And the whole thing was made even more disconcerting by the fact that two of the strangers looked so much like Wiley.

Rae-Anne had worked hard for a long time to chase even the memories of Wiley Cotter away. And now she was faced not only with Wiley himself, but with two other long-legged, dark-haired men whose casual stances and faintly mocking smiles probably masked minds just as razor sharp as Wiley's.

She had every reason in the world to be on her guard against that sharpness as Wiley introduced his brother Jack. She still didn't know what Wiley's reasons were for coming back into her life like this, but one thing was very clear—making love to her last night had been just a frill, a diversion.

She'd let herself imagine—foolishly, illogically—that he'd come back because of her. And now it turned out to have something to do with the FBI. Squaring her shoulders and staying calm as she shook Jack Cotter's hand and listened to him introducing his colleagues was one of the hardest things Rae-Anne had ever had to do.

"My boss, Jessie Myers," Jack was saying, turning to the tall, serious-looking black woman at his side. "And Mack MacGuire, who's also working on the case."

She needed to know so many things about how she'd managed to get caught up in a federal investigation. She needed to think about Rodney, and about the baby, and about what she was going to do if any of Wiley's accusations about her fiancé turned out to be true.

But her thoughts kept wandering to Wiley's handsome face, and to the other stranger in the room, who had taken a chair near the door and seemed to be hanging back at the edges of the meeting, watching them all with observant dark blue eyes.

"My other brother, Sam," Wiley said, noting the direction her gaze had taken. "Although why he's here—"

"He's pushy," Jack put in.

Sam grinned. "Try inquisitive," he said.

Jack glared at both his brothers. "Try remembering who's running this show, all right?" he said. "This isn't a Cotter Investigations special here."

"Nobody said it was, Jack." Wiley sounded almost bored, a sure sign, Rae-Anne knew, that he was covering up an intense interest.

And Sam sounded exactly the same way. "Hey, I'm just along for the ride," he said, leaning back in his chair.

That slow drawl was so much like Wiley's. Rae-Anne frowned, wishing she could stick with one mystery at a time. Ten years ago, Wiley hadn't known where his brother Sam was. And he'd certainly never bothered to introduce her to Jack. But beneath their wrangling, it was clear to her that the three Cotters formed a close family unit. When had that happened? And how?

She didn't like the feeling that everyone in the room knew more than she did. She cleared her throat, grateful that she'd bothered to scrub her face and pull her hair into a ponytail. She felt slightly less disheveled and in control of herself as she asked, "Who's in charge of this meeting?"

"I am," Jack Cotter replied, "and I'd like to get on with it. If Wiley had checked in with us last night the way he was supposed to—"

"I said I'd call as soon as I could," Wiley cut in. "Circumstances change, little brother. You know that as well as I do."

"They seem to change pretty drastically whenever you're in the picture," Jack muttered as he turned to Rae-Anne.

He was the most buttoned-down of the three brothers, she thought, contrasting Jack's close-cut dark hair and neatly rolled-up sleeves with Wiley's rougher style and Sam's half-untamed look. Jack wouldn't have looked out of place in a boardroom, while Sam might have been lifted straight out of a rodeo somewhere on the back roads of Texas.

And Wiley? Where did Wiley belong, and what kind of game had he been playing with her yesterday and last night? His dark gaze stirred her as strongly as ever, but she resisted the temptation to let her eyes linger on his before she turned to listen to Jack.

"I'm extremely pleased to meet you, of course, Ms. Blackburn," he was saying. "But I admit I'm a little surprised to see you here. According to the plan—which Wiley did *not* draw up, I might add, in case he's managed to give you that impression—we just wanted to sound you out about your fiancé's business operation, to see if there was anything you might be able to tell us."

Rae-Anne's frown deepened. "Sound me out?" she repeated. "I don't understand. How was dragging me away from my own wedding supposed to do that?"

She didn't miss the quick look between Jack Cotter and his boss, or the way Mack MacGuire had started to tap the end of his pencil on the table next to his chair. "Maybe you should fill us in on exactly what happened," Jessie Myers said slowly. "Your friend Mr. Cotter seems to have been less than forthcoming with us."

Oh, God, Rae-Anne thought. She wanted to bury her face in her hands and be alone with her own thoughts, the way she'd done the moment she'd closed the bedroom door between her and Wiley a little while ago. But those thoughts were just going to keep heading wildly off in all directions until she found out what was going on.

That didn't mean she was going to share everything that had happened between her and Wiley last night. Hoping she could keep from blushing as she edited out the racy parts of their evening, she gave the group a quick version of yesterday's adventures.

When she was done, there was a long silence.

"He just drove off with you," Jack said at last.

"That's right."

"Without even mentioning that he was there in cooperation with the FBI."

"I didn't hear anything about the FBI until just before you all showed up."

Jack's broad chest rose and fell in a sigh that seemed to be exaggerated for effect. This wasn't the first time he'd butted heads with his stubborn older brother, Rae-Anne thought. She wished she could take more comfort in the fact that other people were mad at Wiley, too.

"You want to tell us what you're up to, Wiley?" Jack turned to the corner of the room where Wiley was leaning nonchalantly against a windowsill.

He shrugged. "I was operating on instinct," he said. "Rae-Anne looked scared. And the evidence against Dietrich was pretty damning. That was enough to convince me it was better to get her out of the way first and explain things to her later.''

"Except you *didn't* explain things to her, apparently," Jessie Myers put in.

Wiley shrugged again. The motion looked easy and unconcerned, and Rae-Anne found her attention being drawn to the breadth of his shoulders under the weathered blue T-shirt he wore with his jeans this morning.

"She's getting the explanation part now," he said.

Jack started to say something, and so did Mack MacGuire. Rae-Anne could hear Jessie Myers's tight sigh, and suddenly she felt as though this was all slipping beyond her, into a realm she didn't understand and couldn't control.

"Hold on," she said, summoning up the voice that had cut through a lot of barroom arguments in her checkered career as a bartender. All three FBI agents turned to look at her, seeming startled by the new edge to her tone.

"I still don't know what started all this," she said. "Why is the FBI investigating Rodney? And why did you think I would be able to help you?"

"We're not just investigating Rodney," Jack said. "This operation is part of a statewide crackdown on illegal gambling. Rodney's involved in laundering money for the mob, which you may or may not know."

"I'm not sure I believe it, but Wiley did mention it."

Jack shot his brother a pointed look. "I'm glad to hear he did *some* of what he told us he would do," he said. "Did he also mention that Rodney's hotel business was propped up by mob money when Rodney expanded things too fast a few years ago?"

"Yes." She sat down on the neatly made bed, silently relieved that Wiley had thought to tidy things up somewhat. "And he said something about Danielle—about Rodney's first wife—"

She still had to force herself to think about it. Rodney could be indecisive sometimes, even vague, when it suited him. But in the two years she'd known him, she'd never seen any signs of violence in his character. The closest he'd ever come was the tight-lipped coldness he'd shown whenever she'd pressed him to discuss something he didn't want to talk about. And it was hard to imagine that his silence about Danielle's death might be covering anything as awful as a knowledge of her murder.

"The evidence on that is pretty circumstantial," Jack Cotter was saying. "But we *do* know that Danielle Dietrich had instituted divorce proceedings and was going after a big slice of Rodney's pie."

"Did she know—about the mob being involved in his business?"

"It doesn't look that way, at least at the beginning. Our guess is that when she got down to making actual demands, Rodney came out and told her why he couldn't hand over the settlement she wanted, and she threatened to blow the whistle on him in retaliation. We think that Rodney—or maybe one of his silent partners—had Danielle taken out of the picture to protect their working arrangement."

Rae-Anne shivered in spite of the warmth of the sunny air. She hated this—hated the casual menace and constant threats that were such a part of Wiley's everyday working life. She didn't want any part of a world where a woman's death could be referred to offhandedly as "being taken out of the picture," or where Rae-Anne herself was just another pawn in a game being played for dangerously high stakes.

But she had become a part of that world, at least until she could figure out what to do about Rodney.

If she'd been alone, and free, she'd have had no hesitation at all about hitting the road until she'd found a place she could start again. She'd spent her whole adult life that way, searching, without success, for a place she could feel at home.

But now everything was different. She had no intention of telling the FBI that she was carrying Rodney Dietrich's child, but it did make her more willing to stay and finish this conversation than she would otherwise have been.

"What will happen to Rodney if your investigation goes the way it's supposed to?" she asked Jack Cotter.

"He'll go to jail."

"For how long?"

"A long time, with luck."

No one in the room seemed even a little bit sorry about that. None of them, Wiley least of all, seemed to realize how badly her life had been thrown off its track by the FBI's intrusion into it.

That made her voice sharper as she said, "And what exactly am I supposed to be helping you with, assuming I'm willing?"

"We've lost our contact inside Rodney's organization, and so far we haven't identified who the new mob courier is. Wiley thought you might help us pick up the trail."

"Why did he think I would do that?"

Jack held her eyes steadily. There was something about the middle Cotter brother that she liked, Rae-Anne thought, something that she instinctively recognized as honest and straightforward. She had the feeling that Jack, unlike his older brother, wasn't in the habit of high-handedly taking over other people's lives and deciding what was best for them.

"He thought you would want to know if there was anything shady in Rodney's background," Jack was saying. He paused, then asked, "Was he right?"

"Probably." She hated to admit it, but Wiley *had* been right. She could never marry Rodney if she was certain he'd been lying to her about so many important things all along.

But she wasn't certain about it yet. And she needed to be, for reasons she wasn't about to share with the FBI. "What if I agree to help you look for evidence and it turns out Rodney isn't the guilty party, after all?" she asked.

Jack looked skeptical. "I'd say you're pinning your hopes on a star that was likely to fizzle out," he told her.

"Even if I am," Rae-Anne returned, "they're *my* hopes. Please," she added, her voice sounding more urgent than she'd intended. "I need to get to the bottom of this for my own satisfaction. If Rodney's only peripherally involved, or if the evidence you've got is somehow misleading—"

It could be, she thought. Rodney tended to be easily influenced by people he admired. He'd lost one fortune early in his career by teaming up with the wrong partner. Maybe he wasn't the criminal the FBI thought. Maybe he'd just wandered into something he didn't understand, the same way Rae-Anne had.

She thought about the searing heat of Wiley's loving last night, and swallowed hard. No matter whether he turned out to be a criminal or not, Rodney had never aroused anything like that kind of passion in her. Even if he turned out to be innocent, she was still going to be marrying a man she loved with less than her whole heart.

But at least her child would have a father, and a home, and a shot at stability. And there was no way she could dream of a future with Wiley anyway, under any circumstances. He'd seduced his way back into her life for all the wrong reasons, and he didn't even have the grace to sound sorry about it.

What he did sound, when he broke into the conversation, was irritated. "I didn't haul you out of Rodney Dietrich's way just to have you head straight back there," he told her.

"No," she answered. "You hauled me out of Rodney's way so I would be more likely to help your brother and his colleagues. Aren't you happy now, Wiley? You've got what you were after."

She didn't miss the flicker in his dark eyes, and knew her double meaning had reached him. He'd been after more than just her cooperation, judging by how he'd acted last night. He'd been looking for a quick recap of the lovemaking they'd once shared so potently.

And he'd gotten it, too. That was what was making her so angry now. She was still in the grip of the sense of hurt and loss she'd felt when she'd wakened to see that indifferent look on Wiley's handsome face.

He crossed his arms over his chest. Rae-Anne could see the corded muscles in his forearms.

"Jack's made it clear that what he wants and what I want aren't necessarily the same thing," he said. "I wanted to see you free of all that wedding hoopla so you could make up your mind and get on with your life."

"I *am* making up my own mind. I'm deciding to go back and find out what I can about Rodney's operation, and about his first wife."

"The hell you are!" His anger flared suddenly, and she knew she'd been right about how tightly he'd been keeping it in check. "It's too dangerous, Rae-Anne. The man had his wife murdered for bringing up exactly the kinds of questions you're talking about asking."

"You don't know that for certain."

"I don't need a videotape to convince me. It's not safe, and I don't want you getting involved in it."

"Did someone make you my official watchdog when I wasn't looking?" She could feel herself breathing harder as she held his glittering gaze. Damn it, she thought, it was happening all over again. Whether they were angry or aroused, there was no denying the strength of the connection that sparked between them.

"You *need* a watchdog, if you're thinking about doing something as crazy as this," Wiley said. "If you had any sense—"

"Humor me." Rae-Anne tried to rein her temper in, tried to slow the pounding she could feel in her temples. "Pretend I *do* have some sense. Pretend I might have my own very good reasons for wanting to get this straightened out to my satisfaction."

Pretend I'm pregnant and scared and I can't imagine what else to do. It was tempting to add the words out loud, just to watch Wiley's jaw drop as the realization sank in of just how badly her life had been scrambled over the past couple of days. *Pretend the man whose baby I'm carrying might be the worst kind of liar, and the man whose simplest touch turns me to jelly inside is up to something I'm only beginning to understand. How likely does that make me to trust anybody's judgment but my own?*

She didn't say it out loud, but Wiley seemed to have understood the turmoil in her face. His voice was gentler as he said, "I'll come with you, then."

"You will *not*." She felt her cheeks redden as she answered him. The thought of being anywhere near Wiley was too distracting even to consider.

"Jack?" He turned to his brother. "You can't possibly agree to this."

Jack shook his head. "It's Rae-Anne's call," he said. "If she feels safe—"

"Of course I feel safe." She said the words quickly, wishing they were truer. "I'll tell Rodney I just had a bad case of cold feet, and that's why I didn't show up at the wedding.''

And Rodney knew, although no one else did outside her doctor's office, that even if Rae-Anne had had a very good reason to bolt away from the wedding, she had an even better reason to come back. Surely that would be enough to keep him from suspecting that the FBI might be involved with her disappearance, or with her return.

She *was* worried that if Wiley was anywhere near the Dietrich ranch, her attention would be so divided that she might not be able to maintain the facade she was going to need. The tremor that went through her when she met his angry brown eyes was proof enough of that.

"This is a mistake, Rae-Anne," he told her tightly.

"If it is, I'll take the consequences of it," she retorted. "Damn it, Wiley, this is the man I agreed to marry. He's the—prospective father of my children." She got the word *prospective* in there just in time, but no one seemed to notice the slip. "I need to do this, and I *don't* need your help, no matter how much you think I should want it."

Wiley's low snarl sounded more bearlike than ever. Rae-Anne watched him jam his hands into the pockets of his jeans and half turn so that he was glaring out the window instead of at her.

It should have been a relief to be free of the weight of his gaze. It should have been easier to turn to Jack and the other FBI agents and start talking about details and logistics now that Wiley was seemingly ignoring her.

But it wasn't.

His brooding presence kept nagging at her, demanding her attention, reminding her inescapably of how powerfully the two of them acted on each other. Was he feeling the same things, resisting the intuitive tug that connected them?

Well, if he was, it wasn't her problem. She didn't want his high-handed interference in her life, and if she just put her mind to it, she knew she would be able to clear away the troubling memory of how it had felt to be clasped in his arms last night, rocking to the rhythm of their shared desires.

Desire wasn't the same as commitment. And attraction wasn't any guarantee of happiness. Nothing that Wiley Cotter could offer meant anything in the long term, not to Rae-Anne or her unborn child. And the long term was what she had to keep her mind on.

She sat up straighter on the bed, resolutely keeping her eyes away from Wiley's side of the room, and said, "I'd just as soon get moving with this, if it's all the same to you. What exactly am I supposed to be after, and do you have any idea where I should start looking for it?"

Chapter 6

He had to try one more time.

Wiley had listened in on all of Jack's briefing, trying to keep the details of Rodney's financial affairs straight in his mind. He'd heard all this once, and it had been hard to concentrate then, too, because he'd been thinking so inescapably about Rae-Anne.

He was doing the same thing now.

He had stayed put in his corner of the room for as long as he could, and then his restlessness had made him start pacing, from the window in the corner to the bathroom door and back.

That had helped a little, although it was still impossible to look at Rae-Anne's pale, composed face without wanting to run across the room and shake her until she admitted that the only wise thing to do was walk away from Rodney Dietrich and let somebody else sort out the details.

It hadn't taken long for Jack to call a halt to Wiley's pac-

ing. ''You want to take a hike or something, big brother?''
he'd said. ''This is like being in a tiger cage.''

''I couldn't agree more,'' Wiley growled.

It had been tempting to go and walk off at least some of
his tension, but he didn't want to miss any of Jack's briefing. So he'd crossed his arms and gone to lean against the
window frame, holding himself still by main strength and
trying to keep his eyes away from Rae-Anne's serious,
thoughtful features as much as he could.

He'd stayed there while Mack MacGuire went out and got
a bunch of sandwiches, and he still hadn't moved when the
meeting resumed after lunch. Sooner or later, he thought,
he would get a chance to talk to Rae-Anne alone. She
wouldn't just walk off and leave him without saying *anything,* not when he'd made it so clear that the idea of her
heading back into Rodney Dietrich's life was making him
half-crazy.

He finally got his chance, although Rae-Anne didn't exactly seem to be going out of her way to seize the opportunity to speak to him. It was midafternoon, and the three
FBI agents had gone out to their car, leaving Wiley and Rae-
Anne to gather their belongings in the cabin. Sam was outside, too, indulging in one of the cigarettes he was allegedly
trying to give up. Rae-Anne had vanished into the inner
bedroom, but it didn't take long for Wiley to follow her in
there.

''Rae-Anne, listen to me.'' He shut the door behind him,
ignoring her protest. ''We need to talk about this.''

She looked steadily at him for a long moment, then
turned to the small suitcase he'd brought for her. ''You
missed your chance, Wiley,'' she told him. ''We should have
talked about it last night, before we—got sidetracked.''

He sliced one of his hands through the air in what he intended as a sharp, frustrated motion. He hadn't realized he

was heading for Rae-Anne until his fingers were actually touching her thick auburn hair.

She went just as still as he did, and Wiley could feel her trembling slightly. He was shaking, too, with the sudden realization of how much it had been costing him to keep his distance from her all day.

"Don't do this, Wiley." Her voice was low and unsteady, but she didn't move.

She didn't really mean it, Wiley thought. She was trying to talk herself into something she didn't really want, the same as she'd been trying to do with this plan about Rodney Dietrich. All he needed to do was reinforce her reluctance, her doubts.

He eased his hand over the elastic band that held her hair in a ponytail and circled the back of her neck gently, persuasively. "I was convinced yesterday when I picked you up in the limo that you didn't really want to marry Rodney Dietrich," he said. "And I'm just as convinced now."

She had closed her eyes. He could see her fighting against something. Just at the moment, it was hard to tell which way the battle was going.

"And if you don't want to marry him, why the hell go back there?" he went on, massaging the too-tight muscles of her neck with his thumb. "Why not just cut your losses? Jack'll find a way to wrap his case up with or without you. You don't need to take this risk."

Her eyes opened suddenly, and Wiley stopped moving. "I *do* have to do this," she told him.

"Why?" He could feel her starting to pull away, but he kept his hand where it was, insisting that she meet his eyes and answer his question. "Why not just leave? You've done it before. You did it when you thought I'd died, did it so thoroughly I couldn't find you in forty-eight states and three countries."

"Is that what this is about?" Her voice was thick with tension. Wiley wanted desperately to wrap his arms around her and hold her against his chest, keeping every kind of danger and doubt away from her.

But that unsettling combination of anger and doubt in her eyes stopped him. "Are you just trying to wrap up old unfinished business here?" she was asking. "You couldn't find me after you disappeared ten years ago, so you're trying to make it up to me by fixing everything in my life now. Is that what's going on, Wiley?"

He growled an expletive and finally loosened his hold. He turned away from her with the same restlessness that had been shooting through him all day, and moved toward the curtained window, listening to the faint sound of his brothers' conversation in the parking lot.

He didn't *know* exactly what was going on. Of course he couldn't magically make their happy past come back to life. And even their happiest moments had been stolen ones, seized in the face of Wiley's uncertain job and Rae-Anne's longings for all the things Wiley knew he could never give her.

None of that had changed. But there was so much more between them than just some unsettled memories. The way they'd made love last night had proved that. Wiley didn't know where it might lead, but he'd be damned if he would let Rae-Anne cut things off just as they'd finally found each other again.

"I'm not trying to fix everything in your life," he said roughly. "Just the parts I know are wrong. And I *know* your heart isn't in this marriage, Rae-Anne. You can't make me believe it is."

They looked at each other for what felt to Wiley like a very long time, and then Rae-Anne sighed. Her face was pale in the dim light of the bedroom. He saw a resigned look come into her wide blue eyes, and felt something hopeful springing to life inside him. Was she finally admitting he was right?

She was, but she looked so unhappy about it that Wiley couldn't feel any satisfaction as she said, "You're right. Rodney isn't exactly the man of my dreams. But I have to go back there anyway."

"*Why?*"

The word exploded out of him as his frustration reached its limit. She'd just admitted that Rodney didn't mean the moon and the stars to her. Then why was she doing this? Why couldn't she admit that Wiley *did* mean something? He wasn't sure where that could lead, but maybe—slowly, gradually—they might be able to pick up where they'd left off ten years earlier.

Her answer shot all of that to pieces.

"I have to go back because I'm pregnant with Rodney's child," she said.

At first Wiley laughed. He couldn't imagine what else to do. It was ridiculous—it was impossible. The body that had had him on his knees in adoration last night had been so perfectly, so exactly the same as he remembered it. The idea that she could be carrying another man's child was one that his mind simply refused to grasp.

"Now do you understand?"

It wasn't her words, but her tone, that got through to Wiley. She sounded resolute, and even more serious than she'd been while she'd listened to Jack and the other FBI agents outlining the case they were building against the father of her baby. She'd had more to grapple with than Wiley had imagined, and she seemed to have come to terms with it in her usual determined style.

"How long—" He couldn't find the words to complete his question.

She finished it for him. "How long have I been pregnant? Not long. About six weeks."

"Six weeks." He repeated it mindlessly.

"That's why the wedding arrangements were—a little rushed."

Wiley's thoughts kept scattering away on him, refusing to fall into place. But isolated parts of the picture were snapping into focus in spite of his confusion.

That protective gesture of Rae-Anne's that he hadn't understood, when she'd wrapped her arms around herself... The dawning, protesting awareness on her face when she'd wakened in his bed this morning... Her refusal to admit that Rodney was guilty until she'd proven it for herself...

"Damn it, Rae-Anne—"

He didn't know what he had started to say. There were no words for the sudden sense of loss that was carving him up inside, no way to tell her how hollow he felt at the realization that she would never be his—that she would always belong to the father of her child in a way she could never belong to Wiley.

He hadn't known how desperate he was to win her back until this very moment.

"If Jack gets the evidence he needs—" Jack suddenly seemed like as much of an enemy as Rodney Dietrich had been just moments ago. Rae-Anne was hemmed in, he saw suddenly, surrounded by far too many grim possibilities.

She was nodding. "My baby's going to have a father who's in jail," she said. "That's why I have to be sure, Wiley. I have to do what's best for this child. I thought I knew—"

She covered her face suddenly with both hands, and Wiley felt something wrench inside him at the helpless thought that he had no right to comfort her now. He'd only added to her turmoil by stirring up all the old feelings that lay unresolved between them.

When she looked up, she had settled her shoulders in a way that seemed to be warning him away. "I don't want to talk about this anymore," she said, looking him in the eye again. "I'm only telling you this because I had a horrible feeling you were never going to get off my case otherwise."

He had a horrible feeling she might be right.

It was disturbing to see himself from Rae-Anne's point of view all of a sudden. He'd thought he was making things easier for her, and instead he'd been charging around in her already complicated life like a rodeo bull run completely out of control.

"And if you breathe a word of this to anybody—"

"I won't." At least that was easy to promise. Wiley held up one palm and fought the urge to pull her close to him, to offer her whatever strength and comfort she might be able to draw from him.

Strength and comfort had turned all too quickly to lust and longing when they'd touched each other last night. And now Wiley could see why she'd looked so miserable when she'd wakened this morning and remembered what had happened.

He couldn't think of a single apology that would do any good. And he'd never been a man to offer excuses.

So he jammed both hands into his jeans pockets again, amazed at how nothing—not his brothers' presence just outside the cabin, not the bombshell she'd just dropped on him, not the danger she was intent on walking into—could keep his body from responding to Rae-Anne's soft white skin and heartbreaking blue eyes. He would have to be half-dead, he thought, before he could stop himself from wanting her.

"You're sure you know what you're doing?" he said gruffly.

"I'm sure."

In spite of the stubborn tilt of her chin, she didn't sound sure. She still sounded scared, and everything in Wiley's bloodstream was telling him to carry her off someplace safe, someplace sheltered.

But that's what he'd been trying to do yesterday, and he'd only succeeded in snarling things up even more. He gave an angry, inarticulate sound that was half profanity, half apology, and started for the bedroom door when he heard his brother Jack demanding from the other room whether Rae-Anne was ready to go yet.

"It's the next gate on the left."

Rae-Anne was almost as nervous going toward the Dietrich ranch as she'd been driving away from it yesterday. She smoothed her hands against her jeans and glanced at Sam Cotter, who was driving.

"How did you manage to get a car from the cab company in New Braunfels, anyway?" she asked him.

Sam gave her the slanted grin that seemed to be his stock response to any and all questions. "We've got a lot of contacts in the area," he said.

"'We' meaning Cotter Investigations?"

He gave her a slow nod and flicked on the turn signal.

"How long have you been working there?"

"Eight, nine years now."

"What did you do before that?"

His grin had turned ironic. "Anything," he said, "and everything."

She hadn't quite been able to stifle her curiosity about the Cotter brothers. She still hadn't gotten a very clear answer about why Sam had come along to this morning's meeting.

She did know he had offered to see that she got safely to Rodney's home, and that Jack had taken his brother up on it, agreeing it wouldn't hurt to have someone make sure she would at least be welcome at the Dietrich ranch.

"Might be more plausible for her to show up in a cab," Jack had said.

"No problem. I can borrow one."

So now, as the sun started to dim in the western sky, she was rolling between the same tall limestone gates that Wiley had driven her through yesterday afternoon.

"You remember the plan," Sam was saying, as the car started up the long driveway toward the low stone ranch house. "You tell them you don't have any money on you, and you need to pay the driver. Then, when you come out, if you're even slightly worried about the reception you're getting, I can get you out of here in no time."

Part of her wanted to tell him to get her out of here right now, before she had to face her jilted bridegroom. She wasn't used to maintaining any kind of pretense, and she wasn't sure she was going to be very good at it. What if she couldn't come up with the answers she needed and was left with this nagging sense of uncertainty about the father of her child?

It was only the thought of that child that kept her voice steady as she said, "I remember."

"Think Rodney's likely to be home?"

"That's his pickup in the yard." Rae-Anne nodded toward the gleaming dark blue truck parked next to the house. "And he generally spends Sundays getting things done on the ranch."

Or rather, making sure his employees were getting things done. Rodney belonged to the fourth generation of Dietrichs to live on this hill-country ranch, but he preferred to see himself as a gentleman farmer, retreating to the country after working all week in the city hotel business his father had bought fifty years earlier.

"You like it out here?" Sam was asking her.

She nodded. "I love it," she said. "My mother's family came from the hill country, and I always seemed to end up drifting in this direction whenever I was on the road."

"According to Wiley, you were on the road a lot."

She looked sharply at him, but his casual manner hadn't changed. Had Wiley been discussing her with his brothers? She felt a blush creeping over her treacherously fair complexion as she wondered what Wiley might have said about her.

He wouldn't have shared the news about her pregnancy. She was certain of that. He was one of the most intuitive men she'd ever met, and when she'd broken her news to him, he'd seen immediately what a bind she was in. In fact, the perceptive look in his dark eyes was still with her as she tried to answer Sam levelly.

"Wiley should talk," she said. "He's always been harder to pin down than a tumbleweed on a windy day."

The corner of Sam's mouth quirked upward. "True enough," he admitted. "All the Cotters seem to have inherited a kind of footloose gene somewhere along the line."

Rae-Anne wished he hadn't brought Wiley's name into the conversation. She'd been working at keeping him out of her thoughts, because the last thing she needed on her mind this evening was the memory of his eloquent eyes, or the echo of how he'd called her name in the heat of their loving. Just as she thought she'd banished him to the back of her mind, though, Sam mentioned him again.

"You know," he said, in the easy drawl that was like a slow-motion version of Wiley's voice, "Jack and I put our heads together about Wiley while you all were packing up this afternoon."

She turned to look at him, not sure what he meant.

Sam spun the steering wheel, gradually easing the car around the long curve of the lane. "We were trying to remember if we'd ever seen Wiley let anybody sass him the way you were doing at that meeting this morning."

"He had it coming to him." Rae-Anne didn't want to go into details about why she and Wiley had been sparring so heatedly.

Sam's grin had widened. "I believe you," he said, "but mostly women don't come out and tell him so. Either they can't be bothered, or they're too head-over-heels about him, or they haven't got the nerve."

Rae-Anne felt a jealous little jolt go through her at Sam's words. So there were other women in Wiley's life, were there? Well, she supposed it wasn't surprising. What *was* surprising was the way she was reacting to the news.

You were head-over-heels enough yourself to completely miss the point about why Wiley came back, she reminded herself sternly. *And you're supposed to be over that now. Grow up, Rae-Anne.*

"Your big brother might be better off if somebody rapped him upside the head every now and again," she said. "He seems to think he knows what's best for everybody, without bothering to consult them about it."

"You're right." The cab was coming to a halt in front of the steps Rae-Anne had descended in her fairy-tale dress and shoes yesterday afternoon. "The only thing is—"

He was out the door before he finished the sentence, leaving Rae-Anne far more impatient to hear the end of it than she wanted to admit. She had to wait until they were both outside the cab before he finished.

"The thing is that every once in a while Wiley *does* know what's best for other people," he said. "He tracked me down when even *I* didn't know where the hell I was. And maybe the Cotters aren't exactly all over each other, but if you tried to pull us apart, you'd have a hell of a fight on your hands. Wiley gets the credit for that. He put us back together, and he's what keeps us together."

He was lifting her small suitcase out of the back seat. Rae-Anne frowned at him.

"Why are you telling me this?" she couldn't help asking.

Anyone watching from the house would have assumed from Sam's casual stance that he wasn't talking about anything more urgent than the cab fare. But the slight glint down deep in his blue eyes told Rae-Anne a different story.

"He'll drive you crazy at times," he said, "but I'd hate to see anybody hurt him. That's all."

The comment was timed so perfectly that Rae-Anne didn't have a chance to come up with a retort. If she was going to play her part convincingly, she couldn't very well stand here on the ranch house steps arguing with the cab-driver.

So there wasn't time to say there was no danger of her hurting Wiley Cotter because she didn't really mean anything to him.

Were all the Cotter brothers so self-contained, so hard to know? she wondered, as she turned toward the house. Wiley, as Sam had said, could drive you crazy at times. Jack had at least seemed straightforward, but then, she'd only been dealing with him on a professional level. She wondered if his manner would change if his heart was involved.

And now Sam was adding to the Cotter mystique, as though there wasn't enough of it going around already.

"One thing at a time, Rae-Anne," she reminded herself as she pushed the doorbell next to the big green door. "You can only worry about one thing at a time."

It was Renee, the housekeeper, who opened the door. Her round, lined face was a complete blank for a moment, and then she lifted her hands in the air.

"Oh, my," she said, almost laughing. "I told Mr. Rodney you would come back. He didn't believe me, but I told him, with that little one on the way—"

She stopped herself, then seemed to decide the damage was done. "I know I'm not supposed to know," she said, putting a hand on Rae-Anne's forearm, "but I'm right, aren't I?"

As she admitted that Renee's guess had been on target, Rae-Anne decided she couldn't possibly take Sam Cotter up on his offer of a quick escape. She was committed to sorting out the mystery surrounding Rodney Dietrich, if only because the child growing inside her gave her an undeniable connection to this place and the people who lived here.

So she returned Renee's hug, and asked if she could borrow some money to pay off the cab. She would tell Sam the coast seemed to be clear, she thought, and she would face the rest of this adventure on her own.

"You can't possibly be serious about going in to work."

"Why not? We were only going to take the weekend off for a honeymoon, anyway. And I'll be better if I have something to do. You know I hate sitting around—I think maybe that's one of the reasons I got so antsy last week. I'm always happier if I'm working."

They were sitting in the big dining room of Rodney's ranch house, with the remnants of breakfast between them. It was another hot day, and Rodney's newly washed sandy hair looked sleeker and more prosperous than ever in the bright sunshine that flooded the room.

His face, though, was anything but sunny. "You should be resting," he insisted. "Renee, tell her a pregnant woman needs all the rest she can get."

The rotund housekeeper was clearing the dishes, but she paused as her employer appealed to her. She looked from Rodney to Rae-Anne, who was wearing a bright yellow shirtwaist dress with a wide white belt and cotton espadrilles, and feeling like anything but a pregnant woman in need of coddling.

"In my experience, Mr. Rodney, sometimes being pregnant gives a woman *more* energy, at least at the beginning," she said. "And I don't know about Rae-Anne, but I'm always happiest when I've got something to occupy me, and that's the plain truth." She hid her quick smile. "Sorry I can't tell you what you wanted to hear."

Rodney waited until Renee had left the room, then cautioned Rae-Anne, "I don't want you working a full shift. You still look tired."

They hadn't gone much beyond the obvious subjects last night. Rae-Anne had explained why she'd lost her nerve before the wedding, and Rodney had told her he understood, and felt bad for insisting on a big wedding when he'd known it wasn't her first choice.

He'd also said he'd been doing some hard thinking in the twenty-four hours she'd been gone. "When I had to face the possibility that you wanted out of this whole thing, it put things into a different perspective," he'd said. "The one thought I kept coming back to is that we could be so happy here—you and me and the baby. I hadn't realized until yesterday just how much I was looking forward to showing a fifth-generation Dietrich around his—or her—territory."

He'd told her before what a wonderful place to grow up the ranch was. And that sense of belonging—of connection with a place—was one of the things Rae-Anne most wanted to offer her child. After eighteen years of being moved from one country to another, from one ornate embassy to the next, she was determined that her child would never have to make a new set of friends only to lose them two years later, or come to know the feeling of being at home just in time to start packing for the next move.

They'd been small tragedies, those childhood uprootings, but they still loomed large in Rae-Anne's memories. She loved the thought of settling down on this hill-country ranch, with the quick-flowing river winding through stands of cypress trees and the rocky, open landscape of the scrubby grazing land. And she'd been happy to hear Rodney's enthusiasm for it last night.

"Did I tell you I was having that old barn rebuilt this week?" he'd asked. "I can't count the number of hours I spent down there when I was a kid. I learned to ride in that paddock when I wasn't much more than four years old. I want to fix it up so our kids can enjoy it when they get old enough."

Last night she'd been too tired to press any of the uncomfortable questions she needed to ask Rodney. Today, though, she knew it was time to remember the real reason she'd come back here. Without settling the question of Rodney's guilt or innocence, there wasn't much point to dreaming about a happy hill-country childhood for her baby.

"I've been wondering," she said, as she finished the last of the enormous glass of orange juice Renee had brought her. "Why didn't you and Danielle ever have kids? Didn't she want them?"

He stiffened a little, as he always did when she asked him about his first wife. "Let's not talk about Danielle," he said.

"But that's one of the things that's been bothering me."
She looked into his hazel eyes, trying to read his thoughts.
"One of the reasons I got such cold feet was that I felt as
though you and I don't really know each other in a lot of
important ways. I don't know anything about Danielle, or
how you felt about her—"

"I loved her. Obviously, since I married her. We didn't
have children because we didn't feel the time was right yet."

"And her death—that accident—"

"Do we have to talk about this, Rae-Anne?"

It had been barely two years since Danielle's death, Rae-
Anne knew. And it was entirely plausible that the sudden
strain in Rodney's voice was due to the fact that it still hurt
him too much to talk about what had happened.

But it could also be caused by an uneasy conscience. Rae-
Anne wished there was a simple way to tell guilt from grief,
but if there was one, she wasn't coming up with it.

"I just—wish I knew more about it, that's all."

"Hell, I do, too." He drained his coffee cup. "I had the
police go over that damn ski boat with a fine-tooth comb,
looking for some reason the towrope broke, but they
couldn't come up with any answers. Just a freaky accident,
they called it."

Jack Cotter had called it something quite different. And
Rae-Anne had to wonder whether Rodney had deliberately
mentioned the police search because he'd detected a hint of
suspicion in Rae-Anne's manner.

She didn't have time to decide. Rodney was looking at his
watch and standing up briskly. "I have a meeting at ten,"
he said. "I need to get going."

This was the first she'd heard of any meeting at ten. She
could have sworn he cut off the conversation to avoid talk-

ing about his deceased wife, but she couldn't think of a way to continue her questions without sounding too obvious.

And during the forty-five minute drive to San Antonio, he kept the conversation firmly on social matters, talking about a barbecue he wanted to host for the new work crew who would be rebuilding the old horse barn on the ranch. When they reached the downtown hotel that was the flagship for Rodney's chain, Rae-Anne still hadn't figured out whether she needed to be pushier or gentler in going after the answers she needed.

"How about a late lunch, and then head back home?" he asked as they entered the impressive three-story lobby.

"Sounds good." With luck, she would be able to gather the information she needed by then.

"Don't wear yourself out."

"Stop worrying. You sound more like a mother than my own mother ever did."

"Just figured I'd supply some of what you'd missed, that's all."

He gave her a quick kiss and a casual wave as she stepped into the elevator on her way to the bar on the top floor.

Rodney *could* supply so much of what she'd missed in her own childhood—a permanent home, a sense of belonging, a stable parental presence in the life of her child. If only she loved him more . . .

Without any warning at all, the image of Wiley Cotter's suntanned face pushed itself into her thoughts, smiling and suggestive and sexy as hell. "Get out of here, Wiley," she said out loud, shaking her head to chase the mental picture of him away. "Why the hell should I be thinking of *you* in the same breath as home and stability and all that good stuff?"

It couldn't have been because she was also thinking of love....

The thought distracted her as the elevator glided to a halt at the twentieth floor. Love wasn't really the issue here, she told herself firmly. The issue was Rodney's guilt or innocence. And if she was going to set her mind at rest about that, she needed an excuse to go digging around in the central personnel files for the hotel chain.

She was still trying to come up with one as the elevator doors slid open and she started to step out, turning automatically toward the long, carpeted corridor that led to the rooftop lounge where she'd presided as head bartender for the past two years. But the two businessmen in front of the elevator door weren't moving aside to let her pass, as she'd expected them to do.

In fact, they were heading straight for her.

By the time the first one had shouldered her toward the open elevator door, it was too late to protest. The second man grabbed her elbow, and the two of them hustled her into the elevator just as the doors were closing.

It all happened too quickly to make sense of it. The elevator started smoothly downward again, adding to the plummeting feeling in Rae-Anne's stomach as the two men muscled her into one corner of the small, enclosed space and leaned in on her.

She felt suddenly three feet tall, and utterly helpless. The certainty that that was how they wanted her to feel didn't help even a little bit.

"Heard you're in the family way." The man who spoke sounded casual, almost genial.

"Who told you that?" Her voice was sharp with anxiety. "Did Rodney tell you?"

There was a pause, as though the two men were exchanging glances over her head. Then the second stranger said, "No. And he doesn't know anything about this visit, either. This is just between you and us. Best to keep it that way, all right?"

"Why?" She had to force the word out.

"Because, Rae-Anne, that fiancé of yours is already in a world of trouble. You don't want him losing his temper, and digging himself into an even deeper hole, do you?"

Dear God in heaven, what were they talking about? All of Rae-Anne's vague suspicions about the Dietrich family business came alive in her mind again, more insistent and ominous than ever.

Had Rodney been talking to these strangers about her pregnancy? If he hadn't—

Rodney's housekeeper Renee knew about the baby. And that meant Renee's husband probably knew, too. And perhaps the rest of the ranch staff, for that matter.

Suddenly the circle of suspicion around her seemed to widen, taking in people whose names she didn't even know, people who seemed to know a lot more about her life at the moment than she knew herself.

Just like Wiley did...

Wiley... She mouthed his name silently, half-turned in on herself beneath the looming shoulders of the two men. The thought of Wiley Cotter—his unfailing nerve, his devil-may-care smile—was enough to give her some extra strength, some extra courage.

But it wasn't enough to keep her knees from shaking badly. And there was nothing she could do to hold in her gasp of fear as the second man leaned a little harder on her and pressed something flat and hard against her belly.

"Now listen up," he said. His slow, hoarse voice made Rae-Anne shiver. "It doesn't matter where we found out about the baby. The point is, it'd be a damn shame for anything to happen to the little guy. Wouldn't it."

It wasn't a question. And Rae-Anne was beyond answering anyway, because she'd just turned her head enough to look down and see what was in his hand.

It was a knife. A long, gleaming knife, with the blade pressing flat against the part of her body next to her unborn child. All he had to do was twist the blade a quarter turn—

His words made the thought even more chilling. "Poor thing," he said smoothly. "So little, and so helpless."

"What—why are you doing this?" She couldn't make her voice operate as anything more than a whisper. And she couldn't get her hands free, no matter how hard she struggled, because the brawny bodies of the two strangers had her blocked completely. Everything in her mind was screaming at her to cover her belly, to protect her child.

And she couldn't do it.

Just as she thought the tension might tear her apart, she heard the soft bing of the elevator bell announcing that they had arrived wherever they were going. Rae-Anne braced herself to fight, in case they tried to drag her out of the elevator. But instead she felt the pressure of their weight lessening.

That didn't take away the threat in what the first man was saying. He moved his face very close to Rae-Anne's just for a moment and said, "Remember what we're telling you, all right? And don't go asking questions about what doesn't concern you."

They were out of the elevator almost as soon as the doors slid open. Rae-Anne leaned against the back wall, fending off her sick feeling of helplessness and the curious stares of a family of tourists who were waiting at the parking garage level to get on. It took her a moment to realize that someone in the elevator was asking what floor she wanted, and another few seconds to get her voice working well enough to tell them to push the button for twenty.

Chapter 7

Wiley had always hated rooftop bars. He liked to keep his feet on the ground and all his escape routes open, and he couldn't do either one to his satisfaction on the twentieth floor of this upscale hotel.

But he made himself stay in his place at the end of the long polished wooden bar, because this was where Rae-Anne was. Or at least this was where she was *supposed* to be.

He'd watched her leave the ranch house with Rodney earlier and had busted his tail to get to his vehicle and arrive at the downtown hotel ahead of them. He'd been sitting inconspicuously next to a potted palm in the lobby when they'd come in, and was in the very next elevator after the one Rae-Anne had taken. Ordering a drink at the classy top-floor bar hadn't taken long.

But Rae-Anne hadn't shown up yet, and Wiley was beginning to wonder if he should go looking for her. He'd told himself he was going to keep an eye on her, even if she didn't want him to. And he couldn't very well do that if he was just sitting around nursing a beer he had no real intention of drinking. Yet the elevator she'd been on had come straight up to the twentieth floor—he'd watched the lit numbers with his own eyes. She should be here, somewhere.

The hotel was far too big for him to do a floor-by-floor search for her. Wiley gave a frustrated growl and decided that if he was going to be stuck here, he might as well get on with the next part of his plan.

The daytime bartender was a young man with jet black hair and a relaxed gait. Wiley caught his attention with an upraised finger, and said casually, "I heard there might be an opening for a bartender around here. Any chance of applying for it?"

The young man looked him over. "You got experience?" he asked.

"Sure do." With luck, the guy wouldn't ask for particulars, since the experience Wiley was referring to consisted mostly of popping the tops off beer bottles for his brothers at their occasional backyard get-togethers.

"Where'd you hear we were looking for somebody?"

"I kind of deduced it." Wiley put on his most self-deprecating grin. "Heard your head bartender was getting married to the owner of the hotel chain last weekend."

The young man shook his glossy head. "If you're talking about Rae-Anne, I don't think she has any plans to quit her job," he said. "In fact—" He paused.

"In fact what?" Wiley pounced on the hesitation.

The bartender put down the glass he was polishing and picked up another one. "I'm not sure she has any intention of marrying the boss, either," he said. "I heard she didn't show up at their wedding ceremony this weekend."

"No fooling." Wiley whistled. "What's this boss of yours like, anyway? To work for, I mean?"

"Mr. Dietrich? He's okay."

"Meaning . . . ?" Wiley let it turn into an open question.

The bartender shrugged. "It's not a bad place to work. I guess it used to be kind of—" He cut himself off. "Well, that has nothing to do with working here, really."

"Used to be kind of what?" Wiley prompted. He'd questioned a lot of witnesses over the years, and he'd discovered that the things people wanted to leave out almost always turned out to be the most interesting.

"Well, I've only worked here for a few months. But I heard that until the last couple of years the place was sort of party central, if you know what I mean. The chain's sort of changed its direction recently. You know, more families, more business trade, not such a high-rolling crowd."

"Why the change?"

The young man shrugged again. Wiley was glad he'd found a Dietrich employee willing to gossip about his boss. On the other hand, everything the bartender was saying confirmed Rae-Anne's insistence that Rodney had reformed his high-living ways. And that left Wiley feeling more torn in two than ever.

He'd run into plenty of conflicts in his twenty-year career in law enforcement. But even his final DEA case, with all its dangers and distractions, hadn't pulled him apart the way he was being pulled now.

He'd launched himself into this case certain that Rodney Dietrich was as guilty as the FBI believed him to be. But then he'd heard Rae-Anne's side of things, and started to see Rodney through her eyes. Was it possible that she was right, that Rodney *was* a reformed character, that Jack and his colleagues were off track and threatening the best chance at happiness Rae-Anne had ever known?

After the meeting with Jack and Rae-Anne's staggering announcement that she was pregnant, Wiley had had to think hard and fast about where he stood. It hadn't been easy, with loyalty to Jack tugging him in one direction and all his renewed feelings for Rae-Anne trying to haul him in the other.

But he'd finally sorted it out.

He stood just where he'd always stood. He would do everything he could to see the truth out in the open, and then he would step aside. If Rodney Dietrich was the lawbreaker Jack thought he was, then Wiley would see that it came out. If the guy turned out to be a sweetheart, Wiley would air that just as wholeheartedly.

It wasn't going to be easy for him no matter which way it turned out. But he couldn't screw around with the truth, not for Jack, not even for Rae-Anne.

So he gritted his teeth and told himself he needed to hear what this junior bartender had to tell him.

It wasn't much. "I guess Mr. Dietrich's getting older, wanting to settle down," he said. "He seems to have calmed down a lot, from what I hear."

Rodney Dietrich was one year younger than Wiley, but Wiley let that pass. He was more interested in this corroboration of Rae-Anne's point of view.

Was Rodney truly in love with Rae-Anne? Was that the reason for his seeming change of heart during the time Rae-Anne had worked here? Had she inspired things in Rodney no one else had been able to?

Hell, she'd done that in Wiley, too. The difference was that in return, Rodney could offer her all the things she'd lacked in her life. Like security. And a home. And domesticity. Wiley couldn't guarantee her any of those things.

The most domestic thing Wiley had done in the past ten years was to build a deck on the back of his house. And even then he was seldom home to enjoy it. Rodney Dietrich, with his five hundred acres of hill country and his comfortable family home, could answer Rae-Anne's hopes in a way Wiley never could.

And besides, Rodney was the father of her child. Wiley couldn't overlook that little piece of information.

He glared at his untouched beer. Rae-Anne had every reason to be hoping that her fiancé was innocent, and every reason to want Wiley to stay out of her way while she was trying to prove it. If Wiley had been the noble, self-sacrificing type, he'd probably have *stayed* out of her way, too.

But he wasn't.

He was just a stubborn, skeptical man who'd only ever loved one woman in his whole life. And he couldn't walk away from her again until he was certain she was going to be all right.

"And where the hell is she now?"

He hadn't realized he'd spoken out loud until he saw the bartender's startled look. A moment later the young man's glance swiveled toward the entrance to the bar.

"If you mean Rae-Anne," he said, "she's right here."

Even before midday, the light in the bar was dim. The few patrons sitting by the big plate-glass windows could enjoy a sunlit view of downtown San Antonio, but in the interior of the big open room, low lighting and dark varnished wood prevailed. In the doorway, Rae-Anne's yellow dress was eye-catchingly bright. She seemed to be floating in the midst of the soft fabric that swirled around her legs.

It took Wiley a moment to realize that the fabric was only swirling that way because she'd stopped so abruptly. When he took a closer look at her, it was obvious that something was very wrong.

He knew that expression. Her face was serious, her blue eyes narrowed, her soft mouth pulled into a thoughtful frown. Rae-Anne was thinking hard, and not coming up with anything.

Thinking about what? What had made her so serious so suddenly? Wiley was powerfully tempted to get off his bar stool and go over to meet her, but he knew it would be the wrong thing to do. Scowling, he stayed where he was, one hand wrapped around his glass.

She hadn't seen him yet. He watched her glance over her shoulder toward the brightly lit hallway. Whatever she saw—or didn't see—out there seemed to convince her that the lounge was where she wanted to be, after all. He saw her shoulders settle and her chin lift slightly as she moved into the big room.

"Hey, Rae-Anne." The bartender's voice seemed to startle her. It startled Wiley, too, making him realize how completely he'd been focused on Rae-Anne.

Wake up, Cotter, he warned himself. *You're supposed to be staying on top of things here. How can you guard Rae-Anne if your attention never gets beyond the look on her face and the way her dress swirls when she moves?*

He looked away from her, listening to her greet her co-worker with some noncommittal answer to the comment that she was at work earlier than she'd been expected.

"Could you find me the bar inventory sheets, Tony?" She sounded as distracted as she looked. And there was something else trembling at the edge of her words as she added, "I figured I'd do the bar order while I was here."

Wiley knew that sound.

It was fear.

He frowned as the younger bartender started toward the office behind the big central bar. What in hell had happened to scare her between the first floor and the twentieth?

Tony remembered Wiley's presence at the last moment. "You want to talk to that guy down at the end of the bar?" he said. "He was asking about a job."

Rae-Anne finally glanced in Wiley's direction. As their eyes met, she seemed frozen to the spot, and he had a sudden sense that this was one thing too much for her, that she wanted to turn on her heel and run.

Why?

But just as he was about to stand up, to head off her escape if necessary, he saw her gather herself together, straightening her spine as she faced him. She wasn't exactly greeting him with a big smile and a wave, but at least her blue eyes were flickering with that spirit he loved in her so much.

"I'll handle it," she said slowly, and made her way to where Wiley was sitting. She lowered her voice as she reached him, demanding, "Wiley, what in *hell* are you doing here?"

Her voice was still quivering. And she was keeping it low, so that Tony and the bar's few patrons couldn't possibly overhear her. Wiley could still see the troubled look on her face, the too-serious expression that told him something was wrong.

She'd looked that way when he'd first picked her up in the limousine on Saturday.

And when she'd found out about the FBI's investigation into her fiancé.

He wanted to know what was making her look that way now.

"You keep asking me that question," he told her, pitching his voice so it wouldn't be overheard.

"And you still haven't given me an answer I like. Why won't you just leave me alone?"

There it was again—that edge of panic, that hint of fear under the self-possession she was working so hard at. Wiley wished he could vault over the bar and take her in his arms, smoothing her dark red hair and reassuring her that whatever was going on, he would help her handle it.

He couldn't, of course. For one thing, he was trying to come off as a casual job applicant, not a long-lost lover or a caped crusader. For another, Rae-Anne didn't want his comfort. And he couldn't promise her the happy ending she deserved, anyway. At best, he was limited to doing what he could to make sure she stayed safe.

"Are you all right?" He leaned forward, trying to meet her eyes again. The troubled way she was avoiding his gaze seemed to answer his question.

And her words contradicted it. "If I say I'm fine, will you accept it and go away?"

"Hell, no." He leaned back. "Like your young friend said, I'm here to apply for a job." He looked around the room, with its old-Texas wooden bar and comfortable, leather-upholstered chairs. "This is a pretty fancy joint, isn't it? Not much like D'Angelo's."

She moved a tray of clean glasses out of her way and started sliding them into the racks above the counter. Whether it was the mention of the bar outside Austin where they'd met, or the fact that he'd watched her doing exactly this at the end of her shift so many times, Wiley felt something in his chest tighten as he followed her back-and-forth motions.

"D'Angelo's was a dive." Her voice was a little steadier, as though the familiar routine of racking glasses was calming to her.

"You didn't think so at the time. You liked it because it was so funky."

"Funkiness was still a novelty for me back then. I'd had all those years in fancy embassies, remember? I thought anyplace without marble floors was just great."

"And now you're back to marble floors again."

Pointedly, she directed his attention to the carpeted floor under his bar stool. "I'm happy to settle for wall-to-wall these days," she said. "The clientele here is pleasant, the pay's good, and I finally got tired of moving all the time."

"So you compromised."

"Of course I compromised. It's what happens when you grow up, in case you hadn't figured that out by now. Living at the extremes is just too exhausting. And those funky little joints I used to work at were pretty extreme. So you can be nostalgic for D'Angelo's if you want to, but I've put those days behind me."

He'd known that already. And he'd never really felt nostalgic for D'Angelo's until just now. But somehow, it was almost unbearably poignant to be sitting here at the bar while Rae-Anne finished stacking glasses and reached for a couple of limes.

He'd been drifting from one extreme to the other, too, in those days. He'd been as alone in the world as Rae-Anne, and he'd given up any idea that he might ever be any other way.

And then, straight out of the blue, simply because he'd stopped in for a drink one night after a bone-crackingly stressful day of pretending he was someone else, he'd found her, cutting up limes and arguing with him just exactly the way she was doing right now. In spite of the lingering look of fear in her eyes, she'd settled quickly into their old pattern of sparring over anything and everything, and it made Wiley want to stretch the moment out, enjoying the familiar give-and-take.

I've put those days behind me. Wiley stifled a sigh and told himself he would do the same thing, if he was smart.

If he could just forget the joy of discovering another human being who seemed to understand the loneliness he felt inside sometimes . . .

And the longing for something more . . .

And the gut-level fear he had of reaching for that something, whatever it might be . . .

He pushed his beer glass away from him almost angrily. Rae-Anne had overcome her fear of reaching for her dreams. That was what she was trying to tell him, and he should be listening, not wallowing in memories that weren't going to do anybody any good. Maybe she was right. Maybe you had to compromise if you were ever going to get what you wanted.

He didn't want to compromise. He wanted Rae-Anne, and he couldn't have her. The thought made his voice rough as he said, "So how about that job I was asking about?"

"How about it?" She looked startled. "I figured that was just an excuse to follow me down here."

"It was an excuse to get into the personnel department with you. Isn't that what you're supposed to be doing?"

She blinked, as though she'd forgotten all about it. Then she made a quick recovery. "I can do it on my own," she said.

"But wouldn't it be easier with somebody to distract the personnel director while you look through the files?"

"How do you know we even *have* a personnel director? Or that I was planning to look through the files?"

"Come on, Rae-Anne. Give me some credit here. I did my homework. I do this all the time, remember?"

Her face set into that serious frown again. "I remember," she said. She didn't sound very pleased about it. She went back to slicing in silence, cutting through the limes so forcefully that Wiley got the definite impression she was trying to send him a message about something.

"I'm not going away," he said finally. "You might as well take me up on my offer."

Her blue eyes were still flickering with tightly concealed anxiety, but her voice was less wary as she answered him. He had the sense, just as he'd had in that moonlit moment when he'd kissed her last night, that she was having a hard time hanging on to her anger at him.

"You'd be a lot easier to take if you weren't occasionally right about things," she muttered, splitting the final lime wedge with a particularly fierce downstroke.

Wiley couldn't stop the slow grin that spread across his face. "Only occasionally?" he said.

"Don't push it, Cotter." She scraped the limes into a bowl and turned to call to the younger bartender that she was going to take their visitor down to the office to fill out an application form.

"If he can sling drinks half as well as he slings baloney, he's a natural for this job," she added. If she heard Wiley's quiet chuckle behind her as she led the way out of the bar, she didn't let on.

"Heseltine. H-e-s-e-l—"

Rae-Anne shook her head. It was hard for her to picture Wiley Cotter under any other name, especially one like Raymond Heseltine, which was how he'd introduced himself in the hotel's personnel department.

He was in the outer office now, giving his particulars to Jerry, the director of personnel. Normally a casual applicant would have been given a form and told to complete it on his own. But Rae-Anne had made a fuss over the so-called Raymond Heseltine, introducing him as an excellent possibility for the next bartending job that came up, and the personnel director had taken her cue.

Once she'd gotten over her resentment at the way Wiley had stampeded her—again—she'd realized that he was offering her the excuse she needed to go rummaging through the personnel department's files. Without the distraction, it would have been much harder to get around Jerry in the office while she looked for the information she wanted.

And she couldn't deny that after her scare in the elevator, Wiley's strong presence was more comforting than she would have believed possible.

She glanced at him and saw him apparently engrossed in applying for a job. The photocopier was right next to the file cabinet she was after, and she figured she had about ten minutes to copy the pertinent files.

"The courtesy van driver—the guy who died so conveniently—was making regular pickups of illegal cash out at Intercontinental Airport," Jack Cotter had told her during yesterday's meeting. "Mob runners would get in the van at the airport, ride downtown to one of Dietrich's hotels and just 'forget' their briefcases on the van. Ellis Maitland, the driver, would take them inside, where the money got counted and shoved along to various bank accounts in various people's names."

"Wait a minute," Rae-Anne had said. "I noticed Ellis doing that once. He was coming in from his shift with an expensive-looking briefcase in his hand, and I asked him whether somebody had forgotten it."

"What did he say?" Jack had wanted to know.

"That a client had left it, but he knew which hotel the man had gotten off at, and he was going to deliver it on his way home. He seemed very cool about it."

"He should have seemed cool. He'd been running the same route with the same couriers for years, ever since the mob bought into Rodney's hotel chain and had Rodney set up the money-laundering angle as part of the payback for what he owed them."

"Ellis could have been doing this on his own," Rae-Anne pointed out. "You still don't have hard proof that Rodney is involved personally."

"No, we don't," Jack conceded. "Not yet."

To get the proof the FBI needed, Jack had to find out who was delivering the cash in the mob money-laundering scheme now. "It's probably still an employee in the hotel," Jack said.

"A *new* employee," Mack MacGuire had put in.

"Right. If something's working, these folks don't usually change it. Our guess is that among the people who've been hired at the hotel chain since Ellis Maitland's death there will be one who's been planted there by the mob. What we need is a name."

And to come up with one, Rae-Anne was going to need the application forms for everyone who'd recently been hired at the hotel. Luckily, she was somewhat familiar with the filing system and knew that new employees' files were kept together at the front of one of the drawers until the information could be put into the computer system. Finding the dozen-or-so folders she needed didn't take long.

She didn't bother to read the forms as she copied them. She'd said she wanted to look over the applications on file for wait staff positions, and she didn't want to have to explain why she was nowhere near the right cabinet for that, in case Jerry came into the inner office before she was done.

He was still busy with Wiley, though, when Rae-Anne emerged with her file folder of copies slung into the back pocket of her purse. "Find what you were after?" Jerry asked, looking up.

"Yes, thanks." She looked at Wiley, feeling the magnetic pull of his dark gaze as she did every time she met his eyes. "I hope we find you a position, Mr. Heseltine," she told him. "And don't worry about those youthful indiscretions you were telling me about. This isn't the kind of place that would hold a thing like that against you, especially seeing as you were never even formally charged with anything."

She saw Jerry frown and shot Wiley a pointed look over the top of the personnel director's head as she left the office. Let him weasel his way out of that on his own, she thought, since he was so good at pretending to be people he wasn't.

The look in his eyes—affronted and amused at the same time—stayed with her as she went into the lobby and stood waiting for the elevator with a reassuring-looking group of women. And then her amusement faded.

He'd been playing a role for the DEA when she'd met him, and she'd seen the toll it had taken on him then. He'd been working on a case involving a big drug ring out of the Port of Houston, and although he'd always been sketchy about the details, it had been clear that any slip could cost him his life.

As, in fact, it almost had.

That heart-stopping danger hadn't seemed to convince him that law enforcement wasn't a safe place to be. True, impersonating Raymond Heseltine in the hotel office wasn't exactly a dangerous assignment. But she was still chilled by how automatically he slid into his professional role, and how good he was at his hazardous job.

She thought of how much it had hurt when he'd disappeared from her life. And how terrified she'd been just now—how terrified she *still* was, when she let herself remember the feeling of being hemmed in by the two strangers in this very elevator.

She wasn't cut out for the danger and drama that made up Wiley's everyday life. And she didn't intend to raise her children with any hint of that kind of dread hanging over them.

She shuddered uncontrollably as she stepped into the elevator with the other women. She rubbed one fist vigorously against her stomach, but it wasn't nearly enough to erase the memory of that long knife blade pressing against her, or the fear that one quick flick of a stranger's wrist might bring a hideous end to her dreams for her unborn child.

Still distracted by the strangers' threats, and by the knowledge that Wiley Cotter might turn up again at any moment, she helped Tony with the start of the lunch rush, then settled down to do her bar order at the little desktop behind the bar. Or at least that was what she intended to do.

First, she thought, she might as well glance over the personnel files she'd copied. Something might jump out at her, something that would point the finger at the mob and away from Rodney.

She scanned the photocopies, mentally noting the names of the eleven recent employees. One was a new courtesy van driver, replacing the late Ellis Maitland. Rae-Anne wondered whether the people behind the money-laundering scheme would do anything as blatantly obvious as simply replacing one hired hand with another.

Wiley had told her that Ellis Maitland had agreed to testify for the prosecution in exchange for immunity on another charge. And that he'd been killed because he was a security risk to his real employers. Surely they would cover their tracks a little more carefully than that.

Of the remaining ten, five were chambermaids, two were laundry workers, one was a front desk clerk, one a market researcher and one a banquet coordinator. Rae-Anne was inclined to wash out the last two, who wouldn't come into casual contact with the general public as much as the money-pickup scheme seemed to require. Of the others, two of the chambermaids were former employees returning after absences, which made them seem less likely, as well.

Three of the files caught her attention. Ruth Garcia, another of the chambermaids, had given only a very sketchy employment history, something Jerry was usually a stickler about. But she'd been hired anyway.

And one of the laundry workers, Armand Grant, seemed to have qualifications that suited him for something a lot more upscale than washing sheets in a hotel basement. Truck driver, airplane pilot, charter boat organizer... Why would a man with so many abilities take on such a low-end job?

The third oddity was the front desk clerk, who'd written "also known as Randy Melrose" next to his real name, Randy Mountjoy. Unless he was an aspiring novelist looking for any available publicity for his nom de plume, it seemed strange. She looked at the employee ID picture she'd copied for each of the three, and wondered if one of them could be the person Jack Cotter was looking for.

"What have you got there?"

Rodney's voice cut into her thoughts, cultured as always but enough of a surprise that Rae-Anne jumped. "You scared me," she told him, hoping she could hold his attention away from the personnel forms by pretending to be annoyed. "Damn it, Rodney, you know I've been on edge lately. Please don't sneak up on me like that."

"I'm sorry."

He leaned one linen-clad hip on the corner of the desk and stroked her cheek gently. "I just didn't recall ever seeing you so engrossed in a bar order before. It looked like you were getting too far back into work, and I figured I'd jolt you out of it."

"Well, you managed that, all right."

Shaking her head and hoping he didn't notice her trembling fingers, she shuffled the forms into line and closed the file folder on them. She hadn't had time to work through all the implications of the two men's threats in the elevator in the past half hour, but they started coming to her again now as she looked at Rodney.

Had the two strangers been telling her the truth when they'd said Rodney knew nothing about their visit? She wanted desperately to ask him straight out, to clear the air between them before anything else could go wrong.

But something in Rae-Anne was sure that Rodney would never do anything to threaten his own child. And if he *hadn't* had anything to do with the two men in the elevator—if they were emissaries of some criminal operation that Rodney wasn't a part of, or was trying to free himself from—

The thought made her tremble all over again as she put the file folder in her purse. "I was just looking over what we've got on file for wait staff applications," she said. "If we stay this busy, I'm going to need more help on the evening shift."

"You shouldn't be worrying about that now." Rodney stood up and shook the creases out of his tan trousers. "You've got other things on your mind, remember?"

She didn't need his significant look at her belly to remind her. She put one hand down on her stomach, and wondered why she suddenly felt like crying.

Was it because she'd always thought that pregnancy would be a magical time, a time to revel in the sense that a new life was growing inside her? Now, instead of making happy plans for the future, she was less and less certain what that future might hold.

"Rodney," she said, suddenly determined to force the issue into the open, "we've never really talked about the business side of our getting married."

"What do you mean?" He was frowning at her.

"I mean that this hotel chain is a big corporation. And as your wife, I'll have an interest in it. Right?"

He didn't answer right away. When he did, though, his voice was careful and neutral. "Are you saying we should have some sort of prenuptial agreement?"

"I'm just saying I think I should know more than I do about how the hotels operate. I mean, you had that big expansion a few years ago. Has the corporation recovered financially from that? Is the organization as healthy as it seems? That's the kind of thing I just wish I knew."

She didn't like the change that was coming over Rodney's good-looking features as she spoke. When she'd first known him, he'd sometimes dealt with his responsibilities by letting them slide off him like rainwater rushing over a dry riverbed. She'd seen a big change in him since she'd started working here, and it had been a while since she'd met that blank gaze that told her that even though he was still standing here, he'd essentially withdrawn from the conversation.

"It's all pretty complicated," he said.

"Meaning you think I won't understand it?" she challenged him.

Her tone of voice seemed to startle him, but only for a moment. His face had that masklike composure again as he said, "There's not that much to understand, really. Everything's running on a pretty even keel at the moment, and I don't see why things shouldn't stay that way. We're fully booked most of the time, and the convention business is still growing. Why are you worried about this? Why don't we just go and get some lunch?''

Oddly, it was his last question that finally threatened to crack the smoothness in his voice. Rae-Anne could hear the quiet sound of alarm in it, just as she'd heard fear in her own voice not long ago. If Rodney was trapped in something that wasn't his own doing—if he was in some kind of danger, and being watched over by people who would turn the events of his private life to their own advantage—

"Rodney, what's going on?" Impulsively, she put a hand toward him, but he didn't return the gesture. "There's something the matter with the business, isn't there? Did you have to borrow money you can't pay back? Is that what's wrong?"

She almost wished he would show anger, or anxiety, or anything at all. The evenness of his voice as he answered her and the glassy calm in his eyes were more unnerving than any argument could have been.

"Everything's going to be okay," he said. "I can make a good home for you and the baby. We're going to be happy together. You'll see."

"How can I believe that when you won't be completely honest with me?"

"*Please,* Rae-Anne." For a moment she thought his facade might finally open up, but he got himself in hand almost immediately. "Please don't ask me about this again. Everything's going to be fine."

Oh, God, Rae-Anne thought. She wished she could believe him, wished it was just as simple as trusting that Rodney knew what he was talking about. Part of her was longing to settle down, to ignore life's hard questions and to enjoy the work and the rewards of raising her children in the part of the country she loved best.

But there were those two men in the elevator.

And the FBI's accusations.

And the way Wiley Cotter kept showing up, dark and insistent, like a reminder of everything that was wrong and unsettled in Rae-Anne's mind.

And Rodney's only answer to all of this was to refuse to answer her questions, and to draw a bland and unmovable cover over whatever was bothering him.

Something *was* bothering him. She was certain of that. And she had some vague and unpleasant ideas about what it was. But what Rodney was telling her was that as far as he was concerned, they were going to have to stay vague.

And that made them seem more menacing than ever.

Chapter 8

"I can't stay long." Rae-Anne dropped the manila file folder on the table between her and Jack Cotter. "Rodney thinks I just came into town on a quick shopping trip."

It was Tuesday afternoon, the day after she'd copied the personnel files, and this was the first chance she'd had to get the files to Jack. They were sitting in a coffee shop in New Braunfels, at a corner table from which, Rae-Anne sincerely hoped, no one she knew would recognize her and wonder who her companion was.

"You think he suspects anything?"

"He might."

She had debated whether to tell Jack about the two men in the elevator and had decided against it. Rodney's manner, remote and ambiguous, had made her think more than ever that he might have gotten involved in something that was far beyond his depth. And that seemed to argue for his innocence overall.

But she knew Jack had a stake in proving Rodney guilty. And he would undoubtedly see the incident with the two men as proof of that. So she'd decided only to share hard, concrete evidence, like the photocopied personnel files. She would keep the doubtful facts to herself, for now.

He nodded as he scanned the files she'd given him. "There's no real need for us to stay and finish this coffee," he said. "Might be less suspicious if—"

"There *is* one other thing."

She'd been debating with herself about this, too. She'd tried to concentrate on the problem of Rodney, tried to put Wiley out of her thoughts altogether. She'd told herself she didn't care about Wiley's past since he couldn't possibly have a place in her future.

But none of it had quite worked. And now the sight of Jack Cotter's long limbs and dark, watchful eyes made it impossible to forget about the man who'd stalked in and out of her dreams in the few hours she'd managed to sleep last night in Rodney's guest room.

Maybe her mind would be more settled if she could fill in a few of the blanks that were bothering her about Wiley, she thought. And Jack Cotter was just the person to help her out.

So she pushed past her hesitation and said, "I was wondering about you and Sam. And Wiley."

Was it her imagination, or did his hawklike eyes sharpen a little more at her question? He tapped his thumb against the closed file folder, the way she remembered him doing during their meeting on Sunday, and said, "What about me and Sam and Wiley?"

She paused again and finally decided just to plunge in. "When I knew Wiley before, he gave me the impression that the only family he had was scattered to the winds," she said.

"But the three of you are obviously very close now. What happened? How did you get back together?"

"Why don't you ask Wiley?"

"I'm not sure he'd tell me."

He looked steadily at her for a moment. "Well, if he doesn't want to tell you, I don't know if I should jump in."

Jack not only looked like Wiley, he was starting to affect Rae-Anne the same way, minus the pulse-boosting attraction that always got in her way whenever Wiley was around. Wiley had always touched her temper in a hurry, as well as her heart, and Jack was starting to do the same thing, without any apparent effort at all.

"What is it with you guys?" she demanded, leaning across the table so their nearest neighbors in the coffee shop wouldn't be able to overhear her. "I'm not asking for a state secret, Jack. I just want to know why the three of you get so darned laconic whenever the subject of your family comes up."

The rhythmic thumping of Jack's thumb on the tabletop was more pronounced now. "Why do you want to know?" he asked finally. "Aren't you busy trying to clear Rodney Dietrich's name so you can marry him?"

"This has nothing to do with Rodney."

Jack gave her a quick version of the grin that was so laid-back on Sam's face and so incredibly sexy on Wiley's. "Rae-Anne, the Cotter brothers may be laconic, but we're not stupid. Anybody can see you and Wiley mean a lot to each other."

"*Meant* a lot," she corrected quickly.

"Are you sure about that?"

She thought about the nights she and Wiley had spent in each other's arms, and the way she had instinctively seemed to recognize him—mind, body and soul—as the answer to so many of the persistent, echoing questions in her life.

He wasn't the answer to the question of who was the father of her baby.

And he wasn't the answer when it came to giving that baby a home free of upheavals and uprootings, either. Rae-Anne frowned across the table at Wiley's younger brother and said, "Yes, I'm sure. Whatever Wiley and I shared is in the past. But now all of a sudden I seem to be surrounded by Cotter men, whether I want to be or not. And I'm curious about how you all got split apart and how you got back together again."

She paused and saw that she'd been right in her guess about Jack. When something touched him closely, he could be just as infuriatingly aloof about it as Wiley.

"Come on, Jack," she said. "Humor me. I'm doing you a big favor here. How about a small one in return?"

He snorted and gave her another quick grin. "You know," he said, "you really don't seem like Wiley's type. He says he gets enough contention out of his job without having to go looking for it after hours."

Sam had said nearly the same thing. Rae-Anne frowned and said, "I told you, this has nothing to do with me and Wiley."

"If you say so." She could tell he wasn't convinced.

And his silence after he'd spoken was starting to get on her nerves. "All right," she said finally. "You don't have to tell me if you don't want to."

"I don't." He reached for the casual suit jacket he'd draped over the back of his chair. "But that doesn't mean you can't ask Wiley about it."

"I've told you, I don't think he'll—"

He leaned forward quickly, as though what he had to say was important and he wanted to make sure it wasn't overheard. "I learned a long time ago not to take too many things about Wiley for granted," he said. "Push him the wrong way and he'll clam up on you, it's true. But if you find the right way—" He mimed the motion of cracking open a clamshell. "He's all yours." His grin was sudden and dazzling. "And don't tell him I told you so," he added as he stood up.

More cryptic Cotter wisdom, Rae-Anne thought as she slung her purse over her shoulder. They'd agreed to leave the coffee shop separately, just in case they were seen by someone outside, and she preceded Jack to the front door, wondering how he'd managed to make a simple question so convoluted.

It was only after she was out in the afternoon sun that she remembered that their meeting was supposed to have been about Rodney Dietrich, and not about Wiley, at all.

Rodney had announced his intentions of working short days this week, so that he could spend time at the ranch with Rae-Anne. And while she'd been in New Braunfels, he'd decided that tonight would be the time to stage the cookout he'd talked about yesterday.

"I always like to do this when we've got new people working on the property," he said, reminding her of the work crew who had started work on the horse barn the day before. "You know—show a little hill-country hospitality and all. Want to ride down with me and let them know about it?"

She suspected he was also hoping that a full, blowout, Texas-style barbecue might remind Rae-Anne just how good life in the country could really be. But she was always glad of a reason to be outside on the ranch, and as soon as she'd changed into more casual clothes, she was happy to join Rodney in the late-model Jeep he used for transportation around the property.

And besides, being out in the country would take her mind off Wiley Cotter and her ongoing curiosity about what his life had been like before she met him. She hadn't wondered about it ten years ago—maybe it had been clear that what they'd had was only for the moment, and never meant to last. And she wasn't sure why she was wondering about it so inescapably now.

But she was, and she still hadn't chased it out of her head as the Jeep bounced to a halt behind the half-fallen stone barn. This was getting out of hand, she thought. It was bad enough to be dreaming of Wiley at night, bad enough that he seemed to be lurking around every corner she turned. Now she seemed to be having problems clearing her mind of him even when he was nowhere around.

"You didn't bring a hat." Rodney looked over at her.

"I forgot."

"You can borrow mine. Here." Rodney pulled a navy blue baseball cap from the back seat. "You know you get sunburned just *thinking* about being out in the sun."

It was true. It was also true that she hated being fussed over, and she wished Rodney wasn't doing it now.

Wait a minute, a voice at the back of her mind cut in. *What about all those fantasies of having a happy, relaxed pregnancy and enjoying putting your feet up for a while? Doesn't that imply letting people fuss over you?*

Rae-Anne adjusted the baseball cap over the hair she'd braided into a thick single strand, and slipped on the sandals she'd kicked off. Maybe she just didn't want *Rodney* fussing over her. She stopped moving, struck by the idea.

Rodney had a way of hovering over her that had only happened since she'd found out she was pregnant. He was acting as though she had suddenly become breakable, and Rae-Anne didn't like it.

Wiley would never treat her that way, she knew. She remembered how he'd reacted two days ago when she'd told him about her pregnancy. He'd been as blunt as usual—blunter, even. He hadn't tried to smooth things over for her or pretend the situation was better than it was. Suddenly, in contrast to Rodney's careful solicitude, she found herself missing Wiley's rough honesty.

Damn it, she was thinking about him *again*.

It was getting almost laughable. She squinted against the late-afternoon sun and told herself she had to get him out of her thoughts. For heaven's sake, even the strangers on Rodney's work crew were starting to remind her of him now. The broad-shouldered, lean-waisted man lifting one end of that big beam, for instance—

Was Wiley Cotter.

It wasn't just her imagination. It was Wiley in the flesh, all six-foot-three of him, soaking up the hot October sun and sweating along with the rest of the crew on the tumble-down barn. Rae-Anne caught her breath and paused halfway out of the Jeep.

"Something wrong, Rae-Anne?" Even behind Rodney's dark sunglasses she could see his expression of concern.

"No," she said quickly. "Just a stiff muscle."

Rodney took that as a signal to help her out of the vehicle and keep hold of her hand as they walked closer to the barn. Rae-Anne could feel her heart beating harder. And her heart wasn't the only part of her responding to the sight of Wiley's magnificent, half-naked body in the sunlight.

He was wearing old jeans, a pair of work boots and nothing more. His upper body was covered in a sheen of sweat, so the impressive planes of his chest and shoulders were highlighted in the sun.

She could tell how heavy the big beam must be, but Wiley was holding his end of it without apparent strain. Rae-

Anne's eyes were drawn inescapably to the hard curve of his upper arm, and the way his tightly corded muscles shifted as he changed his grip slightly.

He'd held her in exactly the same way—effortless, but infinitely strong. In spite of the shade of Rodney's hat, she felt suddenly as though she'd had far too much sun. Her whole body was overtaken by the memory of how it had felt to be held against Wiley Cotter's broad chest, how those powerful arms had cradled her, possessed her.

He looked in her direction without warning, almost as though he'd heard the erotic current of her thoughts. At first she thought he was glaring at her, and tried to summon up her usual spirited reaction to any and all opposition from Wiley.

She couldn't do it. He was too beautiful, with his dark hair in a sweat-dampened tangle over his forehead and his smooth, tanned skin radiating the glow of the afternoon sun.

And after a moment she realized he wasn't frowning, anyway. He was just squinting into the light. After the briefest of glances, he looked away again, making some comment to the workman who was struggling to do something with a chisel at the other end of the beam.

Even that momentary eye contact was enough to shoot Rae-Anne's pulse sky-high again. Wiley's dark gaze was so heated, so sensually alive. She was amazed that she seemed to be the only one aware of it, or of him.

Rodney certainly didn't seem to notice anything out of the ordinary. "See?" he was saying, pointing beyond the spot where Wiley stood. "You can still see the outlines of the old paddock. I'm going to get Abel to fence it in again, when the barn's done."

"Where did the work crew come from, do you know?" Rae-Anne couldn't help asking.

"Abel hires them. He uses mostly local odd jobbers, so far as I know. Why?"

"Just curious. You know I'm interested in the ranch."

Fortunately, that was the truth. And it seemed to be enough to satisfy Rodney as he greeted the workmen and extended his invitation to a barbecue at the main house that evening. Rae-Anne stood silently, aware that the half-dozen men were checking her out with varying degrees of subtlety.

She guessed she couldn't blame them. Aside from Renee, she was the only female on the property. And in her jeans and a cool white cotton shirt over a red tank top, with not a trace of her pregnancy showing yet, she supposed a hard-working man near the end of a long, backbreaking day might consider her worth a look.

But only one of those masculine stares mattered to her. Only one stayed with her as she and Rodney got into the Jeep, keeping her nearly silent all the way to the house as she grappled with the memory of a serious, suntanned face and a smoky, dark-eyed gaze.

It was the same damn dream.

He was standing on the shore of the lake, listening to the breeze in the trees that ringed the shore. And across the water he could see the child playing on the beach, patting the sand into castle-shaped piles.

The sense of urgency was worse this time for some reason. Wiley found himself pacing to the edge of the water and back, trying to work up the courage to jump in and swim across.

He didn't know why it was so hard. There was just something about the lake that terrified him. He tried to push past his absurd reluctance as he stood at the water's edge and found himself grappling with old, illogical demons.

He thought about being pulled under, seized from below by creatures he couldn't even imagine.

He thought about sinking, drowning in icy, bottomless depths, in unfathomable darkness.

He couldn't do it. And yet the child was still over there, with some vague threat hanging over its head that Wiley had to defuse if he could.

A hand shook him, and he jumped as though an icy wave had, in fact, just closed over him. "Time to go, Cotter," a voice said, and Wiley opened his eyes.

Napping. He was taking a nap, worn-out from his day's work on the ranch. He was supposed to go up to the main house with the rest of the crew, and he'd fallen asleep without meaning to.

And had that dream he hated.

"Yeah, I'm coming," he growled, and stumbled into the bunkhouse bathroom to splash some cold water over his face.

The regulars on old Abel's work crew had already told him that Rodney enjoyed playing lord of the manor from time to time, and that eating up at the ranch house beat the heck out of doing their own cooking at the end of the day. Wiley wasn't sorry for the chance to check Rodney Dietrich out at close quarters, and of course it would get him close to Rae-Anne for the evening, which was his primary reason for having wangled a place on the work crew at all.

He wished he wasn't so damn tired, and that the rest of the crew would stop talking about Rae-Anne as they walked up the gravel road toward the big house.

"I heard they were supposed to get married last weekend and she split on him," one of the men said.

"I don't blame her. Guy's a nobody."

"Yeah." Someone else snorted. "A rich-as-hell nobody."

"Any woman looks like that has gotta be able to do better. You check out that body?"

Wiley didn't want to think about these guys checking out the body he'd touched and loved so intimately just two nights ago. He was glad when they reached the big flagstone patio at the back of the ranch house, and gladder yet when Rodney, who was presiding at the barbecue, deputized Wiley to go down to the freezer in the cellar and bring up a couple more bags of ice.

What made him glad about the errand was the sight of Rae-Anne, cool and lovely in a soft white Indian cotton dress, already leaning over the freezer. He'd been wanting a chance to talk to her alone.

And now that he'd gotten one, he was wasting it by taking a long look at the way the folds of her dress outlined her body. For some reason, the belted dress, loose and gauzy though it was, seemed almost sexier than the curve-hugging jeans and shirt she'd worn this afternoon.

The dress hinted things, that was why. It accented the soft slope of her breasts and the slenderness of her waist. Given the nature of Wiley's imaginings when it came to Rae-Anne Blackburn, hinting was a thousand times more potent than any obvious display could have been. He had to fight his impulses hard to keep from thinking of how it would feel to pull that soft white fabric back slowly, inch by inch, and replace its light touch with the touch of his lips.

Her words brought him to earth in a hurry. "I wish you would stop following me around," she said.

Wiley raised both hands. "I'm innocent, honey," he said. "Just doing a favor for old Rodney. And speaking of Rodney, have you gotten anywhere with him since yesterday?"

"Not really."

He looked sharply at her. The light in the cellar was bright, and he couldn't tell whether she was as strained as she looked, or whether it was just the harsh shadows the fluorescent bulbs cast on her face.

"Not really as in nothing's happened, or not really as in you don't really want to tell me about it?" he asked.

She hesitated a moment before answering. "Both," she said. "Wiley, what are you doing here? This is complicated enough without you being underfoot all the time."

Underfoot wasn't exactly a compliment, but he'd been called worse. "Just keeping an eye on things, honey," he told her. "You go out to meet Jack this afternoon?"

She glanced toward the open bulkhead that led toward the patio, but apparently felt reassured that they were far enough from the party that no one would notice them talking. "How did you know that?" she demanded.

"Lucky guess. He going to check up on those new employees?"

"Yes." She closed the door of the big freezer, but before she could reach down to pick up the two bags of ice, he'd done it for her.

"Allow me," he said.

She didn't seem to want to allow him. She stood there with her hands stretched toward the bags, frowning at him. "Don't *you* start treating me like an invalid, Wiley, just because I'm pregnant," she said.

"Rodney treating you like an invalid?" Wiley considered it. "I did think he looked sort of fussy this afternoon." He looked at Rae-Anne's still-slim waist and hoped like hell he sounded as casual as he wanted to as he said, "I didn't get a chance to ask you—how're you feeling? Being pregnant, I mean. Are you okay?"

She brushed a fine strand of hair away from her face toward her thick braid. "I'm fine," she said. "My body seems to like being pregnant, when it gets a chance to relax."

She hadn't had much of that in the past few days, Wiley thought. He felt suddenly fierce on Rae-Anne's account, angry that she was caught in the middle of all this.

"Does the rest of you like being pregnant, too?" He wasn't sure why it was so hard to ask her these things, or why the whole subject made him feel vaguely the same way as the dream he'd just awakened from—restless and ineffective and responsible in some way he couldn't quite define. "Are you happy about this, Rae-Anne?"

She looked toward the cellar stairs, then at Wiley. "I'm not happy about the situation," she said. "But I *am* happy about the baby—happier than I can tell you."

She put her hands over her stomach, and Wiley felt his stomach tighten suddenly as he watched the easy, nurturing motion. *There's your answer, Cotter,* he told himself. He could protect witnesses and corner bad guys and find missing people, but never in a million years would he feel as confident about producing a child as Rae-Anne's gesture proclaimed her to be.

"You never said anything about wanting children when we knew each other before," Wiley said slowly.

"There were a lot of things we never said to each other," she replied. "I mean, you probably only ever said twenty-five words to me about your family—just enough to tell me your father disappeared and your mother died when you were still a kid."

"There's not much more to say about it."

Something flickered in her blue eyes that made him think she disagreed with him. And her voice had a deliberately gentle quality to it that made him wonder whether she'd been waiting for a chance to ask him about this.

"Oh, come on, Wiley," she said. "What was your father like? And your mother?" When he didn't answer right away, she prompted him, "Why did he leave?"

"She kicked him out." Somehow, she'd seemed so open and revealing just a moment ago that Wiley couldn't think of a good enough reason to close up on her. "My father was the world's ultimate con man," he told her. "He loved the word *tomorrow*. Things were always going to be better tomorrow."

"And they weren't."

"No. They got worse and worse, until my mother stopped believing in all the tomorrows and just threw him out."

He'd intended to stop there, but Rae-Anne kept prodding him. "How old were you when that happened?"

"Eleven."

"So Jack would have been—"

"Nine. And Sam was seven." He drew in a breath, amazed that he was telling her about this. He was amazed, too, at the way Rae-Anne's sympathetic blue eyes made it easier to dredge up these memories.

"How much longer did your mother live?"

"Only a couple of years. She drank." He said the words bluntly, because he couldn't see much point to softening them. "And she kept taking up with the wrong man, one right after another. I had a couple of temporary stepdaddies I'd be happy to settle a few old scores with, if I knew where they were today."

Rae-Anne was frowning. "What would be the point of that?" she asked. "It's all so long ago."

Not in my mind, Wiley wanted to tell her. In his memory, in spite of—or maybe because of—the way he'd kept his past a secret all these years, it was still as fresh as it had been that night when he was eleven years old. He could see himself so clearly—a scrawny kid with big ideas about how the world could be when his father's ship finally came in— leaning out of the upstairs window in that rickety house in

Abilene, watching his father storm out to the family's old truck in the wake of the worst fight his parents had ever had.

And he could see the skinny little ankle and foot poking out from under the burlap bag in the truck bed, too, letting Wiley know a minute too late that his seven-year-old brother had stowed away. He'd gone pelting downstairs, yelling that Sam was gone, but his mother had been wailing too loudly to hear him, and Jack had taken refuge in the tree house out back when the fight had started to escalate.

Only Wiley had seen it happening. And there hadn't been a damn thing he could do about it. Sometimes he thought that night—that single moment, in fact—had shaped everything he had become thirty years after the fact.

He'd forgotten what Rae-Anne had just asked him. He'd been wrong, he thought—it *wasn't* easy to talk about this even when he was looking into Rae-Anne's beautiful blue eyes.

"We better get this ice upstairs before it melts," he said curtly. "Let's go."

"Wiley—"

He didn't stop to let the questioning sound in her voice distract him this time. He'd just remembered the feeling he'd sometimes had when he'd first met Rae-Anne—that this was a woman whose love would demand everything and give everything and threaten the whole foundation that Wiley had built his solitary life on.

He turned immediately toward the patio when he emerged from the cellar, astonished at the way one brief conversation with Rae-Anne could leave him feeling that he'd hit more emotional highs and lows than he'd experienced in the past year. She came up the steps after him and was starting to head into the house when Renee, the housekeeper, called Rae-Anne's name and held out a parcel she was carrying.

"There you are," she said. "This just came by express mail. It's from Rodney's aunt, addressed to both of you."

Rae-Anne took the package, which was marked Perishable Goods, and started across the patio with it.

"She usually use typed labels for her mail like that?" Wiley asked.

"I don't know. I've never gotten any mail from her before."

Wiley wasn't sure what it was about the package that put him on his guard. He skirted around the patio toward the cooler, but even while he was dumping the ice into it and getting into a conversation with one of the other workmen about barbecue, part of his attention was focused on Rae-Anne and Rodney and the parcel.

Fortunately, Wiley had a standard lecture that he gave people when they asked him about barbecue, and it was easy enough to launch into it now. "There's some folks say that anything you cook on a grill constitutes barbecue, but to an aficionado..."

He could hear Rodney's words under his own. "Might as well open it," Rodney was saying. "She sent me a whole case of hot chili pickle once, right out of the blue. If it's food, we'll dish it up right here and now."

It wasn't food.

At first Wiley couldn't tell *what* it was. But his uneasiness had prompted him to cut off his barbecue sermon and move closer to the grill as Rodney tore off the tape that held the box closed. It was the label that seemed funny, he thought. Aside from the anonymous typewriting, the word *Perishable* was guaranteed to make someone open the box quickly.

"What the hell—"

Rodney's last word turned to a startled yell, and suddenly he was flinging himself backward, shouting something panicky and unintelligible.

Wiley was already on the move. Rae-Anne was his first thought. He reached her in two long strides, relieved to see that she was already getting out of the way on her own. With his body between the woman he loved and the threat he still couldn't see, Wiley felt free to act.

And then he saw the snake.

It must have filled the whole shoe box, judging by its uncoiled length. It was sliding toward Rodney, half-lost in the melee of running feet, pausing when it came to an open space.

And it was rattling.

"Wiley—"

He heard Rae-Anne's voice behind him, but put it forcibly out of his mind. *Damn it,* he wanted to say, *don't let on that you know me. It's too dangerous.* The irony of worrying about that while heading toward an angry rattlesnake didn't strike him until afterward.

At the moment, he needed all the concentration he could muster to locate a weapon. Time seemed to slow down while he was doing it, and the dry, quick rattling got louder and louder as the frightened voices on the patio receded and Wiley's focus narrowed to the space between him and the snake.

This was the way any fight felt, he recalled—first everything got very slow and very clear, and then, suddenly, you were in the middle of things and there was no time to think at all. He looked to his right and saw only flowerpots and stone benches. To his left there was the white blur of Rae-Anne's dress—damn it, he wished she was farther away—and the fallen plates and paper cups of several of Rodney's guests.

And there was the barbecue. He spun around quickly, grasping the long-handled tongs and the lifter.

The tongs were broad enough to pin the snake down for the couple of seconds he needed. And the lifter, though far from ideal, was lethal enough when Wiley put all his strength behind it, lashing into the rattler the way an autumn hurricane lashed into the Texas coast.

And then it was over, and Wiley was left with his chest heaving as though he'd just run all the way from San Antonio.

"It's okay, folks," he said. "It's dead."

"Are you—all right?"

Rae-Anne was the only one who spoke, and he could tell from the trembling in her voice that she'd remembered only just in time that she wasn't supposed to know him from Adam. He gave her a weak nod and tore his eyes away from hers before the frightened concern in them could tip him into doing something that would give the whole show away.

It had been a hell of an evening so far, he thought.

He'd had to fight his long-buried memories first. And then the damn rattlesnake. And now the longing to move close to Rae-Anne and pull her into his arms to comfort her in the way Rodney Dietrich was so conspicuously *not* doing.

At the moment, it was hard to say which of the three struggles had taken more out of him. As far as Wiley was concerned, things could calm down anytime, and he wouldn't complain about it.

He was disappointed almost immediately.

Chapter 9

"You have to have some idea who sent it, Rodney." Rae-Anne paced from the fireplace at the end of the long, low living room. "One of us could have been killed, for heaven's sake! And you're treating it like it was a prank."

"Because I'm sure that's all it was." Rodney was sitting on the sofa, as imperturbable—or as glazed—as he'd been for the past half hour. "No one dies from rattlesnake bites in this day and age, Rae-Anne. Even if we *had* been bitten, which was unlikely. Rattlers are more interested in being by themselves than they are in sticking around and biting people, and—"

She'd heard all this once before. She'd been angrily insisting that Rodney be more open with her about his business, about his first wife, about *everything,* and he'd just gotten more and more genial, as though she was being temperamental and he'd decided to wait until she calmed down.

His geniality was aided by the hefty snifter of brandy he'd drunk, on top of the beers he'd had at the barbecue. Rae-

Anne had known him to drink a lot when she'd first met him, but he'd cut back on alcohol since then.

Until now. Was this Rodney's way of coping with whatever stresses he was refusing—blankly and utterly—to share with her? She shook her head at him, frustrated and fearful, yet certain there *was* something he could tell her and she just needed to keep asking until he finally opened up.

"Why not call the police, if you think it's just a prank?" she asked. "Surely—"

She was interrupted by a quiet knock on the living room door. Rodney got up to answer it, commenting over his shoulder as he went, "You're making too big a deal out of this, Rae-Anne. The snake's dead, thanks to that workman of Abel's. The whole thing is over."

Rae-Anne closed her eyes. She couldn't get rid of the mental picture of Wiley's big form hurtling toward that snake, one strong arm raised, his expression fierce and focused. If he hadn't been so quick—

She shook her head, willing the thought away. But it wouldn't go. In the confused few seconds between Rodney's startled yell and the realization that the snake was dead, she'd been caught between two impulses so strong she'd felt nearly pulled in two.

I couldn't stand it if anything happened to Wiley Cotter. That had been her first thought when she'd seen him heading her way, planting himself between her and the danger. She'd loved him once and mourned him as dead. She wasn't sure her heart could stand to go through that kind of anguish again.

And the other thought was just as potent, just as heartbreaking. *Danger attracts him like a magnet.* That was so clear in the way he'd thrown himself toward the threat that had arrived out of the blue. Wiley had always been recklessly confident and absolutely headstrong.

Sooner or later, he would throw himself into a situation he couldn't walk away from. And Rae-Anne didn't want to be there to watch.

That was why she was working so hard to keep things together with Rodney. Rodney, no matter what mistakes he might have made in the past, seemed to be trying to put his life together.

And Rodney's life included her child—*their* child. Frowning, she tried to forget about Wiley. What she needed to know—*had* to know—was what was really going on in Rodney's life.

What seemed to be going on right now was a visitor from the hotel. "I told him it was too late for business calls," Renee was saying outside the living room door. "He said he'd wait in his car and just take a minute of your time. It's that same man who came a couple of weeks ago, I think."

The phrase made Rae-Anne stop her restless pacing. Rodney had disappeared into the foyer, and she couldn't help following him, drawn by the fear that this might be some follow-up to the terrifying package that had arrived earlier.

She could hear voices from outside, but by the time she reached the front steps, the visitor was climbing into his car and Rodney had crossed the driveway toward his truck.

It was hard to make her eyes work in the darkness after being in the lit house, but there was something about the curly-haired driver of the car that struck Rae-Anne as familiar. It wasn't either of the two men who'd threatened her at the hotel, but she could swear it was someone she'd seen recently in connection with this case.

She didn't get a chance to figure it out. The curly-haired man had started the station wagon and was heading down the drive before she could get a better look. And Rodney, when her gaze found him, was at the open door of his truck.

The big blue pickup was parked with the other ranch vehicles in the lot next to the house. Rae-Anne could see her fiancé moving quickly, doing something in the front seat and then turning toward the house.

"What's going on?" she demanded, crossing the gravel distance between them quickly. "Who was that guy?"

"There's been a theft at one of the hotels, and the manager wanted to let me know about it." Something had changed Rodney's mood, she realized. He took hold of her shoulders, turning her toward the house. "I've got to go out for a while. We'll talk when I get back."

"Why wouldn't they just call you on the phone, if there'd been a theft? And why call you at all? Can't the manager—"

"Rae-Anne, listen to me." She didn't like the way he was cutting her off. It was almost as though she wasn't there. "It's a delicate matter, and they want me to handle it personally. Which I'll do, as quickly as I can." He was frowning at her as he climbed into the truck cab. "You go in and get some rest, all right? You look tired to death."

It wasn't the happiest choice of phrase, Rae-Anne thought as Rodney's truck took off into the darkness, its headlights cutting a long beam into the open black space around the ranch. *"Damn,"* she said, as she put her hands on her hips and watched the red and white lights of the disappearing truck.

The second truck engine starting up startled her. She'd assumed she was alone and that all the other vehicles in the little parking lot were empty. The quiet roar of one of them coming to life made her jump and put one hand on her suddenly pounding heart.

And then she recognized Wiley.

He was at the steering wheel of a battered black pickup, his face lit starkly in the light of the dashboard as he turned the truck's lights on. He must have seen her arguing with Rodney, she thought. But he didn't look her way, just slammed the truck into gear and started to ease it out of the lot.

Rae-Anne didn't stop to think. Too much was still going on that she didn't understand, and she'd be damned if she was going to let *everybody* ride off into the night and leave her mystified. Cursing the way her flat-soled leather sandals slipped in the gravel, she flung herself toward Wiley's truck and managed to grab hold of the tailgate as he paused to shift from reverse into first gear.

Getting her foot onto the bumper wasn't easy, but she did it. She swung one leg over the tailgate just as the truck started to move forward, and caught a glimpse of Wiley's startled face in the mirror as she half walked, half fell across the empty pickup bed.

Her outstretched hands broke the impact of her collision with the back of the cab. She scrambled to get a grip on the rain channel along the edge of the cab's roof, and was glad she was holding on to it when Wiley braked suddenly and rolled down the driver's-side window.

"Are you out of your *mind?*" She wasn't sure she'd ever heard him sound so furious. "Get out of the truck, Rae-Anne."

She shook her head. "If you're following Rodney, I'm going with you," she said. "I'm tired of being left behind."

He gave a frustrated snarl and launched himself out of the cab. Rae-Anne moved to the other side of the truck bed, out of his reach.

"I'm serious, Rae-Anne." His cowboy boots crunched on the gravel as he came around to meet her.

"So am I. And if we stand here arguing about it much longer, you're going to lose track of Rodney."

She nodded toward the farm road beyond the ranch. Rodney's truck had already disappeared over the first rise. In a moment even the dim glow of its taillights would be gone.

Wiley conjured up a few curses that Rae-Anne couldn't recall ever hearing before, even in the roughest cowboy joints she'd worked in. But in spite of his anger, he seemed to see her point. Unless he wanted to take hold of her physically and haul her out of the truck, he was stuck with her.

And he'd never been a man to waste time once his mind was made up. "All right," he growled. "Get in the cab, then. I don't want to have to worry about you rattling around loose back there."

She didn't wait to be asked twice. She slid over the side and hit the ground moving. The truck was in motion again almost before she'd climbed into the passenger seat and gotten the door closed behind her.

"I thought pregnant women were supposed to get all passive and placid." Wiley was still grumbling as he jammed the truck into gear. "What's the matter with you, anyway?"

What *was* the matter with her? Why had her heightened heartbeat changed from fearful to excited with no warning at all? Why, all of a sudden, did she feel so exhilarated, so alive?

It must be because she was on the move, she told herself. She'd found a way to keep from being left behind this time, and it felt good after all the cautious maneuvering of the past day or two. That must be why she was so revitalized, so charged with all this unexpected energy.

It couldn't be simply because she was sitting next to Wiley Cotter.

Could it?

If it was, it certainly wasn't because Wiley was going out of his way to make her feel as though he was glad to see her.

"It isn't bad enough you have to be right in the middle of whatever's going on around here," he was muttering as they reached the end of the long driveway. "Now you're climbing onto moving vehicles, as well."

"Hey, I figured you owed me one, after that trick you pulled with the wedding limousine." Her sense of elation made her flippant. She couldn't resist shooting Wiley an unrepentant grin when he turned to look at her before steering onto the farm road.

His look gave her more of a jolt than she'd expected. His eyes were nearly black with fury, or excitement, or both. He seemed agitated, almost menacing, as electrified as Rae-Anne but not nearly as pleased about it.

"Don't push your luck, Rae-Anne." He shifted into fourth gear and urged the truck to go a little faster. "Things are starting to heat up, in case you hadn't figured that out for yourself."

The warning reminded her of how serious this excursion could turn out to be. Her light-headed mood started to ebb, although she still felt charged and stimulated by Wiley's presence and by the speed of their headlong progress into the night.

"Of course I figured it out, or I wouldn't have bothered hitching a ride on your truck," she told him. "Or *is* this your truck?" The question had only just occurred to her.

"It's Sam's." He didn't elaborate.

"And why are you following Rodney?" Another thought followed on the heels of the first one. "How did you get into this truck so conveniently? I didn't see you there until you started the engine."

"I've been—monitoring the place."

"Looking for what?"

"Whatever I could find. When I found Rodney coming out to pick up a briefcase from that guy—"

"I didn't see any briefcase."

"They didn't exactly waste a whole lot of time over it. I didn't hear what they said, but I *did* get a nice clear shot of the handoff."

He put a hand briefly on the long lens of the camera that lay on the seat between them, and Rae-Anne realized that in spite of her attempts to break through Rodney's facade, Wiley had been far more prepared than she was to take advantage of any lapse in the pretense her fiancé had built up.

And it seemed more and more likely that it *was* a pretense. Rodney's sudden change of mood, his almost absurd refusal to take the snake in the box as a serious threat, the vaguely familiar outline of the visitor in the car—they all added up to more than Rodney had admitted to her.

But until she had some hard evidence to replace her vague suspicions, she didn't want to admit any of this to Wiley.

"It still isn't proof," she muttered, as he raised his hand to the steering wheel again.

She wasn't prepared for the sudden way Wiley cranked the wheel around. She realized that up ahead, Rodney had turned onto a side road without her noticing it. Wiley looked grim, as if he was trying to marshal all his concentration and finding it very difficult to do.

"Proof," he said tautly, "is the name of the game here. You might want to do up your seat belt, honey. Your boyfriend seems to be taking the scenic route to wherever he's going." Neither of them spoke again until they'd bounced their way along several miles of open countryside. Wiley hadn't rolled his window up, and the breeze was cooling after the unseasonable heat of the past few days. He noticed Rae-Anne wrapping her arms around herself and thought about smoothing her bare arms with his palms, bringing the warmth into that porcelain skin of hers.

Can it, Cotter, he ordered himself. For one thing, Rae-Anne seemed farther from his reach than ever tonight, and more stubborn about refusing to yield an inch until she had definite confirmation of Rodney's guilt. For another, Wiley needed his concentration if he was going to do a careful job of tailing Rodney Dietrich. He couldn't do that if he was picturing Rae-Anne's skin, the color of light cream and twice as smooth.

"At least that dress is better than what you were wearing last time we took off together." He made his words deliberately blunt.

She frowned at him. "We are *not* taking off together," she told him. "We're collecting evidence, that's all."

Wiley snorted and looked at the road. He stayed silent, watching as Rodney's truck turned onto a bigger road and then took an exit for a small town Wiley had heard of but never been to.

He kept well back until the two vehicles had almost reached the town square. His whole body, from the kink in his neck to the tight knot where his heel hit the floor of the cab, was feeling the strain of sitting this close to Rae-Anne Blackburn without touching her.

Keep your hands around the wheel, he told himself. *And your eyes on the road.*

At first he thought it was all going to go off without a hitch. They arrived at the center of the town, which was designed, like so many Texas hill towns, around the hub of a broad town square with a tall limestone courthouse rising out of the middle of it.

Dietrich had chosen a parking space across from the courthouse entrance, and Wiley could immediately see why. "The automatic teller machine," he murmured. "Just what

I figured." Surely the sight of her boyfriend depositing pile after pile of cash through this small-town teller machine would convince Rae-Anne that she'd been wrong about Rodney.

"He told me he was going to San Antonio." Her voice sounded pensive.

"Kind of taking the long way around, isn't he?"

"Don't rub it in, Wiley. Where are you going?"

Wiley had spotted a narrow alleyway—more like a gap between two buildings, really—right next to the bank. If he could get into that from the back, he thought, he would have a clear sight of Rodney at the teller machine. He jockeyed the truck into a small parking lot behind the bank, explaining to Rae-Anne what he was after.

"A picture of him at a teller machine won't prove anything by itself," she told him.

"No. But a picture, plus my testimony, plus the transaction record for an account with Rodney's name on it, should get any jury beyond the reasonable doubt stage. Wait here, all right, honey?" He said the words quickly, hoping she might listen to him for once.

She didn't, of course. She was out of the truck almost before he'd finished speaking.

"There isn't room in that alley for both of us," he told her.

"I don't care. *Please*, Wiley."

Wiley had already started toward the end of the alley, but the intensity of Rae-Anne's voice stopped him.

She never begged for things. The pleading sound in her words now, and the struggle going on in her blue eyes, hit him hard.

Suddenly he felt the way he had when he'd seen her crying that first day outside the limo. Rae-Anne never cried, either. She argued as fiercely as anybody he'd ever met, and she negotiated, and she fought when she had to. But she didn't cry, and she didn't beg.

She'd done both in the past few days. And both times it had been on Rodney Dietrich's account. Wiley ground his back teeth together and wished like hell that smooth-talking swindler had been worth even half of what Rae-Anne clearly felt for him.

"I have to know the truth about this," she was saying. "I'm tired of trusting other people's versions of things. Please, Wiley. Let's not waste time."

Her dark red hair was still pulled back in a loose braid, but a few strands had come free in the breeze. They swirled around her face, making her look even more uncertain and vulnerable. He could see that faint scattering of freckles across the bridge of her nose, over the gentle slope of her cheekbones. Those remnants of her girlhood only showed themselves when she was very pale for some reason.

He'd kissed the delicate curve of her temple so many times, following the trail left by those almost-invisible freckles. He'd done it on Saturday night, when he'd held her in his arms and caressed the color into her too-white face. He wanted to do the same thing now, to soften the tight, unhappy line of her lips and see her turn into his own stubborn Rae-Anne again, with the flash of pure spirit in her blue eyes.

He had no right to do any of those things, because he was one of those people whose versions of things Rae-Anne had learned not to trust. The pleading note in her voice made him uncomfortable because he knew all too well why it was there.

And anyway, she was right that they were wasting precious time. "All right," he muttered, and led the way toward the alley.

Chapter 10

They managed to slide along the alleyway side by side, their backs flattened against the wall of the building next to the bank. When they got close to the street, though, they ran into trouble.

"I want to see what's going on," Rae-Anne insisted.

"I know you do," Wiley whispered, "but this whole thing is going to be a waste of time unless I can get a shot at him with the camera. Here—"

They finally compromised by having Rae-Anne tuck herself against Wiley's chest, half-sheltered by one of his arms, while he leaned toward the street with his camera in his hand. He didn't want to lean as far as the opening of the alleyway until he was certain he had a clear sight line, but he needed to keep track of what Rodney was up to.

So far it seemed to involve sealing up deposit envelopes and writing on the outside of them. Judging by what Wiley knew of the amounts of cash involved in this operation, this part of it could take a while.

"What's he doing?" Rae-Anne demanded.

"Depositing money."

"Depositing it? Are you sure?"

"See for yourself."

It seemed safe enough to let her push past him for a quick look. Rodney's back was turned toward them, and aside from some faint noises coming from a bar on the other side of the town square, the place seemed deserted at this late hour.

But safe was a relative term. Wiley groaned at the sensation of Rae-Anne's hips pushing against him, and lifted his arms a little higher to try to get out of temptation's way. If he started letting his desires run away with him again, he could be in serious trouble. He'd felt the stirring of arousal the moment Rae-Anne had moved close to him in the small, enclosed space of the alley, and it was taking all his willpower to keep from touching her now.

She seemed intent on watching Rodney, though, unaware of Wiley's reaction to their closeness. As she moved into her original position, sliding past Wiley's body a second time, she gave a startled half laugh. "It's a good thing I'm not any more pregnant than I am, or this would never work," she said.

Wiley ducked his head toward the street again and decided it was probably worth getting a shot of Dietrich slipping those piles of cash into the deposit envelopes. Even after he'd focused and taken the picture, though, he was still thinking about Rae-Anne's comment.

"You think Rodney'll be a good father?" His chest felt as narrow and constricted as the damned alleyway as he formed the question, but he got the words out anyway.

"He's always wanted children."

"Just like you, right?"

She lifted her chin. "That's right."

"Why did you wait until now?"

She hesitated, but Wiley waited her out. "The time and place never seemed right before," she said finally.

"So having a big house in the country is what makes it practical to have children, huh?"

"Give me a break, Wiley."

"That's not a real answer."

"Well, it's not a real good time to be asking me these questions, is it?" He could feel her flash of temper in the way she turned to look at him. Her white dress swirled slightly as she moved, making her seem ethereal, just barely real.

Why was he needling her about her desire to have children? Did it have something to do with the fact that ever since their conversation in the cellar this afternoon he'd been grappling with the image of himself as a child and with that troublesome memory of the night he'd watched out the upstairs window as his father and brother disappeared into the darkness?

You're conducting a surveillance job here, he reminded himself. *Keep your mind on it.*

He snuck another look at the bank machine, and saw that Rodney was beginning to make his deposits. Wiley steadied the camera with both hands, focused carefully and got a couple of shots that not only showed clearly what Rodney was doing, but even included the town clock in the background as an extra added bonus. It was one of the reasons he'd chosen this hiding place. The evidence of a specific place and time would add some punch to the case against Rodney, he knew.

Rae-Anne demanded to know what was happening, and he pressed himself flat against the brick wall to let her slide past him again. He'd heard a car drive by and park in the town square a few minutes ago, but everything was quiet now, or so he thought until Rae-Anne suddenly gasped and drew her head in.

"What is it?" Wiley's voice was as soft as he could make it.

"Those men—"

He could feel her whole body shaking and slid an arm around her shoulders before leaning cautiously to his left and sneaking a look at the town square. There were two men in casual suits, their collars open, their walk relaxed, sauntering along the sidewalk toward the bank.

"You know who they are?" he whispered.

She nodded tightly. "They backed me into an elevator at the hotel yesterday and told me to stop asking questions about Rodney's business."

He bit off the expletive that came immediately to his mind. This wasn't the time to demand why the hell Rae-Anne hadn't told him about this before. If these were the mob's knee breakers come to check up on what Rodney was doing, he needed to get the encounter on film, and on tape, too, if he could.

"What is that?" He heard Rae-Anne's soft murmur at his ear as he pulled his trusty microcassette recorder out of the pocket of his shirt. He held it up for her to see, then plugged in the microphone and unwound the cord to its fullest length. If they had to retreat down the alley in a hurry, he wanted to be ready.

The two sets of footsteps were almost at the bank. Wiley heard them pause and then heard the soft tapping of knuckles against glass.

"Wiley, what if they hurt him? What if—"

Wiley put his finger over his lips, and Rae-Anne stopped speaking. He could see anxiety brightening her eyes even in the dimness of the alley.

He wasn't sure what he was going to do if the two guys were here to rough up Rodney, or worse. He couldn't stand the idea of Rae-Anne watching, but the past few days had taught him that it was a waste of time to try to make her do things for her own safety, her own good. If Rodney was in trouble, and Rae-Anne tried to intervene—

He clamped down on his molars again and told himself this was the very last time he was ever going to combine work and pleasure, if pleasure was the right word for it. Trying to be on his guard against what the two strangers might do on the one hand, and how Rae-Anne might react, on the other, was like being caught in a tractor pull.

He could hear the bank lobby door opening, but at first he wasn't sure whether Rodney was coming out or the two men were going in. He set the little microphone down at the mouth of the alley just in case and carefully laid the cord along the edge of the building where it wouldn't be noticeable.

A moment later he was glad he'd done it, as he heard three voices getting closer and closer to the mouth of the alley.

"How did you find me?" That was Rodney. He sounded perplexed, but not worried.

One of the tall men chuckled. "We can always find you, Rod," he said. "We like to keep track of the people we do business with."

"Traced the truck, huh? I thought you trusted me more than that, after all this time."

The second man cut in, "Never mind that."

They'd almost reached the alleyway. It was a natural place for them to head, Wiley realized. Away from the light of the bank lobby, they would be able to talk in the same shadows that had made him see the spot as a good hiding place.

"Hell," he said, almost soundlessly. "Let's go, honey."

They'd gotten halfway down the alley when the three men stopped at the other end of it. Wiley took hold of Rae-Anne's wrist and held her still. If they kept moving, they risked catching someone's eye.

It was only slightly less risky to stay motionless. Wiley held on hard to Rae-Anne's arm, trying to impress the danger of their situation on her.

She was barely breathing, and he knew that she was listening, as he was, for the slightest word from the men at the end of the alley. *Don't let them look down,* Wiley prayed silently. *Don't let them notice the microphone on the ground.*

"So why'd you come all the way out here?" Rodney was asking. "Armand made the drop all right. There's nothing to worry about."

He felt Rae-Anne stiffen for some reason, but she didn't make a sound. Wiley wouldn't have noticed the movement if she hadn't been pressed so close against his side.

"Armand said you didn't invite him in to count the cash like you usually do."

"I was in the middle of something. It wasn't safe."

"We'd like to know what you were in the middle of."

Wiley was keeping his face averted. He was wearing dark clothing, and he knew the back of his head was a heck of a lot less noticeable than the flash of his eyes might have been. But he wished he could turn around long enough to see Rodney's face and get some idea whether the man was operating out of bravado or whether he really was as calm as he sounded.

"I was having a hard time with Rae-Anne. She just isn't letting this thing drop."

"She's got to go, Rodney. She's just too big a risk."

"No!" The word was quick and definite. "If anything happens to Rae-Anne, the deal is off. You know that."

"Then find a way to shut her up."

"I've found one. I'm going to suggest that she and I go away for a while."

There was a pause. The man who spoke sounded almost amused as he said, "Long-range planning never was your strong suit, Rod. How does going away solve anything?"

"It'll give me a chance to talk up the family angle—you know, get her thinking about the baby instead of the business stuff."

The silence this time made Wiley think the two men were exchanging looks. "Sounds iffy," one of them said finally.

"It's not!" Rodney *was* on edge, Wiley realized. He'd just been covering it up well, keeping up an act, the way he'd been doing with Rae-Anne all along. "Look, you don't have to worry about Rae-Anne. I told you that already."

"What if your little getaway doesn't work the right kind of magic?"

"Then I'll think of something else."

There was one good thing about the edge of panic in Rodney's voice, Wiley thought. It meant Rae-Anne's fiancé was genuinely concerned about her. It was the only positive thing Wiley could see in the whole situation.

"We had to step in and bail you out the last time, remember?" one of them was saying.

"You think I'm likely to forget?" Rodney sounded bitter about it.

"Yeah, well, just don't screw up over a broad this time, too, all right? We're happy to see you hard at work putting that cash where it belongs, Rod, but we'd be even happier if you could put a lid on that girlfriend of yours."

"I'll do it." Rodney's voice was lower now, more subdued. "Leave Rae-Anne to me. I'll do it."

"Good. And while we're talking, we've got another piece of news for you."

"News?" Rodney sounded uneasy, and Wiley didn't blame him.

"We've got out-of-town visitors coming to check over the books. You know who I mean."

"When?"

"They're flying in first thing in the morning. We told them you'd be happy to arrange accommodations for them. A suite downtown oughtta do it."

"Sure. You know I will."

"We also told them you'll be happy to go over your figures for the past quarter."

"Hey, you guys know me. I'm a businessman. When have I ever tried to back out of—"

The first man's voice cut him off. "That's the news, Rod. Get a suite ready for them, and be there to meet them by nine. You got that?"

"Yeah. I got it."

"No..."

It was almost inaudible, barely a breath on the cool evening air as the word escaped Rae-Anne's lips. By itself it probably wouldn't have reached the men on the sidewalk. The soft protest seemed to come from deep inside, from the sheltered place where Rae-Anne had nursed her hopes that this time her happiness might last.

Rodney Dietrich had destroyed those hopes. And Wiley could understand why Rae-Anne hadn't been able to restrain that small, anguished sound as she understood how wrong she'd been to pin her hopes on the man who'd fathered her child.

It was that empathy that undid him. He turned toward Rae-Anne, constricted in the narrow space of the alley, and one of his boot heels scuffed against the pavement under his feet as he moved.

"Hold on. What was that?"

Wiley winced at the words and gripped Rae-Anne's arms as tightly as he could, willing her to stand absolutely still. If they were lucky—

They weren't. He could hear steps shuffling at the mouth of the alley and felt sinkingly certain that one or both of the strangers was peering into the darkness, looking for the source of the sound.

"There's somebody down there." The man's voice had gotten quieter. Wiley didn't like the cool, brisk sound of it. If he was the one at the open end of the alley, he knew exactly what he'd be doing now. He'd be taking up a cautious stance with his back against the bank building and getting his gun out.

He had no doubt that was what was happening. If the two hired hands figured they'd been overheard—if they had time to notice the microphone—they would shoot.

And they would barely need to aim. One bullet loose in this narrow space would do damage Wiley didn't want to think about.

There was almost no time to counter the threat. As silently as he could, he reached into the pocket of his jeans and extracted the keys to Sam's truck.

"Get out of the alley." He spoke with his lips right against Rae-Anne's ear. "If anything goes wrong, get the hell out of here. All right?"

"Wiley..."

She didn't make a sound this time. But he could see the alarm in her wide eyes and read his name on her lips.

He couldn't help it, any more than he could restrain his instinctive movement of sympathy just a moment ago. He leaned forward and kissed her, hard, briefly, urgently. Then he pushed the truck keys into her palm and gave her a gentle shove toward the rear of the building. His head was swimming with the taste and feel of her, and he reckoned he wasn't going to have any trouble at all putting on the act he'd decided to stage.

"Wassa matter?" He slurred his speech deliberately as he started to lurch unsteadily toward the three men at the other end of the alley. "A guy can't relieve himself in peace in this town?"

The only thing that kept Rae-Anne going was the knowledge that things would be worse if she went back.

If Rodney saw her, there was no telling what might happen. It was bad enough that he might recognize Wiley as the man who'd killed the rattlesnake earlier tonight. Her one hope was to defuse this situation somehow before that could happen.

She edged out of the alley as quickly as she could, wanting to be gone by the time the two men checked to see if Wiley was alone. She felt sure they *would* check. Her brief encounter with them in the elevator at the hotel had been enough to convince her that these were people who did things thoroughly.

She could hear Wiley's voice raised in protest as she hurried through the small parking lot at the rear of the bank building. "I was just takin' a leak," he was saying, imitating a drunken drawl to perfection. "What time's it, anyway?"

She didn't stop at the truck. If she was going to hit the road, she wanted Wiley to be with her. And she knew she had to be quick. Wiley might sound genuinely drunk, but if the two men got close to him they would realize that there was no trace of liquor on his breath. And that could mean big trouble.

So she ran, cutting across a couple of lawns and onto one of the four streets that came together at the town square. She was heading for the bar across the courthouse lawn from the bank, feeling grateful that after her years of bartending in too many little Texas towns just like this one, she automatically noticed the local watering holes in any place she came to.

Bandera Red's, the sign outside proclaimed. Rae-Anne stopped in the shadowy doorway, pulling in a deep breath and reminding herself of all the good reasons she shouldn't just go barging in with a demand for help.

"I can't look all flustered," she said out loud, keeping her voice low. "I don't want them to pay attention to me. I want them to get curious about Wiley and those two guys."

She glanced across the square and saw that Rodney's pickup truck was driving away. But the two men and Wiley were still standing where she'd left them. Wiley had his hands raised, palms up, as if protesting his innocence. The strangers didn't seem convinced, and that was enough to get Rae-Anne through the doors of Bandera Red's in spite of her pounding heart.

Conversation came to a halt as she walked in. She'd expected that—counted on it, in fact.

"Well," she said, putting her hands on her hips and looking at the row of curious faces staring at her from the bar, "this is the last time I take some stranger's word about what a good time he's going to show me in his old hometown."

"What hometown's that, honey?" It was the bartender who asked.

"This one. I met this guy at a party up in Fredericksburg, and he told me he was going to take me out for a drink in the place where he grew up. Said it was the prettiest hill town in Texas."

Rae-Anne wasn't exactly certain where they were, but her experience in the area told her that most hill-country towns considered themselves the prettiest in the region. Several heads nodding at the bar confirmed that she'd said the right thing.

"And then the minute we got out of his truck, these two guys jumped him." She put on what she hoped was a convincing pout. "Looked like city types. You know, casual suits and all? Big car with tinted windows. They said something about it had been a quiet night out here in the boonies, and they didn't like the look of the way my friend was walking, or something dumb like that."

"Well, hell." One of the men at the bar frowned at her. "Where they at now, honey?"

Rae-Anne nodded toward the door. "Over the other side of the square," she said.

"You just left him?"

She tossed her head. "I came here for a good time, not to watch some old fight," she said. "If I wanted that, I could have stayed at home."

It was working just the way she'd hoped it would. If she'd played damsel in distress, she'd be fending off half a dozen offers of drinks right now, and she didn't have time for that. But the suggestion that there was a hometown boy in trouble outside—fighting with city types, no less—got several of the men off their bar stools before Rae-Anne had even finished speaking.

"She's right," one of them said from the doorway. "Looks like they're lighting into him pretty good."

Rae-Anne's heart seemed to come up into her throat, and it was all she could do not to urge the men to get out there and do something before Wiley got hurt.

Fortunately they didn't need a lot of urging. A few of them had already spilled out onto the sidewalk, and Rae-Anne went with them as unobtrusively as she could. By the time the patrons of the bar were heading in an unsteady clump across the square, she had ducked down the side street again, and was heading fast for the black pickup truck.

She had to reach for the clutch with the very tip of her sandaled foot, but she managed to get the thing going and drove it around to the front of the bank building without letting it stall. When she got there, she could see that her ruse had been only just in time. There was blood running down Wiley's face, and dust on his knees and hands, as though he'd been knocked down more than once.

But the contingent from Bandera Red's was zeroing in on the two strangers, drawing attention away from Wiley. Rae-Anne could hear shouts and challenges, and she gunned the truck engine to reach the spot in time to take advantage of the moment of greatest confusion.

It worked without a hitch, except that seconds after he'd spotted the truck, Wiley ducked into the shadows of the alley to grab his cassette recorder and the camera he must have let fall before confronting the two men.

One of the strangers noticed what Wiley was up to, and shouted "Hey!" But he was a moment too late. By then, the men from the bar were all around, and Wiley was heading toward the pickup, hoisting himself into the passenger seat as Rae-Anne flung the door open to meet him.

"You're hurt." She put the truck in gear and urged it away from the scene with a howl of tires.

"I'm fine." He wiped at the blood on his face and set the camera and recorder on the seat between them. "That was good going, honey. You've got the instincts of a true detective."

"I don't want to be a detective!" She hadn't realized just how upset and relieved she was until she heard the tears in her voice. "I don't want anything to do with this stuff, Wiley. I want a place where I can feel at home, and people I can count on. That's all I've *ever* wanted—and I seem to be getting farther away from it all the time, instead of closer!''

She nearly lost her grip on the steering wheel as she turned the truck around a corner and had to shift into a lower gear at the same time. She didn't know whether she was cursing or crying as she fought to keep the vehicle under control, but suddenly it all felt as though too much had happened to keep a lid on any longer.

"Are you *sure* you're all right?" She didn't like the way Wiley was holding himself, and there was nothing in the world she could do to keep her voice steady as she thought about those two brawny strangers hitting him.

"I told you, I'm fine. This—isn't the first time this has happened to me.'' She wondered if he'd hesitated because he was trying to find a way to avoid saying the obvious thing— that this world of threat and violence and suspicion was the world he lived and worked in every day.

The thought didn't do anything to slow the frustration that seemed to have lodged itself permanently in her throat. "I hate this, Wiley," she said thickly. "I really do."

He didn't answer right away. Maybe he knew there *was* no good answer, she thought. Wiley had always been perceptive, no matter what his other character flaws might be.

"Do you want me to drive?" He waited until she'd nearly mismanaged another turn in the oversize vehicle.

"No. Yes."

Suddenly she didn't know *what* she wanted. She needed peace, and a place where she could think. "I don't even know where I'm going," she finished, as her tears finally threatened to get the better of her. Her vision started to blur, and she wrestled the truck to the side of the road and put it into neutral.

She wanted to lay her head on the steering wheel and weep until her body was drained of all the tension she'd been carrying around with her for the past days and weeks. It was almost overwhelming, pushing roughly past the self-confidence she'd always prided herself on.

This wasn't the place, she told herself. It was tempting to lean against Wiley's strong shoulders and let herself fall to pieces in his arms, but that wouldn't solve anything. Wiley was part of the problem, not part of the solution.

And he wasn't offering her his shoulder to cry on, anyway. He was holding himself stiffly, looking at her but making no move to come any closer. Probably too sore from the bruising those two thugs had treated him to, she thought. Or maybe he considered this case closed now, and was feeling impatient with Rae-Anne's emotional reaction to everything that had happened tonight.

She dragged in a shuddering breath and let go of her death grip on the steering wheel. "Where were you planning to go?" she asked, not looking at him.

"My office in Austin. I have a darkroom there. I need to make some prints of these pictures and dub a couple of tapes for Jack."

"Can I go with you?" Rae-Anne couldn't imagine where else she might go tonight. It was almost midnight, and there was nowhere in the world she could call home.

"Sure."

Wiley's voice was level as he got out of the passenger seat and came around to take over the wheel. His brief answer gave her no clue about his state of mind. And that suited Rae-Anne, who'd had about all the mental exercise she could cope with for one evening.

Chapter 11

The lights were on in the Cotter Investigations office when they pulled into the parking lot. Wiley would have worried about it, except that the haze of cigarette smoke in the hallway seemed to indicate that Sam—who'd been banned from smoking in the office by a majority vote several weeks ago—was here and working late. His guess was confirmed when he unlocked the office door and saw his brother's lanky figure seated in front of a computer monitor in the center of the big open-plan room.

"For Pete's sake, little brother," Wiley said, switching on a light. "It's one o'clock. Go home, would you?"

Sam yawned and stretched his long arms above his head. "You should talk," he said. "Evening, Rae-Anne. What are you all doing here at this hour?"

"Developing pictures." Wiley stalked toward the back of the office, heading for the darkroom he'd had installed a couple of years earlier.

"Pay dirt?" Sam inquired, looking over his shoulder at Rae-Anne.

"I guess you could call it that," she said.

She sounded bleak, and Wiley didn't blame her. The evidence they'd collected tonight was enough to tie Rodney inextricably to the money-laundering ring and to prove that he'd known his first wife's death was no accident. It was enough to demolish Rae-Anne's wedding plans for good and ruin her hopes that her baby would have the kind of home and childhood she'd missed so desperately herself.

"Who the hell turned the air-conditioning off in here?" Wiley knew his irritation was mostly at himself. He'd helped scuttle Rae-Anne's dreams, and he didn't have a damn thing to offer her in their place. That was why his voice was so sharp as he called to his brother from the muggy interior of the darkroom.

"Come on, Wiley. I didn't figure anybody was going to use the darkroom this time of night." Sam eased his legs out from under the desk and loped across the office. "Too hot for the developer in there?"

"Yeah." Wiley stepped into the big main room again, pushing his hair from his eyes. He was moving cautiously, trying not to show that more blows had managed to land on him than he'd admitted at the town square.

Sam picked up on it, though. "Been dusting it up, huh?" he remarked. "Who won?"

Wiley shrugged the question off. "I need to dub a microcassette," he said, "and develop half a dozen prints. And then I need to get some sleep. You want to get out of my way so I can do that?"

Sam held out a hand. "Give 'em to me," he said. "I'm in the middle of a hell of a long search on the modem. I need an excuse to stand up and stretch once in a while. I'll throw that in the soup for you and drop it off on my way home."

Wiley handed over his camera and cassette recorder without an argument. "It's all yours," he said. "Screw it up and you're a dead man."

"You hear that?" Sam appealed to Rae-Anne. "Do a guy a favor and all you get is threats."

"Well, there've been a lot of threats going around lately." She sounded tired and bitter, and once again Wiley could understand why.

He looked at her pale, troubled face and thought about moving closer to her, tucking those escaped auburn strands behind her ears, smoothing her tousled hair and easing some of the weariness in her blue eyes. But her stance—arms crossed, chin kept studiously lifted—was warning him to keep his distance.

He exchanged a glance with Sam, and saw that his brother had been taking in perhaps more than Wiley wanted him to. "Are you really okay?" Sam's question hovered halfway between Wiley and Rae-Anne. "What happened tonight?"

"Rodney Dietrich showed his true colors, that's all. If you get those pictures and tapes done before morning, we can get them to Jack and wrap this thing up for good. You want to try to grab some sleep before that happens, Rae-Anne?"

"More than I can tell you."

As they went to the parking lot, Wiley knew that for Rae-Anne, "wrapping things up" was no simple matter of handing over their evidence to the right people. She was carrying a part of Rodney Dietrich inside her, and there was no way to escape that fact.

There had to be something he could do to make sure things worked out for her, he thought. Maybe Wiley wasn't the answer to Rae-Anne's dreams, but he'd be damned if he'd let her out of his life a second time without doing what he could to take some of the rough edges off the situation she found herself in. With all his expertise, and all his contacts, surely he could come up with something that would help her out.

If only he wasn't so damn tired....

Rae-Anne woke up disoriented, not sure whose bed she was in. The light in the room was dim, and she thought she could hear rain spattering against the windows.

The windows of her room at Rodney's ranch house had been sheltered by thick shrubs. And at her apartment—the one she'd given up in anticipation of marrying Rodney—the bedroom windows had been so close to the building next door that rain had never reached them.

Then where *was* she? She blinked and stretched in the comfortable bed. And then she remembered.

Wiley's house was in a quiet suburb of Austin, with a small yard in the back that was open to the sky all around. That was why the view out the windows looked so empty.

"Oh, God." She kicked off the covers and swung her legs over the side. She dimly recalled Wiley pulling this oversize gray T-shirt out of a drawer somewhere last night and apologizing for the fact that he didn't have a spare set of sheets to put on the bed.

The sheets she'd slept between were clean enough, but they carried the subtle and indefinable scent of Wiley's body, and that was why Rae-Anne wanted to escape them so quickly this morning. In spite of her confusion, in spite of the gray day outside and the sporadic rattle of rain against the windowpanes, she'd wakened feeling good all over, and she knew why that was.

She'd always wakened that way when she'd slept with Wiley. Apparently even sleeping alone in his bed had the power to make her body hum this way.

And that was all wrong.

Things were getting clearer now. She recalled her glimpse of the rest of Wiley's sparsely furnished home and his off-hand comment, as he'd picked up a week's worth of old newspapers, that he probably spent more time in his car than he did here. And she remembered, only too well, the jaded, mocking tone that both Wiley and Sam had fallen into last night at the Cotter Investigations office.

The office had been bigger than she'd expected, and somehow more permanent-looking. There had been desks for six or eight people, aside from the glassed-in office that seemed to belong to Wiley.

And that was where he belonged, she thought, in the world of investigations and intrigue. His small, spartan house, with its empty, half-used atmosphere, was an extra, a place to camp between shifts. His *real* home was wherever his job took him, and he, like his brothers, was happiest speaking that tough-guy language that turned violence and danger into jokes.

"This is no place for me. Or for *you*," she added, rubbing one closed hand over her belly. "We need to get out of here just as soon as I can figure out where to go." She blinked the sleep out of her eyes as she pushed her fingers through her hair and headed for the bathroom.

She could hear Wiley's voice as she stepped into the hallway. He seemed to be on the phone, but she couldn't hear what he was saying. When she emerged from the bathroom a few minutes later he was still speaking, but her attention was caught by the black-and-white photos spread out on the small table in the hall.

Sam must have dropped these off sometime during the night, she thought. There were seven of them, glossy black-and-white blowups that did more than any words could to prove that Rodney Dietrich was as guilty as Jack Cotter had said he was.

The first picture showed Rodney talking to the curly-haired man who'd come to the Dietrich ranch house last night. Rae-Anne shook her head as she looked at it, marveling that it had only *been* last night. The picture seemed to have been shot just before the curly-haired man—Armand Grant, one of the new employees whose file and ID picture she'd copied—had driven away from the ranch.

Wiley had caught the two men in the act of exchanging a briefcase. That must have been what Rodney had been stashing in the front seat of his pickup before he, too, had driven away, Rae-Anne thought.

The rest of the pictures were as damningly clear as the first one. Wiley had gotten several clear views of Rodney filling the deposit envelopes with cash at the small-town automatic teller machine. He'd even managed to get the town clock in the background, she noticed, tying the event to a specific time and place.

The final picture wouldn't have seemed significant unless you knew that the shiny new pickup truck in it belonged to Rodney, and the long dark car next to it to the two men who'd threatened her and attacked Wiley. Its license plate was clearly displayed in the photograph, and once again the town clock in the background held it all together, showing that the car—which would undoubtedly prove to be registered to someone with a connection to the mob—had been at the right place at the right time.

"Right. First thing tomorrow, then."

Wiley's voice cut through her thoughts, and she wondered for the first time who he was talking to. She'd expected him to be calling Jack, but although his voice had the mocking edge he always used with his brothers, his words didn't make sense. Surely he would want to deliver their evidence to the FBI sooner than tomorrow morning.

His next comment brought her up short. "And listen, buddy, don't do too much of a hard sell, all right?" he was saying. "There's been a lot of stuff coming at her lately, and I think she's more likely to go for this if you don't come on too strong."

He paused, then laughed. "Yeah, I know you, all right," he said. "Just lay it out as a business proposition, and I think she'll say yes."

Rae-Anne didn't listen to the pleasantries that ended the phone conversation. She was too busy feeling furious with Wiley Cotter.

"What was that all about?" she demanded, when he'd hung up the phone.

He was wearing the black sweatpants and white T-shirt he'd pulled out of his dresser before heading out to sleep on the sofa-bed last night. Judging from the stiff way he was moving as he set the phone on its shelf, and the dark shadows under his eyes, he hadn't rested nearly as well as she had.

But he seemed to have showered and shaved already—his hair was damp and newly combed, and there was no trace of stubble on his long jaw. And his voice was assertive and steady as he said, "I called a guy I know who's just starting up a greenhouse business down in Wimberley. Last time I talked to him he was looking for somebody to run the office side of things. I thought you might be interested."

"Why did you think that?"

Wiley moved toward the small kitchen and switched on the coffee maker on the counter. "You're going to need to do something to support yourself," he said. "Obviously you can't go back to working for Rodney. And this'll be nice sedate work—reasonable hours, sitting at a desk instead of standing behind a bar, and the pay's generous."

"Wiley—"

He went on as though she hadn't spoken. "I figured I might as well make use of some of my contacts and see if I could help out," he said. "Wimberley's a pretty little place—a real hill-country town. We can find you a comfortable place to rent and get your stuff moved down there before—"

"Wait a minute." She stepped into the living room. The patter of rain was louder against the big plate-glass window that overlooked the yard. She could see a small wooden deck out there, shiny in the rain, and a black drum barbecue at the far end of the small lawn.

"Who's this 'we'?" she asked.

Wiley didn't miss a beat. He didn't look directly at her, either, she noticed. "I feel kind of an obligation to help you settle things," he said. "After all, I've been in on this since the beginning, and—"

"An obligation?" She cut in on him again, feeling madder and madder as she listened to his down-to-earth tone. *We'll just do the sensible thing, that's all,* he seemed to be saying. As though *sensible* was a word that had any place in their tumultuous relationship.

Obligation didn't belong there, either. And the idea that he could even suggest it—

"You have no right to be making my decisions for me, Wiley," she told him crisply.

"You said the same thing when I hijacked your wedding limousine, but it turned out it was a good thing I did." He seemed to be speaking to the countertop, glowering at its bare white surface as though it had insulted him and all his ancestors.

At the moment, she was just as glad not to be meeting the dark sizzle of his gaze. She had a feeling they were on the edge of saying things that had been lurking just under the surface ever since he'd reappeared in her life, and it was hard enough to keep her thoughts straight without letting the dangerous magnetism between them start acting on her again.

"I'll admit that," she said. "I'm not exactly thrilled about the prospect of being a single mother whose child's father lied to me from the very beginning of our relationship. But I'd rather know about it than not know."

"Or find yourself the victim of some accident, like Rodney's first wife," Wiley muttered.

"You don't need to rub it in, Wiley. I get the picture."

Suddenly she didn't know if she was angry at Rodney or Wiley or at the whole situation. She only knew that something inside her was starting to boil over, and there was nothing she could do to stop it.

"But just because you were right about Rodney doesn't mean I'm going to let you take me by the hand and lead me through the rest of my life," she said. "That's not what I want."

"Good." He looked at her finally, and the jolt of meeting his eyes was just as potent as she'd known it would be. "That's not what I'm trying to do."

Rae-Anne felt another kind of jolt, one that had the hollow feeling of disappointment to it. She swallowed hard and said, "Well, the rest of my life starts this morning. And I'll deal with it in my own way. You have no place in it, not now."

It was happening all over again—that quick, intuitive connection between them. Any strong feeling was enough to ignite it—anger, passion, longing. And Rae-Anne knew, beyond any doubt, that what Wiley was feeling right now was the same hollow disappointment that had just echoed through her frame a moment before.

Why?

She was telling him to stay out of her life, and he was replying that he wasn't interested in sticking around for the long haul. Why, then, was she suddenly feeling as bleak as the rainy day outside? And why was Wiley looking as though he felt exactly the same way?

She hadn't had time to come up with an answer before Wiley stepped out of the kitchen and fired off an angry question of his own.

"This is because I disappeared on you ten years ago, isn't it?" he demanded. "I let you down once, so you've decided you can never trust me again."

"This isn't about trust."

"Isn't it?" His temper seemed to be fraying along with hers. "Are you sure? You spent the first half of your life being uprooted from one place after another, and believe me, honey, I can understand how that makes you want something—anything—that you can count on. But are you sure you haven't gotten to the point where you *can't* trust anybody except yourself?"

"I don't know what you mean."

Wiley's sofa was almost the only piece of furniture in the living room. It sat facing the big window, isolated in the middle of the beige-carpeted floor. Rae-Anne was leaning one hip against the end of it, and she felt herself wanting to retreat when Wiley moved closer to her. But it seemed important to stand her ground, and not to let him see how it affected her when he raised both big hands to her shoulders and rested them there, forcing his presence on her, trying to make his point.

But it *did* affect her, and her quickened breathing was proof of it. She was suddenly aware that she had nothing on except Wiley's T-shirt. And as always, anger and passion were becoming more and more mixed together as they argued with each other.

"Did you ever bother asking my superiors at the DEA about where I'd been buried after they told you I was dead?" he asked, holding her eyes level with his own. "Did you demand to see a copy of my death certificate?"

"You're crazy, Wiley. I had no reason to think they were lying to me. You're being unreasonable."

"Maybe I am. But you might want to consider this, Rae-Anne. Deep down, was there a part of you that *expected* me to run out on you someday? Did you figure anybody you got close to would eventually disappear from your life, the way they did over and over when you were a kid?"

He was touching on things she didn't want to think about. And yet she knew there must be some truth to what he was saying. Why else would she be feeling this sharp ache in her bones, this biting sense of hurt?

"You disappeared pretty fast and pretty thoroughly yourself ten years ago, honey." Wiley's voice had gotten harder. "And it looks to me like you're getting ready to do exactly the same thing again."

It was so tempting to stop fighting and just give in to the warmth of his hands resting on her shoulders. His chest under his well-worn white T-shirt was rising and falling in an unsteady rhythm, and she knew intimately how the beat of his heart would feel if she rested her head against his shoulder and leaned in to the strength of his big body.

She couldn't do that. It was too important that she keep her thoughts straight, for the sake of her baby if for no other reason. She put both her hands over her stomach and glared at Wiley.

"I'm not just thinking about myself," she told him firmly. "In case you'd forgotten, I'm going to be somebody's mother in seven more months. I can't afford to let myself get sidetracked on all these old issues." With an effort, she moved away from him and sat down on the sofa.

It wasn't fair, she thought. Even here the seductive, musky hint of Wiley's body kept teasing her. He'd folded the blanket he'd used last night and set it on top of the pillow that lay on one arm of the sofa, but the faint scent of his skin kept suggesting rumpled beds and passionately tangled limbs to Rae-Anne's mind.

And he wasn't letting her retreat this time. He came around to stand in front of her, then lowered himself until his elbows were resting on his powerful thighs and his eyes were locked with hers again. He took her hands in his, insisting that she think about what he was saying.

"Did you actually believe I'd forgotten you were going to be somebody's mother?"

His voice was rough, but softer. And his eyes, which had been snapping with anger a moment ago, were searching hers with slow concern.

Rae-Anne shook her head. She didn't want Wiley's concern, she told herself. She wanted to be alone, and free.

Except that she wasn't. She'd just finished telling him so herself. "Oh, God, Wiley," she said. "Sometimes *I* forget it. Sometimes I still can't believe this is happening to me. But I have to handle it on my own. Can't you see that?"

"Life can be hard enough, Rae-Anne. Why make it harder by refusing to let people help you?"

Because letting people get too close—even if they were just trying to help—was a prescription for getting hurt, and Rae-Anne couldn't stand to hurt any more than she already did. But she couldn't find the words to tell Wiley that right now. She'd tried to draw away from him a minute ago, and he hadn't let her. It was just too hard to summon up the strength to pull away a second time.

She tilted her head forward in sudden weariness, and felt Wiley's arms go around her. Her forehead came to rest on the strong curve of his shoulder, and suddenly he was surrounding her gently, without his usual air of taking command.

He was holding back, she realized, letting her decide whether she wanted to move closer to him or not. And it didn't seem to be an easy thing for him to do. His body was tense, his breathing quick and shallow. But he *was* keeping himself still, his arms loosely around her waist, his breath lightly ruffling the loose hair at her temple.

She moved a little closer, because she couldn't help it. In spite of her determined words, in spite of all her good intentions, it simply felt too good to have Wiley holding her like this. She felt as though she'd been through a wringer and back these last few days. Now, even if it was just for a few stolen moments, she found herself wanting to be free of all the questions and decisions, just letting herself rest.

Wiley was moving one hand across her shoulder blades, kneading muscles she hadn't realized were quite so tense. She took in a deep breath, startled by how good the slow inhalation felt.

The sense of being sheltered in his embrace was suddenly too comforting to resist. She moved closer, to the very edge of the sofa, and heard Wiley's knees ease onto the carpeted floor as he came to meet her. He drew in a long breath, too, and Rae-Anne couldn't tell if the shuddering release as he exhaled was running through his body, or her own, or both.

"You know—" She was startled by the throatiness of her voice, and by the hint of tears in it. Had she been this close to tears all along, and just refusing to admit it? "You know, my life would be a lot simpler if you weren't in it," she said.

Her head was still resting on his shoulder, and her lips skimmed the warm, smooth skin of his neck as she spoke. She closed her eyes, picturing that deeply tanned skin and the magnificence of his half-naked body the day she'd seen him on the work crew at the Dietrich ranch. He'd turned her knees to water that day, and he was doing it again now.

"How can you say that?"

He was still moving his hand over her back in ever-widening circles. Rae-Anne felt drawn closer to him with every slow curve. Somehow his deep voice had become a part of it, an audible caress that vibrated inside her like a lover's promise.

"How can you say you don't want me in your life, af- ter—what we mean to each other?"

There it was again—that turbulent mix of anger and yearning and sympathy that was unique to the two of them. Rae-Anne could hear the rasp of it in his voice, and see it in his eyes, too, when she raised her head to look at him.

There was no trace of the mockery he sometimes dragged around him like a protective cloak. She could see many things fighting for the upper hand in his eyes, but that high-handed arrogance was gone, leaving emotions so raw and honest that Rae-Anne's whole soul responded achingly to the thought of them.

"What—do we mean to each other?"

She had to ask it. And from the scowl that appeared on Wiley's handsome face, it was clear that he had no simple, handy answer.

But he didn't skirt the question, either. "If you want to come back to bed with me," he growled, lifting his hands to frame her face, "I'll be more than happy to show you."

Chapter 12

Stop thinking, Wiley ordered himself.

Stop imagining that this might be the last time you'll ever make love to Rae-Anne Blackburn. Stop trying to figure out what you can do to keep it from being the last time.

There *was* nothing he could do, he knew. Rae-Anne had only gotten more stubborn in the past ten years, and the harder he pushed her, the harder she pushed back. Until that sudden, sweet moment when she'd finally softened in his arms, she'd been intent on letting him know that she was as ornery as she'd ever been. And as single-minded.

And as beautiful.

Wiley felt the world around him fading into nothing as he eased down on his bed with Rae-Anne. It was like crawling into a nest that nobody knew about except the two of them, a place where they could hide. It was warm and secluded and nearly silent, and even the faint patter of the rain against the window only made the room seem like more of a refuge against the cold realities that had been pursuing them.

He propped himself on one elbow and looked at Rae-Anne. Her face was touched with that rosy blush that always seemed to make her eyes brighter, her lips redder. She must have combed her hair since getting up, because it had that softly burnished look that always made Wiley want to bury his face in its auburn depths and draw in the honeyed scent of her skin until his whole body was suffused with it.

He didn't move, though, because he couldn't bear to cut short this silent moment, this wordless exchange. They held each other's eyes as though they needed to know things that words didn't exist to express. And the longer Wiley looked into Rae-Anne's dark blue eyes, the more deeply he felt himself being drawn into the old magic, the old spell they seemed to cast over each other whenever they were close like this.

Stop thinking, Wiley. You can think later.

Gradually, everything ebbed away except the two of them, and the bed, and the moment. Wiley ran one thumb along the line of her cheek and was rewarded by a slow smile that curved Rae-Anne's mouth upward and erased what was left of the uncertainty in her blue eyes.

When you smile at me like that, nothing else really matters. He wanted to say the words out loud, but didn't. Every time they spoke, they seemed to find something to disagree about, and he couldn't stand the thought of another heated exchange interrupting this sensuous moment.

So he stayed silent, and felt the hunger in his body growing as he gave up even thinking about conversation, or argument, or decision-making. This was a chance moment stolen from time itself, and Wiley was already half-immersed in it.

He lowered his head slowly, barely touching her mouth with his, waiting for her response as he'd waited for her embrace on the sofa. He was already hard and aroused—

had been since he'd put his arms around her in the living room. But it was worth the effort of reining himself in to feel her kissing him, softly, almost tentatively, as though for all the times they'd made love, this one was something new and she was determined not to rush through it.

The teasing exploration of her lips and tongue took care of any lingering desire on Wiley's part to go on thinking rationally, or at all. He was completely lost in the moment, lost in the way Rae-Anne was feathering tiny kisses along his lower lip. He'd never been so minutely aware of how soft and moist the inner reaches of her mouth were, or how tantalizing it could be to hold back this way, reining in his desire to plunge deeper, to taste her more fully.

Rae-Anne's faint moan seemed to connect with the very root of Wiley's body, turning him to liquid inside. He could feel her trembling as he slid his free arm around her. The realization that she was having to work hard at holding back, too, affected him like a shot of pure, hundred-proof moonshine.

He deepened their kiss slowly, still exploring rather than demanding, despite the bone-racking effort it cost him. But it was worth it when he heard another slow moan from deep in Rae-Anne's throat, and felt her mouth open wider to him, welcoming him into that hidden pool of warmth and sensation.

Wiley's libido was clamoring wildly to speed things up, to claim Rae-Anne's whole body as his own, to push them both over the edge of the chasm he knew they were headed toward. But the slow seduction they'd started seemed to be dictating a pace of its own.

And the sheer pleasure of it was unlike anything Wiley had ever experienced.

He'd never known how exquisite it could feel just to lie next to a woman without moving, feeling the long line of contact between their two bodies igniting a chain reaction in his nervous system that left him light-headed and aching to do away with the clothing that came between them. He slid his hands slowly over Rae-Anne's upper body, over the warm swell of her breasts and the indrawn curve of her waist, and finally slipped his palms under the edge of the loose T-shirt he'd lent her and pushed it upward.

She raised both hands to his face, sustaining their slow kiss even while she was arching her back to help him ease the T-shirt off. When she finally broke the contact of their mouths, Wiley felt as though he was suddenly gasping for air, bereft of a nourishment he needed for life itself.

The creamy expanse of her body was enough to make him feel more than alive again. She sat up to pull the T-shirt all the way off, and as she tossed it over the edge of the bed, Wiley started to rise, too, eager to be rid of his sweatpants and shirt.

But Rae-Anne held him where he was, her hands gentle but strong. "Let me do it," she said.

Her voice blended with the soft spattering of the rain against the windows, and Wiley felt irrationally as though the rain was another kind of caress, mixed in with the un-imaginable delight of Rae-Anne's fingers tracing a slow line down over his torso and arriving finally at the drawstring at his waist.

She untied it quickly, deftly, and once again captured his wrists when he made a move to slide himself free of the pants. She seemed intent on studying him, on bringing his arousal—and hers, too, if her flushed cheeks and quickened breathing were any indication—to a slow, rolling boil.

She shifted her position slightly among the rumpled sheets as she pulled his sweatpants free. Wiley stroked one hand over the silky expanse of her inner leg and heard her long, shuddering sigh as his fingertips glanced across the sensitive spot at the juncture of her thighs.

The thought of the sweet dampness within was driving him crazy. But this deliberate rhythm of enticement had him in its grip, and he couldn't have rushed things if he'd wanted to. He rolled onto his back as Rae-Anne grasped the lower edges of his T-shirt, and looked at her as she helped him out of it.

He thought he'd never seen anything so beautiful.

Her eyes glowed with a light that told Wiley she was feeling the same slow rhythm that was pulsing through his body. Her lips were parted slightly, reddened by their slow kisses, and she looked excited and confident and radiant in a way Wiley hadn't seen in far, far too long.

She was still sitting as she jettisoned his T-shirt, and Wiley took advantage of her position, maneuvering himself so that his head lay in her lap. Somehow, suddenly, desperately, he wanted to be at the sweet core of her, surrounded by that feminine strength and warmth and circled by Rae-Anne's arms.

Finding himself there was even more astonishing than he'd known it would be. He breathed in the perfume of her skin and caught the faint scent of the moistness in the center of her body as he did. His arousal was nearly unbearable now, but he was far beyond even thinking of hurrying this moment of peace in the midst of temptation.

What held him in silent amazement as he closed his arms around her waist was the thought of the child she was carrying inside her. Suddenly it seemed irrelevant that the baby's father was a criminal whom Wiley had done his best to condemn.

Here, in the tender circle of Rae-Anne's arms, with his face pressed against her belly and her pulse resonating in his bloodstream, he had a sense of how right it was that Rae-

Anne should be carrying this child, that she should have a new life to lavish her strength on, that after so many years of stubborn solitude she would not be alone anymore.

"Wiley—"

He didn't lift his head at her breathless cry. He was so certain of the bond between them at this moment that he knew why she'd spoken, and knew it wasn't a protest or a question. Her voice had hovered halfway between satisfaction and sadness, and as she wrapped her arms more securely around him, holding him to the core of her for one long, heavenly moment, Wiley knew he was sharing everything she was feeling, the confusion and the longing and the gladness, too, that she was still alive and strong and eager for the motherhood that lay ahead of her.

He wasn't sure what ended the moment. It might have been a suddenly unendurable spasm of need from his body, or it might have been the way Rae-Anne shifted against him, leaving him awash all over again in the unmistakable scent of her arousal.

Whatever the reason, Wiley couldn't wait any longer to push toward the satisfaction he knew they both wanted so fiercely. He slid one hand between Rae-Anne's legs again and let out a groan of raw need at the realization of how wet and ready she was for him. She was gasping, touching him with that combination of discovery and experience that never failed to set off fireworks throughout his body.

Their coming together held none of the slow patience of the prelude to their lovemaking. It was almost as if, in that silent, empathetic embrace, they had each reached for the core of the other and found it, and there were no more layers to strip away between them now.

That was how it felt as Wiley plunged into the body of the woman he loved—had always loved, more than he'd imagined possible. They were meant to be together like this—it was meant to be.

They moved together as though they really had merged and become a single being. And the light that burst in Wiley's consciousness at the moment of climax was partly vision, partly the sound of Rae-Anne's euphoric cry, partly the swell of certainty in his heart that he belonged with this woman as he had never belonged anywhere else on earth.

The damn baby was crying. Wiley could hear it.

It had never cried before. Usually it just sat there on the sand, playing contentedly. But now he could hear the unhappy wails coming across the water, rising and falling with the wind.

"Damn."

He shaded his eyes with one hand and squinted across the lake. Maybe if he swam fast, he thought. It wasn't really that far, now that he thought about it. And he was a good swimmer. He didn't know why he'd never been able to plunge in before now, but somehow things seemed to have changed since the last time he'd had this dream.

The water might feel good, anyway. And he hated standing here listening to the child's panicky wailing. The sound kept catching in its throat, as though its heart was breaking.

He was in the water without being aware of getting there. It felt colder than he'd thought, but he kept his arms and legs moving quickly and cut through the icy lake without feeling tired or chilled.

"I'm coming," he called, when he was about halfway across. "Hold on. I'm coming."

The noise seemed to get fainter once he touched the shore. *Don't fade out on me now,* he thought. He was aware that this was just a dream and that he'd been chasing this particular child for what felt like his whole life. Yet at the same time he felt urgently that he had to hurry, that it was vitally important to reach the baby at last.

He sprinted across the sand beach to the spot where the child sat. He could see the sand castle now, and the little green plastic pail, bright against the drab tan of the beach.

And finally he could reach for the child, whose sobs had diminished to almost nothing.

As his hands closed around the little form, he understood why the sound had stopped. It wasn't a real baby he was holding, but one made from sand, just like the brave little castle with its waving paper flags. Wiley grasped at the memory of the crying child, but it was gone.

He was left at the shore of the silent lake with his hands empty and his heart telling him over and over that he was too late, too late, too late....

"Wiley." Rae-Anne leaned one knee on the bed and shook him. "Wiley, Jack's on the phone. Wake up."

He seemed to wake up all at once, looking dazed and hostile. "What—" was all he could manage to say as he squinted at her.

The rain was pelting harder against the bedroom windows, and Rae-Anne had clicked on one of the bedside lamps when she'd come into the room with the cordless phone. "It's Jack," she said again, "and I wouldn't have answered it except that it rang so long I thought it might be an emergency or something."

"Right. An emergency."

He sank down onto the badly wrinkled bed, pressing one hand over his face for a moment. He'd looked wild-eyed when she'd shaken his shoulder, Rae-Anne thought, as though she'd caught him in the middle of a nightmare.

She held the phone toward him, prodding him with her knee, and he finally reached out and took it.

"Jack." His voice sounded husky. "What's up?"

How could a man look so disheveled and still be so beautiful? she wondered. The dark hair that masked his forehead seemed blacker than ever against his tanned skin, and the length of him—his thighs and torso under the light blanket he'd pulled over the two of them—was making Rae-Anne's body quiver with a longing that should have been slaked by now.

The beginnings of the dark bruises scattered over that magnificent chest should have been more than enough to sober her, to counteract everything Wiley made her feel. But there was something about him that found its way into her bloodstream even when he slept, even when that larger-than-life personality of his wasn't in force.

She'd always loved to watch him sleep. There was something unexpectedly vulnerable about his closed eyelids, something childlike in the curve of his dark lashes under the wide slash of his brows. When he was asleep, it was possible to imagine that Wiley Cotter had once been a child, as confused and lonely as she'd been herself.

Usually, though, he woke up with a little more grace than this.

"I said I would call. For crying out loud, Jack, it's barely nine o'clock," he was snarling into the phone. Rae-Anne was surprised to see that he was right. She had no idea what time they'd awakened before, but it had obviously been very early.

"No. He doesn't know where she is." That probably meant herself, Rae-Anne thought. And "he" was probably Rodney, who might be tipped off that something was wrong now that Rae-Anne had walked out on him a second time.

There was a pause, and then Wiley said, "Yeah, I know. I've got them here. You want to collect them yourself, or wait for me to deliver them?"

Rae-Anne's guess about the answer to that turned out to be correct. "Jack's on his way over," Wiley said, as he pushed the button to disconnect the phone. "Sorry about the rush, honey. But he wants to get the pictures and the tape and put a lid on Rodney as soon as he can. I guess we better get dressed."

He didn't move right away, though he draped one long arm over the side of the bed and reached for his discarded sweatpants. Rae-Anne had already gotten into her bra and panties while he was on the phone, but she hesitated before pulling her white Indian cotton dress over her head.

"What did I wake you from?" she asked slowly. "Were you dreaming?"

He'd always scoffed at her interest in his dreams, but his scorn on the subject had only convinced Rae-Anne that her questions had touched some place in him that he didn't want to expose.

And he wasn't scoffing now, just lying there with one arm across his forehead, looking at the ceiling with eyes that she suddenly couldn't read. She didn't like the way he seemed so distant all of a sudden, and she pressed the point, adding, "It seemed like I interrupted *something* when I shook you awake."

He sighed deeply, then rolled over and grabbed his sweatpants. As he stood up to step into them, Rae-Anne caught her breath at the male hardness of his thigh muscles and the rock-hard ridges of his belly. She couldn't forget the way she'd been consumed by that body of his only a little while before, and she hated the thought that he might be retreating into the tough-edged, lonely world he'd let himself be coaxed out of so briefly, so exhilaratingly, this morning.

"It's nothing much," he said. "Just this dream I don't seem to be able to get rid of."

Nothing much? she wanted to say. Wiley was smart enough to know that recurring dreams were the ones with the most urgent things to say. But he was shrugging the whole thing off as he continued.

"All my life I've had this dream about being stuck on the shore of a lake. And there's somebody on the other side that I have to get to, only I can't."

"Who's on the other side of the lake?" Rae-Anne asked, letting her dress fall over her head and reaching for the ends of the belt.

"A kid." Wiley gave a half laugh, as though he expected her to find this silly and wanted to chuckle at it before she did. When she stayed silent, waiting, he shrugged and said, "It's a baby, actually. Sitting on the beach, playing in the sand."

"Do you have any idea who the child is?"

He shook his head at her. "You've been a bartender too long," he told her. "You're starting to sound like a shrink."

"You're not answering my question," she persisted, in spite of the way his brows had lowered.

"No, I don't have any idea who the child is." He paused. "Unless—"

Rae-Anne waited.

"I guess it might be Sam," he said finally. "When he was little."

"What makes you think that?"

He sighed and pulled his T-shirt impatiently over his head, then pushed his hair back with one broad hand. "The night my mother kicked my father out of the house, I saw Sam go with him," he said.

She felt the quick flicker of interest that Wiley's past always set off inside her. "Your father took a child of—what, seven years old?"

"My father didn't exactly take him. Sam stowed away. He adored my dad. I guess he figured if the family was going to split up, he was going to choose the parent he preferred."

She thought about it for a moment. "You said you saw him leaving," she said.

"Yeah."

"Meaning—"

He dragged the covers over the bed quickly, efficiently, smoothing away the scene of their loving with a few motions. "I don't know what it means, Rae-Anne," he said. "It's just the only explanation I can think of for the damn dream, that's all."

He gave the blanket a final tug and stood up straight, looking hard at her. "Either that or I'm just short on sleep, or some damn thing. Or maybe it's from eating Rodney's hamburgers last night. Your boyfriend's no four-star chef, honey."

Rae-Anne felt something clench up inside her as she watched him, something that threatened the fragile sense of hope she'd felt as she'd looked into Wiley's sleeping face.

She didn't have to ask why he was doing this, why he was saying *your boyfriend* in that harsh tone of voice when he knew beyond a shadow of a doubt that she was through with Rodney Dietrich. She *had* touched something deep inside him, maybe with her questions, maybe in that impossibly secret moment when they'd held each other so close, not speaking, just silently confirming the strength of the connection between them.

The way he was reacting told her he hadn't wanted to be touched so deeply, and he was retreating at full speed. She followed Wiley into the living room and watched while he poured himself a cup of coffee and collected the black-and-white photographs into an envelope.

"You wouldn't be so tight-lipped about this if it wasn't important," she told him.

It worked. He paused, then frowned at her. "Important to who?" he wanted to know.

"To me. To us."

This time he didn't answer. And despite her confidence that she was onto something, Rae-Anne felt a hint of fear fluttering in her chest. Even in their wildest nights of passion ten years earlier, she'd never felt anything as intimate, as tender, as that moment with Wiley just now. She'd never been so sure she was touching the *real* Wiley Cotter, reaching beyond all the defenses he'd built for himself to the lonely but loving man within. But he was digging in, alarmed, maybe—or maybe scared—by what the tenderness of that moment might mean in their relationship.

"I'm looking at a lot of important decisions in the next few days," she told him, when he didn't answer her last comment. "It might be—helpful if I had some idea what your feelings are before I start making those decisions."

Do you love me? In bald terms, that was what she needed to know. But she and Wiley had never discussed love—had never even mentioned the word between them.

Suddenly, that didn't seem like a very good omen.

"I've told you what I think."

Wiley was leaning one brawny shoulder against the doorframe between the living room and the hall. There it was, Rae-Anne thought, that trademark Cotter slouch, covering up whatever tangle of feelings was hidden inside.

"I think you should accept this job at the greenhouse and stay in Wimberley at least until the baby's born. After that—"

"Wiley." She glared at him, starting to feel angry again. "I said I wanted to talk about *feelings,* not about career counseling. I can find a job for myself. I can find a place to live. I can figure out what to do about the baby. What I can't figure out on my own is what to do about *you.*"

Her voice wobbled over the last word, and she caught herself sharply. She'd come this far without breaking down in tears, and this didn't seem like a very good time to start.

"I'll be on hand to help you out. You know that."

"Do I? You mean you'll help me rent a van so I can get my furniture down to Wimberley, and you'll help me set up my VCR and maybe shop for some baby clothes?" He started to answer, but she didn't give him the chance. "Because I just told you that's not what I'm looking for from you, Wiley. If we're going to be together at all—if we're going to be together—"

She couldn't finish the sentence.

Do you love me? was hanging in the air, but she couldn't bring herself to say it.

What if he said no?

"You're asking for more than I have to give."

That wasn't as bad as a blunt negative, but it didn't exactly make Rae-Anne's heart leap with joy, either. "How do you know what I'm asking?" she demanded.

"Because I know you, Rae-Anne. You want a lot from life. You expect a lot. And you deserve it. You know as well as I do that the reason you were having doubts about marrying old Rodney was that you just didn't love him enough."

She took a big breath, feeling it quiver in her throat. This was it, she thought. Wiley had introduced the word *love,* and she needed to follow up on it.

"What if—I *did* love you enough?"

Something flashed in his dark eyes, and she was almost frightened by the intensity of it. It was like seeing a wild horse's eyes roll just before it ran away or lashed out.

"I'm the wrong man for this." He sounded torn, reluctant, as though he didn't want to say the words but couldn't see any way around them. "I'm the wrong man for *you*. I don't know anything about love. Hell, I'm not even sure I *want* to know about it."

"What do you mean?" Fear made her voice sharp.

He sighed and dragged a hand through the hair that had fallen forward over his eyes. "I can't love the way you do, Rae-Anne," he said. "I just don't—believe in it. The kind of love I've known in my life has always screwed things up more than it's fixed them. Sometimes it's a downright dangerous thing. It's not something I know how to handle. It's certainly not something that makes me think I would be a good parent." He gave a short, cynical laugh. "Hell, I can't even imagine it," he added.

She had no good answer for him this time. She couldn't help picturing him looking out the window of that little house in Abilene, watching his father disappear into the dark night and turning to face the slow disintegration of whatever love his family had known. Had something died in his heart at that moment that simply couldn't be brought back to life?

Maybe none of the Cotter brothers knew how to handle love, she thought. Maybe she was crazy even to be talking about this with Wiley.

But the memory of their lovemaking was still so sweet and so vivid. And as for what she'd felt when he'd turned his face toward the unborn child in her belly and held her so close against him—

"I know all about how love can hurt you," she said. "You know I do. But if I really believed there was no point to trying again, I wouldn't be here right now. That's what makes me want this baby, Wiley, even though its father is probably going to be doing ten to twenty for money laundering by the time it's born. My own childhood may not have been so great, but I can still make something good for this child.''

Her voice wavered again. It was harder to come back from the slip this time. Was it because she'd just admitted to herself, in the most hidden depths of her heart, that when Wiley had been holding her earlier this morning, she'd found herself lost in impossible visions of raising a family with him, watching him learn to love again as he held his own children and hers?

She'd never allowed herself these thoughts before. And the bleak look in Wiley's eyes made her think she probably should have kept it that way.

''Maybe this baby won't exactly have the home and stability I was planning for,'' she said, more forcefully because of the tears that were trying to find their way into her voice. ''But it'll be loved. It will always be loved, just as much as I can manage.''

Wiley's silence when she finished speaking was worse than any answer could have been.

She couldn't tell if he was angry, or miserable, or just impatient with the whole turn their discussion had taken. His face was nearly blank when he raised it to look at her again, and his voice was bleak.

''Maybe that's the difference between us, Rae-Anne,'' he said. ''You're willing to go ahead with that kind of hope, and I'm just not.''

His words echoed in her mind like a series of doors slamming. *I'm not.... I'm not.... I'm not....*

''Not ever?'' She couldn't meet his eyes as she asked it.

But she could see him shaking his head, slowly but definitely. "I won't promise things I can't be sure I'll deliver," he told her. "I won't do it, not even for you."

Not even for you had a slightly comforting sound to it. She must mean *something* to him, Rae-Anne thought. That incredible moment of unity in the midst of making love hadn't just been a delusion, then.

But it wasn't enough to dispel the choking sensation in her throat or the hollowness in her chest. She'd laid her feelings open to Wiley Cotter, and he was telling her he didn't want them.

In fact, he was spelling it out in detail, just in case she hadn't already gotten his message. Rae-Anne tried to swallow, gave it up and reached for the handle of the front door next to her. She'd maneuvered herself into a spot right next to an escape route, she realized, and wondered fleetingly whether she'd done it on purpose, whether she'd instinctively known, from the dark look on Wiley's face when he'd wakened after making love, that it was going to come to this.

"Try to understand," he was saying, but her mind had already moved on to how she was going to get out of Austin with no car and no money, and where she could possibly go next. "I'm not like you. I can't think about an unborn child and promise to make it happy. How the hell can anyone promise another person's happiness? I spent my whole childhood listening to promises, and none of them meant a damn thing."

"I know all about empty promises." Her voice was soft and sad.

"Then you should know why I won't take a chance on making one. I'll help you get your feet on the ground, and I'll help settle this thing with Rodney, because those are things I know I can do. But don't ask me to promise happiness, Rae-Anne. Happily ever after is more than I can do.''

She couldn't stand to listen to the ache in Wiley's voice. There was something pleading in it all of a sudden, something that begged her to understand.

But he was saying all the wrong things.

''What if I promise you something I can't come up with?'' Was she hallucinating, or was she seeing the glassy sheen of tears brightening his dark eyes? ''Damn it, Rae-Anne, what if I hurt you again the way I hurt you before?''

She couldn't let herself listen to the anguish in his words, or think about what those unshed tears might mean. Wiley had told her he couldn't love her, and she didn't need to hear it again.

''What would happen?'' She undid the top lock on the door as she spoke. ''I don't know what would happen, Wiley. And unfortunately, we're never going to have a chance to find out.''

Chapter 13

"Have you got a green light yet?"

"No."

"Why the hell not?" Wiley felt impatience eating at him, making him curt with his brother as he stepped into Jack's office. "If that bastard Rodney Dietrich managed to slip through the cracks—"

"Keep your shirt on, Wiley. I know this is hard for you to believe, but occasionally people do manage to get things done without the benefit of your help. We're waiting for Mack to check in, and once all his people are in place, we'll go."

"And find Dietrich's ranch empty, chances are."

Jack sat down behind his desk and shook his head at his older brother. "Sounds to me like you're getting a little short on sleep," he said. "There's no reason for Dietrich to think we're closing in on him."

"There's Rae-Anne—"

Wiley didn't finish the sentence. Suddenly, no matter how hard he tried to convince himself that this was just business, all of his thoughts seemed to be revolving around Rae-Anne.

He'd caught Jack on his car phone and changed their meeting place this morning because the thought of hanging around his house remembering Rae-Anne's words and the soft hurt on her face and the erotic fulfillment of their lovemaking was simply too much for him to take.

And he was antsy because he needed to get this wrapped up, for Rae-Anne's sake. He didn't know where she'd gone or what she was planning to do, but he wouldn't rest easy until he'd completed the one part of this business that he felt competent at. And that meant seeing Rodney Dietrich under arrest at the soonest possible moment.

"Speaking of Rae-Anne—" Jack seemed to have picked up on the real reason for Wiley's anxiety. "Was that who answered your phone this morning?"

"Yeah." He frowned at his brother, daring him to go on asking questions about it.

Unfortunately, Jack had never been able to resist a dare. "What's going on between you two, anyway?" he asked.

"Not a damn thing."

Jack nodded slowly. "That must be why this big old dark cloud appears over your head every time I mention her name," he said.

"Shut up, little brother. My only concern about Rae-Anne Blackburn is to get Rodney Dietrich off her back, the same as it was when this whole thing started."

The phone on Jack's desk rang, and Wiley was spared any more perceptive comments. It had been the same way this morning when he'd met Jack at the Cotter Investigations office to hand over the tape and photographs. Jack had asked after Rae-Anne then, too, and had seemed to see beneath the surface of Wiley's chopped-off comments to the struggle that he was trying to cover up.

It was hell having brothers who knew him inside out, Wiley thought as he leaned back in his chair and propped his boot heels on the edge of Jack's desk.

And at the same time, Jack and Sam were the only family ties he had. Maybe the quiet attachment the Cotter brothers had for each other didn't go far enough to suit Rae-Anne's romantic heart, but damn it, it had been enough for Wiley, these past few years.

Was it still enough? Would it ever feel like enough again, after the past few days?

He wished he knew.

"She's *where?*" Jack's question cut into Wiley's thoughts, startling him until he told himself that "she" didn't necessarily mean Rae-Anne Blackburn. There were other female human beings in the world, after all, even though Wiley's mind was filled with thoughts of one particularly independent, auburn-haired, blue-eyed woman.

But Jack's next words made Wiley sit up straight again, clunking his heels onto the polished office floor. "Why the hell would she go back there?" Jack was asking. "According to Wiley, she was through with Dietrich for good."

"Jack, what the *hell*—"

His brother waved him away, listening hard to whoever was on the other end of the phone. "Yeah, I know. All right. I got it. We'll be there."

Wiley was on his feet by the time Jack hung up the phone. "What is it?" he demanded.

Jack was shaking his head as he reached for the suit jacket he'd slung over the back of his chair. "According to the guy we have posted to keep an eye on the Dietrich ranch, Rae-Anne Blackburn just showed up there."

"How the hell—"

"Apparently she took a cab."

Wiley couldn't get it to make sense. "A cab?" he repeated. "From Austin? That's a hell of a long ride."

"Apparently Dietrich forked over the fare at the door. I thought you said she'd left him, Wiley."

"I'd have put money on it." Wiley reached for his jacket—the rain had intensified during the day, and his dark green windbreaker was still damp to the touch—and followed his brother out of the temporary office the FBI had rented while Jack was working on Rodney Dietrich's case.

"Well, she's back there now. And her timing is way off, big brother, because if Rodney tries to put up any kind of a fight when we go in to arrest him, there could be some bullets flying around that ranch of his pretty soon."

This was all wrong.

For one thing, she'd counted on Rodney being away from the ranch when she arrived. She'd figured he would be meeting with his mob cronies at the San Antonio hotel, and that she would be able to get in and get out without encountering anyone.

But Rodney was home. Judging by the smell of brandy on his breath he'd been reverting to his old manner of relaxing himself.

And while she'd been retrieving her little heart-shaped locket from her dressing table, Rodney had paid off her cab, sending it on its way. Rae-Anne found herself suddenly furious when she saw it driving toward the ranch gates.

"You're wasting your time, Rodney," she informed him. "I only came back because I wanted the locket my father gave me. Now that I've got it, I'm just going to call another cab and get out of here again."

"No, you're not. We're going to go away together and sort all of this out."

The nearest telephone was in Rodney's private office. Rae-Anne headed that way, intent on escaping from here as soon as she possibly could. But it was impossible to bite back her answer to Rodney's words.

"Were you and Danielle trying to sort things out, too, when she was killed?" she demanded tightly.

Rodney shrugged, following her into the office. "Danielle wouldn't listen to reason. She wanted to bring the whole thing down, and she couldn't see that nobody would benefit from that, including her. I know you're more reasonable than that, Rae-Anne. Especially because you've got the baby to think of."

He gave her a confident smile, and Rae-Anne cursed herself for being so blind to that good-natured facade of his. She'd thought his charm had been a part of a naturally easygoing nature, a sign that he'd put his hellion days permanently behind him. Instead, it had been covering up things she couldn't bear to think about.

"I *am* thinking about the baby," she told him. "That's why I'm leaving. It's only *because* you're the father of my child—"

"Our child," he corrected.

Rae-Anne shook her head. "No," she said. "Not anymore. This child is not going to be just a prop to make you feel like you've succeeded in life, Rodney. And with the proof the FBI has, I don't imagine I'll have a hard time getting a judge to give me sole custody."

"Proof?" He said it as though it was a word in a language he didn't know.

"Yes, proof," she repeated. "I was there last night. I saw you making those deposits. I saw you meeting with those two men—the same two who threatened me at the hotel on Monday."

"They threatened *you*?" He sounded genuinely puzzled.

So he *hadn't* known, Rae-Anne thought. It was cold comfort, and it came far too late to save what she had once felt for Rodney Dietrich.

"They threatened me and the baby," she told him. "Now do you understand why I can't let you have anything to do with this child?"

Rodney walked to the office window and then turned to face her. Outside, beyond the thrashing branches of the shrubs that lined the back of the ranch house, the weather was turning uglier.

Just like her thoughts. Rae-Anne felt suddenly caged, caught in a comfortable, expensive trap. She reached for the phone, but before she could lift the receiver, Rodney stretched out one foot and kicked the cord away from the jack. It was a petulant gesture, a child's frustrated revenge, and it made Rae-Anne even madder.

She knew part of her fury was at Wiley, and part of it at herself, for getting mixed up in all of this in the first place. But she didn't have time to sort through it all now. She focused all her anger on Rodney as she spoke.

"You may have gotten away with silencing one wife, Rodney, but I don't intend to help you do it a second time," she told him. "If you're not going to let me call a cab, then you'll have to lend me the keys to one of the ranch vehicles. I promise you'll get it back."

He still looked puzzled. "I would never hurt you," he said. "If I'd known those two had threatened you—my God, the thought of them saying they would hurt the baby—"

She'd found his devotion touching in the beginning. She'd been glad he wanted this child, and relieved at the idea that her son or daughter would have two parents and a permanent home.

Now, the smooth sound of Rodney's voice made the flesh at the back of Rae-Anne's neck prickle with discomfort. He'd needed a wife and a family to complete his image of himself as a gentleman rancher, the son of a well-known family carrying on a proud Texas tradition. And she'd been nothing more than a part of that plan, a piece of his veneer.

At least Wiley was honest with me. She couldn't keep the thought back. Rodney had promised her the world and had been lying through his teeth the whole time. At least Wiley had been honest enough to admit he had nothing to promise.

And maybe that was the best she was going to be able to do. The thought made her suddenly very tired, especially when she realized how much planning she still had ahead of her.

"Spare me the platitudes, Rodney," she said, moving toward the door. "I'll ride out of here on the tractor if I have to, but I'm not staying here to—"

Two things happened at once. Rodney grabbed at her wrist, and she tugged against him to free herself. And at the same moment she heard voices from the hallway, and half fell sideways as Rodney pushed her aside and lurched toward the door, turning the key in the lock.

Except for Rodney, the house had been empty when she'd arrived. Renee always did the shopping on Wednesday afternoons, and the other ranch employees—the crew rebuilding the barn and the men who worked with the livestock—had probably gone into town, too, unable to work in the pouring rain. So who—

She had a momentary hope that it was the FBI, come to make the arrest that Wiley's proof should have made possible by now. The voices on the other side of the door—demanding that Rodney open up, telling him they knew he was in there—could very well mean the official investigation had caught up with her ex-fiancé at last.

But the sudden panic on Rodney's face made her think he knew these particular voices. And his words confirmed it.

"Oh, my God," he said faintly. "We have to get out of here."

"Who is it? Do you recognize them?"

"You don't want to know."

That told her enough. She should have realized right away that if Rodney was at home swilling brandy instead of at his downtown hotel meeting with his silent partners, as he'd arranged last night, something wasn't quite right.

She held a hand over her belly and forced herself to think clearly. There wasn't time to sort through Rodney's dirty business, not if the vehement sound of the men's voices outside the door meant what she thought it did.

"They're going to find some way to open the door," she told Rodney. "We need to surprise them when they do."

"Surprise them?" His face was an utter blank. Rae-Anne realized with a renewed jolt of fear that his facade had collapsed completely, leaving him empty and slack.

She took hold of his arm and shook him the way she'd been wanting to ever since he'd answered the door. "Listen to me, Rodney," she said decisively. "Those bookends are heavy. You take one, I'll take the other. When the door opens—"

She was already on her way toward the bookshelves, reaching for the heavy bronze bookends that held up the expensive leather-bound books she'd never known Rodney to read. A moment later she heard a quick spattering sound that she didn't recognize, followed by Rodney's dismayed gasp.

She pulled down the first bookend and tossed it at him, not caring that he staggered under its weight. She could see the splinters of wood jutting out of the office door now, and knew that the spattering sound had been a muzzled weapon shooting off the lock.

"When the door opens, throw it," she said, positioning herself just out of the line of fire in case their visitors came in shooting.

Luckily, they didn't. And Rodney's aim was off—the bookend he threw went wide of the door and crashed into the glass-fronted barrister cases along the wall—but the distraction worked to Rae-Anne's advantage.

Her own shot was better, and she heard a heavy oomph as one of the two men reeled sideways. He careened into his partner, and the two of them were still scrambling for their footing and looking to see where all the projectiles were coming from when Rae-Anne slipped past them into the hall.

"Get her!"

The voice goaded her to a burst of speed she hadn't known she was capable of. She dashed through the dining room and into the kitchen, her impractical leather sandals slipping on the linoleum floor as she turned toward the back door of the ranch house.

Behind her there was a sudden high yowl of pain, and she felt herself hesitate, hating to leave Rodney to the two shooters' mercy. But then she heard heavy footsteps coming after her down the hallway, thudding closer. It was like listening to a gigantic version of the raindrops pounding on the stone patio outside.

She'd done what she could to give Rodney a chance. If his guilty conscience had paralyzed him to the point that he couldn't take advantage of it, there was nothing Rae-Anne could do to help him. She had two lives to save—her own and her child's—and she knew, as she flung open the kitchen door and sprinted into the rain, that it was going to take all her wits to do it.

"Looks like Rodney's got company."

At the head of the small procession of cars—his plus the three agents detailed to back him up as he arrested Rodney Dietrich—Jack turned in to the long driveway at the Dietrich ranch house. The wipers were on their highest speed, and Wiley could barely see the outline of the dark car parked in the exact spot where he'd picked Rae-Anne up last weekend.

What he *could* see was enough to slam his heart into the wall of his chest. "And I think I know who it is," he muttered. All his vague fears of the past few days suddenly coalesced into one giant wave that threatened to engulf him. "Step on it, would you, little brother?"

Jack was a government employee, and to a certain extent he was bound by government rules. But Wiley had to say one thing for his brother. When things started happening, Jack was a good man to have on your side.

He seemed to hear the strain in Wiley's voice, and he obliged by tromping down hard on the accelerator. "That the car in the last photograph?" he demanded.

"Yeah." *Damn* it, Wiley told himself, he never should have let Rae-Anne out of his sight. He should have taken hold of her, insisted that she stay with him, demanded that she wait until Rodney was on ice before she—

There wasn't time for this. Jack's car was screeching up behind the long dark vehicle, and Wiley vaulted out of the passenger seat even before Jack had gotten the gearshift into park.

At least he'd had the foresight to come armed. He hadn't really expected a lot of resistance from Rodney Dietrich—the man had shown himself to be pretty spineless at the encounter in the town square last night. But something had prompted Wiley to pick up his revolver before joining Jack's party. It rested reassuringly in its shoulder holster as he made a headlong dash up the shallow steps and pulled open the front door of the house.

He heard car doors slamming behind him and was aware of shouting voices, but he didn't wait to see whether they were calling to him. From somewhere inside the big, low ranch house he could hear the moaning sound of someone in pain. It was enough to catapult him down the hallway without caring who might be lying in wait for him. If Rae-Anne was hurt—

But it was Rodney Dietrich he found in the office, whose door appeared to have been shot through. The sandy-haired man was lying on the floor with both hands convulsively grasping his right leg. He'd been shot but not killed, Wiley realized. Now, what the hell did *that* mean?

He didn't have time to find out. Rodney was Jack's concern, not Wiley's.

"Where's Rae-Anne?" He knelt by the wounded man, shaking him roughly by one shoulder in an attempt to get through the pain-induced glaze over Rodney's hazel eyes. "Is she here?"

So slowly that Wiley's whole body ached with the effort of waiting for it, Dietrich's eyes swiveled to see who was questioning him. "Rae-Anne," he repeated, like a child hearing a word it recognizes.

"Is she here?" Wiley refrained—with difficulty—from jostling him again. "Come on, Dietrich, talk to me!"

"The . . . back door."

Wiley didn't stick around to express his gratitude. Jack's men were erupting into the office, guns drawn, faces tense.

"She's outside somewhere." Wiley tossed the words over his shoulder as he headed into the hall. "I'm going after her."

Outside, the rain made it nearly impossible to see or hear clearly. Wiley was soaked through almost immediately, but he barely noticed it, except to shake his head as the water started to run into his face.

He was scanning the familiar landscape, trying to look at it with new eyes. Where would Rae-Anne have headed to escape the men who'd shot Rodney?

There were a couple of guest cabins—too close, he judged, and too easy a target—and the sheds for the sheep and goats. She might be hiding there, although crossing the morass of mud in the paddocks surrounding the shed would have slowed her down dangerously.

No, the gravel road was a better bet. She might have headed toward the river, hoping to hide herself among the big cypress trunks. But if she was still wearing that white cotton dress, she would be an easy target in open territory, and that made him think she would head for cover. In that case, she might have thought of—

The barn. Somehow Wiley felt certain it would have crossed her mind. The old barn he'd been working on with Abel's crew *looked* deserted, but in fact it offered more shelter than the shooters might expect.

He headed that way fast, keeping his eyes open for any sign of movement in the gray, rain-drenched landscape. Aside from a few placid cows waiting out the storm under a live oak tree, he couldn't see another living creature. The whole countryside felt drowned, silenced, empty.

And then suddenly it wasn't.

If he hadn't been in such a state of alert he might not have noticed them. They were off the road, moving through the scrubby trees that dotted the whole ranch. And they were definitely heading in the same direction he was. He could see the pair of dark shapes moving smoothly through the rain, each holding one arm in a characteristic way that made Wiley's heart thud at his chest again.

You knew all this, he told himself. You knew they were armed. You know Rae-Anne's out here somewhere. Get on with it, Cotter, and stop imagining the worst.

The worst got a little closer and a little harder to ignore when he came in sight of the old half-fallen barn. He'd gained ground on the two men, and he could see their confidence in the way they were approaching the roofless building. They knew they were stalking an unarmed woman, and they were being businesslike about it, getting the job done with minimum fuss and maximum efficiency.

The men each took one side of the barn. By the time they were ready to dart around the tumbledown stone wall, hoping to surprise their hiding quarry if she was there, Wiley had reached the shelter of one of the cypress trees that lined the riverbank. He was within shooting distance, and he had a clear view of the interior of the barn.

That was the good news.

The bad news was that he also had a clear view of Rae-Anne.

He applauded her initiative—she'd managed to climb up to a short platform on the second level of the half-fallen building, and even to dislodge the end of one of the beams Wiley had helped to wrestle up there only yesterday. But she was still in big trouble, whether she knew it or not.

He could see her positioning the end of the beam on a jutting stone in the wall, and guessed at her plan. A falling twelve-by-twelve was a formidable weapon, if she timed it right.

But it would only work once, even if she was lucky enough to hit her target. And she couldn't see that the two men had split up.

There wasn't time to get too fancy about things. Wiley waited until the two gunmen seemed just about to spring, and then he loosed off a round directly at one of them.

The rain made it almost impossible to focus, and the bullet didn't hit the target. But at least it redirected the men's attention.

Wiley didn't want to direct it too specifically to the spot where he was standing. He was still outgunned, and Rae-Anne was still in a lot of danger. Getting himself killed wasn't going to help either one of them.

So he crouched low and snaked his way through the saplings that grew between the bigger trees. The ground under his feet was slippery with rain and fallen cypress needles, and the Spanish moss hanging down from the live oaks between him and his opponents made everything seem blurred and unreal.

But it *was* real, and more dangerous than Wiley wanted to think about.

By the time he reached a new hiding place, the two men had each fired at least twice at the spot where he'd just been. He could see their bullets making little explosions in the dirt, scattering twigs into the sodden air.

If he could just distract them from Rae-Anne, there was a good chance Jack and his buddies would be drawn in this direction by the gunfire. But as he prepared to fire and move again, the two men said something to each other that he couldn't overhear, and he saw one of them disappear around the corner of the barn while the second one kept his gun leveled in Wiley's direction.

He fired a quick shot and saw the man duck behind the stone wall for protection. But the other one was loose, skirting behind where Rae-Anne stood on that high wall inside the roofless structure. If the gunman caught sight of her—

Wiley couldn't take a chance on that happening. Aiming his shooting arm as steadily as he could, he burst out of his shelter, firing as he ran, and headed directly for the barn.

He heard the deadening thunk of the beam falling just as he reached it. And there were shots being fired at him, too, diverting his attention. He shouted Rae-Anne's name, and saw her clinging unsteadily to the truncated stone platform she was standing on. Below her the first gunman lay sprawled in the mud, apparently stunned by a well-aimed release of the big beam Rae-Anne had maneuvered into place.

But there were two more dangers now. The other shooter was still on the loose, and Rae-Anne was in trouble. Wiley saw one of her feet slip, and felt a sick lurch of fear as he imagined how slick those limestone blocks would be under the smooth soles of her sandals.

"Hang on!" he shouted, and launched himself toward the spot directly under where she stood.

The second gunman came around the corner shooting, and Wiley felt something hot and sudden stinging his upper arm. He kept moving, suddenly not caring about his own life if it meant saving Rae-Anne's. The whole world had focused to a single point, the place where she would land if she fell.

And she *was* falling. The effort of heaving the heavy beam had unbalanced her, and the rain was making it impossible for her to keep her grip on the smooth stone blocks. Wiley was peripherally aware of a gun firing again, but he couldn't shoot back because he'd tossed his gun aside in his reckless dash toward Rae-Anne.

There was more gunfire, and a sudden yell to his left. And then he saw what he'd been most afraid of—Rae-Anne's white, rain-soaked dress fluttering in midair as she lost her hold on the tiny platform she'd managed to climb up to.

Wiley pushed himself to cover the last few muddy yards between them. He stretched his arms out to break her fall, but the force of it knocked him off his feet. He couldn't keep hold of her. Or maybe it was her own flailing limbs that propelled her out of his grasp and launched her toward the stone wall.

He saw her fall backward as he struggled to his feet in the mud. He reached her in the same sickening split second that her dark auburn head cracked against the limestone.

Wiley was too late, too late to do anything but gather her against him and say her name, urgently, hoarsely. She looked at him with wide, astonished blue eyes for one brief moment, and then Wiley watched the dismay in her pale, drenched face disappear into unconsciousness.

Chapter 14

She's pregnant...

Why were those words running around and around in her mind?

Rae-Anne turned her face against the crisp white pillow-case and wished her head didn't hurt so much. Someone was touching her shoulder, gently but insistently. She wished whoever it was would go away.

Damn it, would you hurry up with that thing?

It was Wiley's voice she was hearing, although she couldn't figure out why. She squeezed her eyes more tightly shut, resisting the hand that was shaking her shoulder. Beyond the dull roar of her headache she could hear—in her memory, maybe?—the grinding of gears. It was all jumbled up with the rain and the gravel path behind Rodney's ranch house and the shouting of voices, too many voices to keep straight....

But Wiley's had been loud and clear. She tried to hang on to it, not wanting to open her eyes to the light.

"Come on, dear. I have to wake you up every hour, to make sure you're okay. It's standard procedure whenever there's a chance of concussion."

There had been gunshots. She wished she could sort it all out, but she just kept remembering the pelting rain and the quick biting sound of the guns firing. And her feet slipping out from under her on that stone ledge.

And then one isolated moment came into clear focus, like an image held in freeze-frame.

Any known medical conditions?

Someone had shouted the words over the spatter of the rain against the hard ground. And Wiley had shouted back, *She's pregnant. Be careful with her. She's pregnant.*

Her eyes flew open suddenly. Her whole skull felt invaded by bright light. She raised a hand to her face to shield it, and saw a nurse in a white uniform looking at her.

"There we go," the nurse said. "How are you feeling now, dear?"

Rae-Anne shook her head at the question, keeping the movement short because it hurt so much to move. Speaking was an effort, too, but she fought her grogginess and the pain that seemed to be spreading all the way through her.

"The baby," she said, focusing her eyes as well as she could on the nurse's face. "Is the baby all right?"

"Oh."

She knew it the moment the woman opened her mouth. Or maybe she'd known it already—known that something was wrong, something was missing inside her.

The blind feeling of protest started low down in her body, tightening her stomach into a knot and making it hard to breathe. *No,* she wanted to shout, making the hospital halls ring with it. *Everything has to be all right. I can't have come this far and then lost—*

"Tell me," she said, struggling to lift her head off the pillow. "You have to tell me."

"The doctor will be around soon—"

"I don't want to wait for the doctor. Tell me what happened, damn it!"

She didn't know if the nurse's hands were pushing her against the bed or helping her get her balance as she sat up. She didn't care how much her head throbbed. What did that matter—what did anything matter, if something had happened to her baby?

It seemed to take forever for the nurse to put it into words. When she did, she sounded apologetic.

"I'm so sorry," she said. "They said you took a bad fall. The baby miscarried. You're not pregnant anymore."

It was like being trapped inside a bad dream.

Outside her window the sky was dark, but the light from the hospital corridor made it hard to sleep. She managed to doze off and on, mercifully escaping from the aching loss that seemed to have settled permanently inside her. But every time she lapsed into sleep, someone would come and wake her up again, shining lights into her eyes, taking her pulse and her temperature.

What was worse was that they kept telling her it was for her own good.

Leave me alone, Rae-Anne wanted to say. *If you really want to help me, just leave me alone.*

It was after daylight before they finally did. She had an impression from a stray comment that one of the doctors was giving her something to help her relax. She swallowed it gratefully, wanting nothing more than to sleep and blot out everything that had happened in the past twenty-four hours.

Her headache was better, but it was still hard to open her eyes.

Rae-Anne half turned in the hospital bed, wrapping her arms around the place in her body where the baby should have been and wasn't. She kept expecting to feel some kind of physical pain, but there wasn't any. The miscarriage had happened so easily, so absurdly. It was almost as though she'd never been pregnant at all.

The only pain was in her heart, where she couldn't bring herself to let go of her treasured dreams of carrying a small, sleeping bundle into a gently lit bedroom, settling it into bed with infinite care, laughing in response to a wide, delighted baby smile.

Her sense of loss was so strong that she moaned out loud.

And heard an answering rustle somewhere in the room.

No more bright lights, she wanted to say. *No more people in white coats.*

He wasn't wearing a white coat. He seemed to be wearing the same dark plaid shirt she'd glimpsed when he'd come around the corner of the old stone barn in the rain yesterday—or had it been two days ago already? She saw dried mud on the knees of his trousers as he eased himself onto the bed beside her.

And then she closed her eyes again, not caring what day it was or how Wiley had gotten here or what he was wearing.

"Wiley..."

She heard her voice shaking, and moved gratefully into the strong circle of his arms, settling her cheek against his thigh. He ran one big hand over her hair, smoothing it. Rae-Anne felt something inside her loosen as his deep voice rumbled into the quiet room.

"Shh, honey... You're all right now."

"I'm *not* all right." Something caught at her throat. "Wiley—the baby—"

"I know. Damn it, I know, Rae-Anne. They told me about the baby."

It was as though a dam had burst inside her. She hadn't realized how tightly she was holding everything in until she felt it all start to spill over into Wiley's embrace.

It wasn't just tears, although those were spilling over, too, feeling even more urgent because she'd been holding them back for so long. But there were words mixed in with her sobs, the kind of words she never let herself give in to, raw and childish words, full of hurt and need.

"Wiley—it isn't fair—"

"I know."

"It hurts so much—I can't believe how much it hurts."

She didn't realize she was crying until she saw damp patches appearing on the dark blue fabric her cheek was pressing against. And then, suddenly, her tears overwhelmed her.

"Wiley, I just want to go *home*...."

What was left of her adult pride vanished with the phrase. She sobbed out all her loss and frustration in Wiley's strong embrace, suddenly needing his silent, stubborn strength more than she needed breath itself.

I just want to go home.... Even in the midst of her tears she knew it was ridiculous. But the words had been dredged up from somewhere deep inside her, some remnant of the child she'd once been, the child who'd never had a home to call her own.

The words had always been there, in her heart. She didn't know where *home* was, didn't have any idea how to go about finding it.

But it was what she wanted.

And the longing for it was so powerful that she felt as though it might break her in two as she cried in Wiley's arms. She felt him stroking her hair, murmuring her name, settling himself higher on the bed so that she was half-cradled in his lap, surrounding her with his strength.

By the time she'd wept all the tears that had been gathering in her for so long, every bone in her body ached with weariness.

She tried to lift her head again, and couldn't.

She tried to tell Wiley how glad she was that he was here, but she couldn't manage that, either. It was all she could do to burrow her face a little closer into the angle of his hip. A moment later she was drifting into sleep in Wiley's sheltering arms, feeling drained but strangely peaceful.

When she woke up again, he was gone.

"You have a visitor."

The nurse who bobbed her head through the door sounded bright and optimistic. And Rae-Anne's mood brightened, too, as she caught a glimpse of broad shoulders, dark hair, long legs standing awkwardly in the doorway.

But it was the wrong Cotter.

It was Jack, looking tentative, with a bouquet of red carnations held uneasily in his hands. He came slowly into the room, setting the flowers on the windowsill before lowering himself into the chair next to her bed.

"I heard about the baby." He didn't bother with small talk, which Rae-Anne was grateful for. "I'm sorry. I— Well, shoot, I don't know if it would have changed things if I'd known you were pregnant. But I'm sorry as hell."

"It's all right, Jack. I'm—starting to come to terms with it."

It was true. The dull sense of loss was still there inside her, but the way she'd let loose all her emotions in Wiley's arms earlier—yesterday? Today? She still wasn't certain—had softened the sharp edges of the pain she'd felt.

Which didn't answer the question of where Wiley was now.

Before she got a chance to ask, Jack had reached into his jacket pocket and pulled out a folded edition of the San Antonio paper.

"Thought you might want to know how things turned out," he said. "It's been in the papers, but I didn't know—"

"I haven't read it," Rae-Anne said.

"Well, you should. It makes a hell of a good story." He unfolded the paper so she could see the front-page headline. Dietrich Tied To Statewide Gambling Bust.

"We picked up Armand Grant, the new mob courier, on his way into Mexico the night before last," Jack went on. "Turns out he'd been told to pay close attention to how Rodney behaved whenever the cash was exchanged, the way it was that night at the ranch house. Rodney's mob colleagues were starting to get uneasy about him, especially after he announced he was going to get married."

"Why should that make them uneasy?"

"Because any wife with her wits about her was bound to feel some interest in her husband's business. And you worked in the hotel chain, which would make you even more likely to start asking the wrong kinds of questions."

"Which I did."

"Right. Rodney kept insisting that he could handle you, but his backers weren't so confident. So when Armand reported that Rodney had seemed edgy and upset, a couple of the boys were sent out to remind him just how serious this all was."

"And Wiley caught it on film."

"Yeah. And I think Rodney's willing to talk, to save his own skin."

"He's alive, then?" Rae-Anne realized suddenly that she felt almost nothing for Rodney Dietrich. But for some reason it was a relief to know he hadn't been killed.

Jack's nod confirmed it. "Shooting him in the leg was a way of incapacitating him—and scaring him—while they went after you."

"Then it really is—all over."

"It really is. Rodney's testimony will be enough to wrap the case up. It went as well as we'd hoped it would. Biggest operation I've ever been a part of. And if we'd been able to get you out of it in one piece, Rae-Anne, I'd be sitting on top of the world right now."

"I'm in one piece. A bit banged up, maybe, but still in one piece."

Jack grinned, and Rae-Anne felt her heart beat a little faster at the way the quick flash of his smile reminded her of Wiley's. Had all the Cotter brothers been issued those devastatingly sexy dimples at birth?

"Wiley said you were made of sterner stuff than most full-grown FBI agents," Jack said, "and now I believe him."

"Where is Wiley?"

She knew her voice sounded breathless as she asked the question, but she couldn't help it. She was beginning to wonder whether she'd just dreamed that moment of sweet solace in Wiley's arms, and she needed to know—*now*— what was really going on around her.

"The doctor chased him out of here a couple of hours ago. Said if Wiley got any tireder *he* was going to need to be admitted to the hospital."

So he *had* been here. And the sky outside seemed to be getting dark again—she'd been here for at least twenty-four hours, then. Rae-Anne frowned, and tried to put it all together.

"Wiley sat up all last night waiting to get in and see you," Jack was saying. "They kept telling him you couldn't have visitors until morning, but—well, you know Wiley."

In some ways, she knew him better than she knew herself. And in others—

She shook her head. Wiley had refused to promise her anything, refused to offer any hope that they might have a future together. Yet he'd been here, refusing to leave her. Jack's visit might have cleared up the details about the mystery surrounding Rodney Dietrich, but at the same time the puzzle of Wiley Cotter was only growing more tangled.

"Do you know when I'm going to be able to check out of here?" she asked.

"Tomorrow morning, they said. If you feel up to it."

"I feel up to it." She didn't stop to consult the various parts of her body that had taken a beating in that fall from the stone barn. She needed to be on her feet, trying to pull together the scattered pieces of her life.

"I'll come by and pick you up, if you want," Jack said. "And deliver you wherever you want to go."

She didn't know where she wanted to go. She didn't really have anywhere she *could* go.

Where was Wiley? What was he thinking and doing? Why had he been so patient, so loving, only to disappear as though he'd never been here at all? Was this a pattern that was destined to keep repeating itself over and over, no matter how close she and Wiley seemed to become in other ways? Some of the bleakness she'd felt after learning about the loss of her baby crept into her now, chilling her.

She accepted Jack's offer, grateful for the watchdog mentality that all the Cotter brothers seemed to share. But it was Wiley she was thinking of as Jack took his leave.

Was she crazy to keep thinking of the silent strength he'd offered her a few hours earlier?

Had he stayed silent because he still refused to take a chance on promising her anything at all?

She knew there were a hundred other more urgent things she should be sorting out. She needed to think about where she was going to go when she got out of the hospital tomorrow, and how she was going to support herself. She needed to come to terms with the fact that she wasn't Rodney Dietrich's fiancée anymore. Or the FBI's informant. Or anyone's employee.

Or anyone's mother.

But even the thought of the baby she'd lost wasn't quite enough to force her thoughts away from the vision of Wiley Cotter's laughing, dark-eyed face. That vision was still with her—dazzling, puzzling, too much a part of her to be banished to the past this time—when she finally drifted into an uneasy sleep much later that night.

Wiley crossed his arms for about the sixth time. His blue sedan was as clean as it ever got—he'd run it through a car wash on the way over here—but it still wasn't any glass coach, and no amount of soap and wax was going to turn it into one.

And Wiley was no Prince Charming. He couldn't guarantee Rae-Anne the happy ending she deserved. Damn it, he hadn't even been able to keep her safe at Rodney Dietrich's ranch two days ago. She'd lost at least one of her shining dreams, and it was partly Wiley's fault.

He should be miles away from her, shouldn't have argued when Jack had mentioned that he was going to pick Rae-Anne up at the hospital this morning.

But he *had* argued. And he was here, in spite of his restlessness, his doubts, in spite of the fact that it had taken all the willpower he had just to get his eyes open this morning.

He was here because he simply hadn't been able to stay away.

And getting himself here had been the easy part. Wiley crossed his arms in the other direction and wished the hospital would hustle itself and let Rae-Anne go.

As though he'd conjured her out of his thoughts, she appeared at last. A nurse in a white uniform was pushing her in a wheelchair, but once they were clear of the automatic doors, Rae-Anne got to her feet steadily enough and turned to thank the other woman with a quick, gracious smile.

When she turned to look at the parking lot, shielding her eyes with one hand against the bright morning sunlight, Wiley's heart turned over.

It wasn't just that she looked so beautiful, with her freshly washed hair glinting red-gold in the sun and her skin so seductively fair and smooth against the simple floral-print dress Jack had brought from her closet at Rodney's ranch house.

It was the way she was holding herself, and the look on her face.

Wiley knew that look. He'd seen it only last week when he'd driven up to her front door in a much more elegant vehicle than the one he was driving today.

Then, Rae-Anne had been gowned and coiffed and made-up until she was as glossy as any bride off the pages of a magazine. But it had been the look in her eyes that had riveted Wiley, that quietly mutinous look that meant she was scared to death, and making herself move ahead in spite of it.

It was what he loved most about Rae-Anne Blackburn. And it gave him the courage now to lift one arm and catch her attention.

"Wiley?"

She said it as if he was the last person on earth she'd expected to see. The slow sound of his name on her lips plunged him into thoughts of the morning Rae-Anne had walked out of his house, announcing that they were through with each other.

Did you figure anybody you got close to would eventually disappear from your life? he'd asked her then. Had he been right? Was it even remotely possible that a woman as wary as Rae-Anne Blackburn could ever hook up with a man like him?

If it wasn't—

He shook his head and pushed the thought away. "Your coach turned back into a pumpkin," he told her, opening the passenger door. "I hope you don't mind."

She looked at him for what felt like a long time, her blue eyes alive with too many different emotions for Wiley to be sure of any of them. She was frowning as she accepted his invitation to get into the car. But she *did* accept it, and Wiley felt his heart lighten a little.

This was only the first hurdle, though. Wiley knew he should be explaining himself to her, telling her everything that had been going through his mind and tearing his heart in two since he'd left her yesterday morning.

But he was too damn tired for speeches.

And too uneasy for pronouncements.

And Rae-Anne was too beautiful, anyway. How was he supposed to keep his thoughts straight when he could feel her cornflower blue gaze resting on him this way? He watched her slender fingers doing up the clasp of her seat belt and wished he could kiss the tips of them, one after the other, until he heard her sighing softly with pleasure.

He growled a little, and started the car.

"Wiley."

"Yeah?"

"Where are we going?"

"You'll see."

She reached over and put one hand on his forearm. He could feel the soft pressure of her touch through the light-weight brown jacket he'd slung on this morning, and it was enough to make him pause before turning out into the traffic.

"We've done this scene, Wiley, remember?" Her voice sounded tired and doubtful—damn it, Wiley wished he could just rock her in his arms without speaking, the way he'd done yesterday. "You've already picked me up and run off with me once this week. If you're thinking—"

He couldn't tell her what he was thinking. Not yet. It had taken him most of the night to come to terms with his real feelings for Rae-Anne, and most of today to figure out what to do about it. He couldn't just blurt it out in ten words or less.

"I have something I want to show you," he said. "And something I want to say to you. And after that—well, you can tell me where you want to go, and I'll take you there."

They were silent as he piloted the car across Austin. Rae-Anne glanced at him only once during the drive, at the moment when he turned onto the side street that led to his office.

He had a pretty good idea what she was thinking. Rae-Anne had always hated the gritty side of Wiley's career, and this past week had given her reason to dislike it even more.

"Don't worry," he said out loud. "This has nothing to do with my work—at least, not with Cotter Investigations."

She looked puzzled, but she stayed silent until Wiley had parked the car across the street from his office building. In the clear morning sun, the garishly painted little barbecue restaurant looked loud and bright. He fished the keys out of his pocket and felt himself wanting to hold his breath as he led Rae-Anne up the sidewalk.

"Why do you have keys to this place?" she wanted to know.

"Because, honey, as of about five-thirty yesterday afternoon, I'm the proud owner of this little joint."

They stepped inside and Wiley clicked on a couple of lights. The turquoise walls seemed more ostentatious than ever, and without anybody around, the open central courtyard looked empty and deserted.

Had he made a mistake? Wiley wondered suddenly. Was he making a mistake right now? He swallowed hard and took Rae-Anne's hand.

"Come on," he said. "The best part is out back."

But even the big drum smoker that had seemed like the restaurant's pride and glory yesterday wasn't enough to raise a response from Rae-Anne. Wiley felt his confidence ebbing, felt himself sliding into the silence and uncertainty that had kept him so far away from this woman for so long.

And then, as clearly as if the words were echoing in the empty space around them, he heard Rae-Anne's voice saying, *What if I loved you enough to marry you?*

She'd asked him that two days ago, and he'd given her a pretty lousy answer.

It was time to see if he could come up with something better.

"Let me get this straight," Rae-Anne was saying, following Wiley toward the painted picnic tables in the center of the courtyard. "While you were supposed to be catching up on some sleep—which, I might add, you look as though you still need—you were out buying real estate?"

Wiley nodded. "Place was going to close down," he said. "I didn't want to see that happen. All of us at the office have been eating lunch here for years now."

"So you're becoming a restauranteur as well as a private eye." She frowned, and barely seemed to notice as Wiley wrapped his hands around her slim waist and hoisted her onto the nearest table, so that their eyes were level with each other.

"No."

A flicker of Rae-Anne's old defiant spirit showed behind the wariness in her blue gaze. Wiley felt his breath quicken at the sight of it, and at the feeling of her forefinger hitting the center of his chest.

"Wiley Cotter," she said, "explain yourself."

"I decided yesterday that I needed a change." He'd practiced saying these words, but it was still hard to get them out. "A big change. I've gotten tired of shooting at people, Rae-Anne. And tired of people shooting at me. And when you came so close to getting killed the other day—"

He couldn't bring himself to finish the sentence. The nightmare image of Rae-Anne's white dress fluttering as she lost her grip on that stone wall would be with him until the day he finally pegged out, he was certain.

But she hadn't died. And that flash of spirit in her eyes was more pronounced now, giving Wiley the confidence to go on.

"I'm quitting the investigations business," he said bluntly. "Sam can take over the agency, although I haven't broken the news to him yet."

"And you're devoting your life to barbecue instead?"

This was it, Wiley thought. This was the final hurdle. It had come up more suddenly than he'd expected.

And yet it felt as though he'd been waiting his whole life to say these words to Rae-Anne. He moved a step closer to her and rested his hands at her waist, gently, not demanding anything as he so urgently wanted to do.

"No," he said, and saw her eyes widen. "If you'll let me—and I know there's no good reason you should, after everything that's happened—I'm planning to devote the rest of my life to *you.*"

Her whole face changed as he spoke, and suddenly he knew she'd been waiting to hear these words as long as he'd been waiting to say them. His hands tightened around the curve of her waist, and his voice was rough with desire and impatience as he went on.

"I know I've been thickheaded about this," he said. "You tried to get through to me, and I wouldn't listen. You wanted to talk about love, that morning at my house, and I wouldn't do it."

"Is that what we're talking about now? Love?" Her voice was so soft, so sweet, that it was a physical effort not to tilt his head and kiss her.

If he did that, the conversation would come to a sudden halt. But he couldn't resist leaning his forehead against hers, drawing her a little closer, as he said, "It's what we should have been talking about all along, honey. But I was so fixated on keeping you safe and solving this damn case and getting you out of Rodney's clutches—"

He shook his head and wondered how it was possible to be feeling elated and furious and uncertain all at the same time. Only Rae-Anne Blackburn had ever been able to do this to him.

"When I saw you falling—when I thought I might lose you—nothing else mattered," he told her. "The only thing that's mattered to me since that moment was that I loved you—that I *do* love you. And I've been such a hardheaded fool that it's taken me this long to tell you so."

It was going to take an entire lifetime to get over the fear he'd felt in that awful moment. It he'd lost the chance to hold Rae-Anne this way, to pull her close to him, to whisper her name against her red-gold hair and feel her whole body trembling in response—

But the welcome way she nestled into his embrace made Wiley think they were going to have an entire lifetime to get over it, to get over everything that had ever gone wrong between them.

"I love you, Rae-Anne Blackburn," he murmured. "I want to marry you and have children with you and run this funky little barbecue joint until we're both old and gray—if it'll make you happy. If it won't—"

She leaned back and smiled at him. "Funky little joints are my biggest weakness," she said. "You know that. I never did belong in that shiny tower Rodney built. And as for the part about having children—"

He'd been rushing her. He'd known it was going to happen. He lifted both palms and held them toward her. "I know it's too soon to be talking about this," he said. "We don't have to—"

"Yes, we do." He *was* seeing tears in her eyes, Wiley thought. And he was seeing joy, too. The look on her face was about the most beautiful thing he could imagine. "We have two unhappy childhoods to make up for, Wiley—yours and mine. We'd better get to work on it, as far as I can see."

She'd said "we" so easily, so naturally, that Wiley wanted to shout with the joy of it. He recaptured her in his arms and held her tight.

"What the hell made you go back to that ranch, anyway?" he demanded, no longer trying to keep his questions in any kind of order. "If Jack's people hadn't been monitoring that place—"

"I left something there—something I couldn't stand to leave behind."

Wiley reached into his pocket and brought out the small locket that Jack had retrieved with the rest of Rae-Anne's belongings. "It wasn't this, by any chance, was it?" he asked.

Her smile blossomed for him as he dangled the thin gold chain in the sunlit air. "How did you know?" she asked.

"I remembered it from—from your wedding night."

He'd nearly said "from *our* wedding night." And maybe that was closer to the truth after all, he thought, as he fastened the little locket around Rae-Anne's neck and let himself slide into memories of how it had glinted against her skin in the soft light of the cabin he'd carried her away to.

They'd pledged themselves to each other that night, and every time they'd ever made love.

And the silent promise of their passion had finally found its voice in the happiest moment of Wiley's whole life.

"It's not a wedding ring," he said softly, "but I'll take care of that the minute you promise to marry me."

"I promise." She looked into his eyes with such unmistakable love that Wiley wasn't sure he could stand it. "And, Wiley?"

He was lowering his head to kiss her, but her soft question stopped him. "Mmm?" he said.

"A promise isn't the same as a manufacturer's guarantee, you know. I'm not going to trade you in the first time the going gets rough."

"I know that now." It was what he'd finally understood in the depths of the night, and what had finally given him the courage to tell Rae-Anne what had been in his heart all along. "A promise just means we love each other enough to try." He shook his head. "Seems so simple now," he said. "I mean, hell, honey, I know barbecue recipes more complicated than that."

"But they don't taste as good, do they?"

The laughter behind the tears in her eyes was making Wiley crazy. And so was his need to kiss her.

"No," he said. "They don't. You hungry now, Rae-Anne?"

"No."

"Good. Me, too." He lifted her effortlessly off the table, amazed at the way that everything he wanted in the world could fit into the circle of his arms this way.

"Remember I said I'd take you wherever you wanted after I said what I had to say?" he asked her.

Rae-Anne nodded.

"Well, the offer still stands. You got any ideas where you want to go, honey?"

"Yes." Her voice broke over the word. "I want to go home. With you."

"Then that's where we're going."

He said the simple words like a triumphant bridegroom claiming the woman he loved. He tightened his arms around Rae-Anne, exhilarated by the idea of sharing her tears, her happiness, anything and everything that life cared to throw at them from now on.

As long as they were together, he thought, they would find a way to make this happiness last.

And as long as they were together, they were already home.

* * * * *

COMING NEXT MONTH

#703 SURVIVE THE NIGHT—Marilyn Pappano
Heartbreakers
Framed! Escaped convict Dillon Boone had no choice but to do the
unthinkable: take Ashley Benedict hostage. Her home provided a
place to heal his wounds, while her arms promised love and
acceptance…if only they could survive the night.

#704 DRIVEN TO DISTRACTION—Judith Duncan
Romantic Traditions
If anything, Maggie Burrows's life was pretty darn sedate. Then
Toni Parnelli moved in next door—and immediately put the moves
on Maggie. He was a younger man, determined to break all the
rules—and more than determined to break down Maggie's reserve.

#705 A COWBOY'S HEART—Doreen Roberts
Sharon Douglass had loved and been left by her cowboy, and
now their son wanted to follow in the footsteps of his rodeo-
riding father…a father he didn't even know. Then Mac McAllister
returned to Sharon's ranch expecting to save the day—but instead he
got the shock of his life.…

#706 BABY OF THE BRIDE—Kay David
Rachel St. James found herself the proud *almost*-mom of a beautiful
baby girl—but with no husband in sight! Desperate for the adoption
to go through, she proposed nick-of-time nuptials to friend
Paul Delaney. Now the last thing the convenient groom wanted was
for their marriage to end.…

#707 BLACKWOOD'S WOMAN—Beverly Barton
The Protectors
Though Joanna Beaumont had learned the hard way about life's
darker side, she still was every bit the romantic. Especially when
it came to cynical J. T. Blackwood. His harsh demeanor beckoned her
to heal his wounds—even as she welcomed his tender protection from
the terror of her past.

#708 AN HONORABLE MAN—Margaret Watson
She'd ruined his life two years ago, and now Julia Carleton had
the audacity to ask for his help. Well, ex-cop Luke McKinley would
just have to say *no*. Only he couldn't. Not when his silence could
mean harming innocent people…or the woman he'd fallen for,
despite the odds.

Silhouette

S P E C I A L   E D I T I O N

™

THE MACKADE BROTHERS

the exciting series by
NEW YORK TIMES BESTSELLING AUTHOR

Nora Roberts

The MacKade Brothers are back—looking for trouble,
and always finding it. Coming this March,
Silhouette Intimate Moments presents

THE HEART OF DEVIN MACKADE

(Intimate Moments #697)

If you liked THE RETURN OF RAFE MACKADE (Silhouette
Intimate Moments #631) and THE PRIDE OF JARED MACK-
ADE (Silhouette Special Edition #1000), you'll love Devin's
story! Then be on the lookout for the final book in the series,
THE FALL OF SHANE MACKADE (Silhouette Special Edition
#1022), coming in April from Silhouette Special Edition.

 These sexy, trouble-loving
men heading out to you in
alternating books from
Silhouette Intimate Moments and
Silhouette Special Edition. Watch out for them!

Alicia Scott's

Elizabeth, Mitch, Cagney, Garret and Jake:

Four brothers and a sister—though miles separated them, they would always be a family.

Don't miss a single, suspenseful—sexy—tale in Alicia Scott's family-based series, which features four rugged, untamable brothers and their spitfire sister:

THE QUIET ONE...IM #701, March 1996

THE ONE WORTH WAITING FOR...IM #713, May 1996

THE ONE WHO ALMOST GOT AWAY...IM #723, July 1996

"The Guiness Gang," found only in—

TRINITY STREET WEST

where danger lies around every corner—and the
biggest danger of all is falling in love.

Meet the men and women of Trinity Street West in the
new Intimate Moments miniseries by

Justine Davis

beginning in March 1996 with

LOVER UNDER COVER (Intimate Moments #698):

Caitlin Murphy was determined to make a
difference at Trinity Street West. Then cocky detective
Quisto Romero shattered her world. He was willing to
risk everything to catch a young boy's killer—and to
conquer the defenses she had put around her heart.

Don't miss this new series—only from

INTIMATE MOMENTS®
Silhouette®

PROTECTORS

by Beverly Barton

Trained to protect, ready to lay their lives on the line, but unprepared for the power of love.

Award-winning author Beverly Barton brings you
Ashe McLaughlin, Sam Dundee and J. T. Blackwood...
three rugged, sexy ex-government agents—each with a
special woman to protect.

J.T. Blackwood is six feet four inches of whipcord-lean man.
And in April, in BLACKWOOD'S WOMAN (IM #707), the
former secret service agent returns to his New Mexico ranch
for a well-deserved vacation, and finds his most dangerous
assignment yet—Joanna Beaumont. The terror Joanna fled
from five years ago has suddenly found her. Now only J.T.
stands between his beautiful tenant's deadly past and her
future...a future he is determined to share with her.

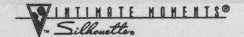

INTIMATE MOMENTS®
Silhouette

BBPROT3